THE HEXED & THE HUNTED

MELISSA MARR

ALSO BY MELISSA MARR

<u>Signed Copies:</u>

To order signed copies of my books (with free ebook included in some cases), go to MelissaMarrBooks.com

<u>Thriller</u>

Pretty Broken Things (2020; psychological thriller)

<u>Fantasy</u>

Graveminder (HarperCollins, 2011)

The Arrivals (HarperCollins, 2012)

Cold Iron Heart (2020; *Wicked Lovely* adult)

The Wicked & The Dead (2020; Urban Fantasy)

The Kiss & The Killer (2021; Urban Fantasy)

Dark Sun (2021; Urban Fantasy)

<u>Young Adult Fantasy</u>

Wicked Lovely series (HarperCollins, 2007-2012)

Made For You (HarperCollins,, 2013)

Seven Black Diamonds (HarperCollins, 2015)

One Blood Ruby (HarperCollins, 2016)

<u>Middle Grade Fantasy</u>

The Hidden Dragon (Penguin, 2023)

The Hidden Knife (Penguin, 2021)

The Blackwell Pages trilogy (with Kelley Armstrong, Little Brown, 2012-2014)

<u>**Co-Edited with Kelley Armstrong (with HarperTeen)**</u>

Enthralled

Shards & Ashes

<u>**Co-Edited with Tim Pratt (with Little, Brown)**</u>

Rags & Bones

AUTHOR'S NOTES

AUTHOR'S NOTES:

The term "hillbilly mafia" is not meant in a pejorative way. My mother was born in a "holler" (that's spelled h-o-l-l-o-w to those of you who aren't coming from barefoot roots like mine). And I grew up thinking everyone had a household gun supply and M80s to toss in the yard.

I've been setting this up in earlier stories with hints of Allie's background. I don't write about where I come from very often. There's both a lot broken and a lot beautiful in places like my home.

The sections of the story in Scotland are based on actual places, as well. One of the first things I did when I was a "baby author" with a royalty check was go to Orkney. I've been back to Scotland often since that trip, and there is nowhere I've been yet that's as lovely as Scotland.

To the best of my knowledge, however, there are no magical artifacts buried there, and in the real world I would never disturb an archaeological site (especially because my kid is an archaeologist, and she's vaguely terrifying when it comes to people who have or are disrupting sites).

PROLOGUE

L ate that night I slipped into bed with Eli. The dead were safely nestled back in their graves, and the *draugr* I hadn't beheaded were vanished to their dens or nests. And Iggy had crawled back into whatever cave he lived with his antiquated notions.

"How was work?" Eli murmured after kissing me hello.

"Dead," I quipped.

Eli, proving yet again that he was the one for me, smiled. "Indeed."

I filled him in, and then snuggled into his arms. I wasn't exactly sleepy, but tonight's magic had left me ready for rest. It was a bit alarming to suddenly need sleep, but that was another question for another week. Tonight was for pre-wedding snuggles.

The next thing I knew, the magical alarm that let us know that Allie was here was blaring. It felt like only a moment after I fell asleep, but the light said it was the next morning.

"Breakfast!" my assistant called as she let herself into the house.

"Did you forget to lock the door?" I grumbled to Eli, pointedly *not* looking at him. I didn't do well with continuing to grumble when I looked at him. My beloved was almost painfully handsome. No human-born was as striking as even the least of the fae. Add ethereal beauty to a body that was temptation personified, and his baffling decision to choose me of all the far-more-worthy people in his world and in mine . . . well, let's just say that the only way I had ever resisted him was by constantly avoiding or arguing with him.

Now that I was fallen, it took more effort than my sleepy ass was willing to expend to stay surly when I even looked at him. Love, man, it messed up years of successful surliness.

"I gave her a key," he said cheerily.

Then he escaped my grumpy morning mood to start to ready himself for the day while I was met with the chirpy "Helloooo, my bridal birdie" of my assistant.

I swore she was cheerful just to piss me off sometimes.

"Come on! Up up up," Allie said, knocking on the bedroom door. "We need to head out so we can get you all beautified. I have a whole team meeting us there."

I jerked open the door. "You're lying, right?"

"Nope."

An hour later when we arrived at Beatrice's estate, where I was to be married in front of my nearest and dearest, my magic instantly reached out to the dead in the soil, absences in pockets of space. Perhaps for some people, starting a wedding with a counting of the dead would be odd—but I took comfort in it.

There were a number of graves here. Three women in the bayou. Six more men in the ground closer to the house. A child in a grave. And a tangle of bones in a field . . . sixty . . . maybe up to eighty bodies. It was as if I greeted them when I visited, reaching out, finding them, knowing where they were. I was a necromantic witch, as well as being the product of a witch-*draugr* relationship.

That particular pairing should never have created life. Dead things don't *give* life, but the dead sperm donor who impregnated my mother knew she was a witch.

As a result, I was an aberration—half-witch, half-*draugr*. . . oh, and because I'd fallen in love with a faery and bonded with him, able to access fae magic, too. The dead were mine to protect or eliminate. The living were mine to protect, and thanks to Eli, that included faeries now. Assuming I had the time between the attempts on my life to contemplate it, the responsibility on my shoulders might be intimidating. For now, I simply let my grave sight roll out to greet the dead in the earth.

In the city, the dead were always easy to find. New Orleans was a city of graves. Out here in what was once called Slidell, the dead were often hidden—except the *draugr*.

My sense of the dead was always humming here at Beatrice's home. Her guards were not all walking dead, but there were enough dead present that I felt hyper-alert the first few times I'd been here. Now, after several visits over the last year, I was getting used to their "signatures." I could even identify some of the guests by the way my magic recognized them.

Beatrice, queen of the *draugr* here, swept out the door, and despite her elegant gown, she still looked like she was a moment from declaring war. She was draped in a midnight blue gown covered with hundreds of small glinting gems that gave her the appearance of royalty—which she was among her kind. She was the sort of old that still made my bones tingle at the chill she radiated. When she died, dust and air would be all that remained of her, but over the recent year or so, I had become surprisingly fond of the fanged woman in front of me. Beatrice was, after all, my ancestor.

She wore no shoes today. In fact, a pair of employees at her door were collecting and tagging all shoes. There would be no footwear allowed at my wedding. Fortunately, this was a small, private event, and none of my guests were the sort to disagree. They knew me.

"Your dress awaits," Beatrice said, motioning us forward.

The hallway was covered with a carpet of moss and flowers. Magic or patience could be responsible. I didn't ask which it was. I merely followed her to a medieval looking room where dresses were hung in waiting.

Light blue and green dresses for my bridesmaids. And for me, a mid-tone blue dress that was cut to look a bit like a mermaid's tail. The material was dyed several shades lighter than my hair. Simple, but narrowing at the calf to highlight my shape. It was fancier than I thought I wanted, and there was nowhere to hide a sword.

"I'll slaughter the world for you," Beatrice reminded me. "Wear the dress. Relax for these hours."

I nodded and slipped into the dress. Few beings could outmatch her in a fight. So far, I knew of only one: Chester, the oldest living human alchemist and her once-upon-a-time murderer. If he decided to appear here, we were all doomed.

Beatrice stared at me. "I have sent Alice's people away to tend the bridesmaids. I know that sort of *primping* is not your style."

I muffled a laugh.

Then the *draugr* queen leaned forward and placed a circlet of gems on my hair. "This is not a veil. It is not a fae crown. It is in place of those things."

Carefully I met her eyes in the mirror. The crown was obviously a gift, but I could not help but suspect that there was more to it. "You're not telling me everything."

Beatrice waved my words away, reminding me of every time my own mother made such a gesture. "Today is not the day to speak of everything," Beatrice said. "Later you may question me. I shall answer."

I nodded. Honestly, there was only so much I could handle, and I was at my maximum stress capacity far too often lately.

"Today you celebrate your love here with your family, yes?" Beatrice fussed with my hair.

Behind me, by way of the mirror, I saw my mother, who had just walked into the room. The three of us stood there for a moment, and I realized that today was significant to both of them, too. My mother had fought for me simply to exist, bringing life out of death, and I was the descendent of a woman who had thwarted death in a different way. Strong women came before me, making a path that I had followed.

Beatrice kissed Mama Lauren's cheek. Then mine. "You are my greatest achievements in these many centuries of un-living existence."

Before we could think to reply to being called achievements, Beatrice *flowed* out of the room. I often wondered if emotion was too much for her in some moments. It certainly was for me.

"She loves us in the way she can," Mama Lauren said. "I remind myself of that often when she is imperious."

"She sounds like you," I teased.

Mama Lauren swatted my arm lightly. "You are lovely, despite that sass."

"Because of it?" I asked.

"Perhaps." My mother's smile was agreeing even if her words were tentative. "From my long-ago bargain . . . to this wedding, there has never been a risk too great when it came to your happiness."

Sometimes I thought this was exactly why I'd been so hesitant to want children. Mama Lauren had set such an example of what it meant to be a mother that I wasn't sure that sort of self-sacrifice was for me—but my bad luck in genetics was good luck on this front. I had a longer life than any human expected to have, and that was only added to by bonding with one of the fae. My longevity was tied to his now, so there was no rush to procreate.

My mother and I talked and finished getting ready in what felt like minutes although it was almost two hours later when we finally walked out of the room and toward the courtyard.

I watched as Allie, Sera, and Christy walked toward Beatrice, who was officiating.

Then, Jesse stepped forward. My "Man of Honor" had chosen to wait at the front with the ring. When I reached him, he would be in place to hold my bouquet of vibrant flowers. My family and my friends were here.

My *reason* was waiting in front of me. Halfway up the aisle was my groom. My already-husband. My bound-unto-death fae prince. Handsome in every way I could dream—and completely mine.

Eli was everything I never dreamed to find. He'd stitched my stab wounds, created a safe haven for me in his home, and waited while I struggled with fears of commitment. Instead of asking me to be less than what I was, Eli stood at my side in conflict and life.

My mother escorted me toward him, and I could not look away. How had someone so amazing, so gorgeous, so strong slipped into my life and stayed? In a world with so much wrong, how did I get so lucky?

"Breathe in and out, Gen," Mama Lauren whispered.

"Trying." I smiled at Eli. "He steals my breath."

I knew there were guests as well, but in that moment, I couldn't tell you who or why they were here. All that mattered was my family, my dearest friends, and this man.

My mother and I reached Eli's side, and she said, "I give my heart into your possession, Eli. Guard her. Love her."

"I shall," he promised.

"I trust you." Mama Lauren stepped away, watching us with a pride that made her glow.

As I placed my hand on Eli's arm, I was trembling. This was it. The last ceremony. The final exchange of vows.

"Three exchanges," I whispered, thinking about the rule of three. We were as bonded as any couple could ever be, but instead of finding that frightening, I was elated. This person, inexplicably, was mine to love and cherish until we died together. Our souls, our pulses, our very lifespans were intertwined, and I was so grateful my eyes teared up.

Eli simply smiled as we walked toward Beatrice.

She looked at us, nodded, and said, "The couple would like to say a few words in the presence of witnesses."

"Eternally yours," he swore. "I've waited years to be able to call myself the luckiest person in either world, Geneviève Crowe."

"I was oblivious so long. I'm glad you thought I was worth the wait."

Friends laughed, but the truth was that we were here because he had the patience to let spark build to friendship build to love. I mean, there were some faery bargains along the way to make me not run screaming into the night. I had always had the sort of commitment fears that bordered on pathological. It took fae patience to get us to this place.

"My heart, my hearth, and my hand are yours, Geneviève Crowe. Unto death I shall live and fight at your side. And in us, the future of my family is bound." Eli stared into my eyes as if we were the only people here. "It is my privilege to love you, and my great joy to be loved by you."

"My heart, my hearth, and hand are yours, Eli of Stonecroft. Not even death could tear me from your side." I swallowed the fear of a world separated from him. Now that we were together, I would never let go. Then I smiled and swore, "I love you and will be honored to be mother to your child one day, partner on the throne of *Elphame,* and the sword at your side."

Then Eli gave me a wicked smile. "I accept your faery bargain, Geneviève of Crowe and Stonecroft. Your terms are acceptable to me."

I laughed at his going off script. "So mote it be, Eli of *Crowe* and Stonecroft."

Beatrice shook her head at our impromptu modification and

then asked, "Do you take this person to be your spouse, your partner, your equal in all ways?"

"Unto death," Eli said.

"Unto death," I echoed.

"By the powers granted me by familial law, as well as my court
and kin, I pronounce you wed." Then she swept her arms open
and stated, "May I present Geneviève and Eli of Crowe and
Stonecroft."

GENEVIÈVE

Three months later

"I HAVE HAD WORSE STUDENTS, HEXEN," IGNATIUS Blackwood, formerly dead Hexen Master and acolyte of Baron Samedi--loa of the dead--stared at me from the other side of my training room in the apartment that was mine pre-marriage.

We were at an uneasy peace that was dangerously close to friendship. I had reluctantly grown fond of Iggy, and even kidnapping hadn't changed that entirely.

"I'm not *that* bad," I grumbled at his faint praise. If I hadn't been so capable, I'd have been dead a dozen times over by now. The problem, unfortunately, was that Chester, the alchemist who had once killed Iggy *and* Beatrice, was not too keen on my tendency to accumulate power, and Chester tended to kill those he found threatening.

Iggy's interest in me, on the other hand, was the same sort that a lepidopterist had toward butterflies. I was a curiosity, and he collected curious things. Treasures were his interest. Whereas Chester wanted to eliminate the anomalies, Iggy wanted to collect them. It was no wonder the two men were at odds.

Chester was greedy for knowledge and power, and Iggy was a witch—a hexen—who had crossed Chester in the 1800s. I wasn't sure how or why, but Iggy had been murdered by Chester.

The formerly dead Victorian man wasn't sharing details, but I had inferred that his death was violent and painful.

All I knew for certain was that when I met Iggy, he was clad in his death garb—vintage 1800s suit, elegant ring and watch, and an ebony walking stick. Unlike most dead folk, he'd stayed after I tried to send him back to the grave. Then, through a mix of my magic and Iggy's treachery, he was brought back to life.

Now I was on Chester's radar, and I suspected Iggy was, too. So Iggy was determined to protect me even if it was against my will—to the point of kidnapping me—and when that had failed, he'd become adamant that he'd train me.

These days, Iggy looked a lot closer to my age, and tended toward designer trousers and shirts that revealed a set of muscles that were out of place with his age at death. Whatever magic it took for him to be able to do so, I could admit that he moved and looked a decade younger.

The new physique *also* meant he could best me in physical fights. So we'd added that to our training. I taught him martial arts, and he taught me a few dirty street fighting tricks.

So I was in witchy boot camp these days.

Six fight dummies were positioned around the room, and just as many illusory versions of Iggy were scattered among them. Through some mix of magic and genetics, six Iggys grinned at me, looking like a flock of a well-dressed, fit, young pirates.

His next hex, from one of the six versions of him, landed me on the ground with legs akimbo and pride wounded. I tried to laugh it off, but my favorite jeans were now . . . ventilated, and I'd pulled a muscle in a place I was not going to massage in front of anyone but my husband. "I didn't know I could still do a split."

IGGY WAS THE BEST HEXEN I'D EVER MET.

Ergo, my current awkward state: sprawled like a drunken giraffe trying to decide *which* Iggy was the real one. His duplicates moved independently. If I could find the *real* Iggy, I could attack him and erase the illusions.

"Do you think Chester will be amused by your quips?" the Iggy on the far left asked.

"No, but—"

"I want to keep you alive, and all you do is mock the lessons." Iggy to the center scowled.

The *real Iggy* was my self-appointed teacher, and I was failing this lesson spectacularly—because to solve it, I had to first counter his duplication hex.

Which Iggy was flesh?

"No one's killed me yet, Iggikins," I muttered as I pushed to my feet. Again. Somehow being splayed out, legs akimbo like Bambi on ice made it harder to sound serious, but I was nothing if not tenacious. I insisted, "That has to mean *something*."

Iggy scoffed, and every one of them said, "It means you're lucky."

I studied the many Iggys, hoping for a clue. I sent out a push of necromantic energy, and this time only one Iggy zinged back: the Iggy closest to me.

Got you! I telegraphed my intent too soon, though. He fired several hexes that promptly knocked me back to the ground.

He didn't crow at his victory or even throw a little snark at me. He simply gave me a smug smile and motioned for me to get back to my feet.

I was starting to think Iggy knocked me to the floor just because it pissed me off.

"So that's how it is?" I asked.

He smiled wider.

So, I retaliated: a volley of hexes and a knife that sailed through the air targeting the real Iggy. I heard the knife hit actual flesh.

The five illusionary Iggys vanished, and the real one still had a fresh wound on his shoulder from the knife I'd launched at him.

"Better." Iggy rubbed his temples like he was as old as he truly might be. "Much better. Not fast enough, but at least you *did* something. I do not understand why a hexen of your caliber is so reticent about attacking."

"Because I'm not heartless?" I stared at him. I understood, objectively, that he was training me, but practicing any of the more dangerous hexes on him seemed . . . *wrong.* The man had died in the 1800s, and he'd been restored to life—by me— recently. I wasn't sure how long he'd lived the first go-round, but he had at least a decade or three on me, not counting the century plus where he was moldering in a grave. Maybe death wasn't as intimidating after you'd done it?

I watched as Iggy muttered hex words for stitching and slow- ing. Or maybe it wasn't as daunting when the fixes were that easy. Iggy made it all look easy.

He gave me a pointed glance as he repeated the hex again.

These were useful hexes, especially with my propensity for getting stabbed, and we both knew he expected me to retain them whether he said as much or not. If he *hadn't* wanted me to learn, he wouldn't let me hear him. So many of the hexes had been lost over time because people weren't eager to pass on their knowledge.

"You are only alive, Hexen, because of luck and an absurd excess of power." Iggy met my gaze.

I preened, though I was certain it wasn't intended to be a compliment. "Powerful and living! I'll take it."

Then, while he was once again glaring at me, I summoned

tendrils of the trailing plant that hung in my main room. That wasn't witch magic. It was a side effect of my marriage to one of the fae. The prince. The heir. My best friend, lover, and soulmate.

The unexpected bonus of marrying Eli Stonecroft was that his magic was now mine to access, as was some of my magic his to use. Currently I was using that fae affinity for nature to stalk my teacher with silently creeping vines.

Cheating? Maybe. Real fights were never about being *fair*, though, so I wasn't about to ignore part of my arsenal when a century or so old witch decided to hex me.

Iggy was about to walk away, so I taunted, "I was strong enough to bring your dusty ass back to life, Iggy Pops . . ."

"Because of my guidance," he corrected.

"Manipulation, not guidance." I stood, put my hands on my hips, and glared.

At the exact same time, I urged the plants to lash out at him like trained vipers. The plants encircled his ankles and jerked him toward the ceiling. Within moments, my teacher was hanging upside down from my ceiling, tethered there like a fly in a spiderweb.

"Excellent! Now, think of hexes the same way: extensions of will. You can do it when you summon the dead. You can do so with plants. What about the rest?" Iggy swung from the exposed beams in my fight room as he spoke. "*Blind* me, Hexen.

"Seriously? Can't you just leave it at 'good job, Gen' or something?" I shook my finger at him, hating that I felt like the cautious one, but I preferred to train with non-lethal and non-disfiguring hexes.

Or swords. Swords were good. Blunt swords and fight dummies, no living things injured. But no, Iggy was determined to push me to uncomfortable places.

"If I wanted to kill you, that would be a logical next move in self-defense. If I can't see you, I can't strike you as easily." Iggy made it all sound so practical, but the thought of blinding him made me cringe. He was my teacher, albeit not by my conscious choice, but still!

"What if I hex one of the dummies so you can still see that I c—"

"Don't worry, poppet. I'll still be able to behold your glory later. Unlike you, I can heal whatever you do to me . . ." Iggy grinned, looking at me with a sort of lecherous gaze that almost made me feel prudish.

I tried to send a stinging hex at his eyes.

"Basic, low-level," Iggy grumbled. "*Blind* me. Or do you just like the sight of me in restraints? Does your husband know about this kink of—"

His words ended with a bellow of pain. Where his eyes had been now was only bloody gouges and empty sockets.

"Iggy!" I released the magic that was binding the plants, dropping Iggy to the ground carefully.

I cradled him in my lap, like a dying kitten. "Monkeyballs. Fucksycles. Dammit, Iggy! I didn't mean to . . . Ugh! I'm not sure how to fix—"

"Hush. That was excellent work, Geneviève." He sat up, wiped his hands over the vacant space, and chanted something in a language I didn't know.

I watched in awe as his eyes grew back, filling those empty hollows with a slow shift as if he'd poured gel into a mold. I'd been beheading monsters since I was a teen, so this ought not disgust me, but it did. Layer after layer of gelatinous goo filled his eyes like pudding spooned into a desert cup.

I resisted gagging, but only with effort.

When Iggy's eyes were back, they were startling ice-blue. He'd regrown his eyes in such a way that they were entirely new. "How . . .?"

Iggy smiled, ignoring my question, and exclaimed, "Now *that* was how you hex, Geneviève. If I were Chester, that would be a great first volley. Could you target your excision hex? Lungs? Heart? Bollocks?

"Are you suggesting I cut out your *heart*? Snip your . . ." I gestured. "Forgive me if I don't think regrowing your heart is in my skill set."

Iggy chortled. "Maybe we don't practice that one on my heart. Hmmm . . ."

Before he could suggest we find a person—or *draugr*—to experiment on, I held up a hand. "I can target it without needing to torture someone *if* I'm not exhausted, but I'm not sure if going *snip snip*"—I made a scissors gesture—"is going to make Chester anything but enraged."

Iggy shook his head. "It would hurt like the devil had his nethers in a vise. That's what you want, Hexen. The goal is to evoke pain and make him pause, so you can escape."

"Or kill him."

Iggy sighed and reached out to capture my hand in his own slimy, bloodied grip. "We've gone over this. You must flee when you can. No killing attempts. He's too strong. He killed *me*, Hexen. Do you think that *you* are trained enough when I was not?"

I scowled and shoved Iggy away. "Trained? No. I have three types of magical heritage, though. I might not have as much knowledge as you, but—"

"He'll kill Eli," Iggy says bluntly. His words were designed to hurt as much as his hexes did.

Few things take the wind out of my fight as that one can.

"Even if you lack self-preservation," Iggy continues, "you care about Eli, don't you? Chester will kill you, and *that* will kill Eli. If you learn no other thing that I try to teach you, understand this: you *cannot* kill Chester. Sheer luck and arrogance are not enough."

I paced away from him, ostensibly to wash the blood from my hands. *His* blood. I'd been bound in a blood bond with Iggy a few months ago, so I wasn't letting his blood on my skin a second longer than I had to do so. I trusted Iggy in ways—but I wasn't fool enough to forget his ill-conceived plot to protect me against my will.

"That's the way, Geneviève. Simply run from Chester the way you do when you see how much I care for you," Iggy taunted.

The truth was that Iggy had no *romantic* interest in me, and we both knew that. His care was friendship, maybe possessiveness. It wasn't romantic or sexual. In truth, Iggy seemed to always flirt with no intent to deliver. I'd watched him flirt mercilessly at the bar with countless people since his resurrection, but he'd never acted on it. Never left with the women who gazed at him adoringly. As far as I could tell, he was basically living like a monk. Flirting was a reflex, possibly a hobby.

"Can you stitch my mouth shut?" Iggy asked, pulling me out of my mental meandering. "Quickly. Efficiently. It won't stop all hexes, but it would limit a lesser hexen, and inconvenience even Chester."

"Stitch your . . ."

"Like such," Iggy said.

He gave me a warning look, and I had the sudden sensation of a thick thread piercing my lips and sewing them shut. I couldn't cut them open, although that was my first thought.

I needed to learn to start with less brute force, more finesse.

Duck dongles. Nothing made sense as my brain could only think "can't speak" and I barely resisted the urge to claw at my own mouth.

My panic must've been obvious enough that Iggy unstitched my mouth, pointed at one of the fight dummies, and started to walk me through the intonations. It was a frightfully easy hex, but one I'd never ever heard of.

"It was from a marriage manual," Iggy said quietly. "One that hasn't survived."

I met his eyes briefly, my question as obvious as if I'd said it aloud.

"Because I saw to it that the remaining copies were destroyed," Iggy said. "There was a woman . . ." He said nothing more, but it was a tidbit of his life I hadn't known, a gesture of friendship.

And it was enough for me to try harder.

GENEVIÈVE

By the time Iggy and I were both sufficiently exhausted by attempting to improve my hexing, I was . . . energized. I found fighting worked a lot like caffeine for me; the more I had, the more I wanted. My teacher, however, was starting to look at me as parents looked at children who had discovered a cache of cake.

"Want to patrol? Or are you too tired?" I asked, bouncing on the balls of my feet as I asked. I was pretty sure Iggy was not up for a patrol, but I had energy to spare.

"Where's your less abrasive half?" Iggy gave me the sort of look that made me remember that he wasn't convinced that I was safe when I was left unsupervised.

"I'm a grown ass witch, Iggy Pops."

"With a murderous enemy," he rebutted.

"True but . . ."

Iggy gave me a look, and then parroted an Allie quote at me: "Friends don't let friends get murdered."

"Fine."

Despite the weirdness of our admittedly brief history, he *had* become a friend. I'd had no desire to add him to my very short list of friends, but there he was, setting up shop in my life. Clearly, I wasn't great at boundaries or grudge holding. My ex-girlfriend Sera was a friend. Allie, a woman who attempted to murder me, was my assistant. Beatrice, the queen of the creatures I'd been killing since I was a teenager, was my ancestor. *She* was the weirdest member of the group: my very un-alive, fanged, witchy grannie—who, because life is weird, had previously slept with Iggy, whom I'd resurrected.

But then again, maybe weird was the way of the world.

My *family* was weird, and my *friends* were weird, and honestly, I wouldn't have it any other way. So if the dead dude I had resurrected was determined to be my babysitter, I might just be stuck with it.

"I expected Eli to come collect you by now," Iggy said in his version of casual questioning. "Might Bea be stopping by? Or shall I escort you to the walled manor of your princely hero? I'm fairly sure the city doesn't require a patrol at this hour."

I laughed. "You suck at subtle."

"I'll have you know that I can be remarkably subtle. You, Ms. Crowe, simply happen to be better at seeing through my subtlety due to that fae thing." He waved his hand at me as if my 'fae thing' was a physical trait. He pressed his lips together then, already lost in a thought, muttering, "Perhaps we can harness *that* to craft hexes . . ."

Iggy paced toward the room that had once been his temporary quarters when he was dead. Of late, it had been his "rental" lodging when he wasn't "renting" a room at my assistant's home. He fancied himself my guard, as well as Allie's lately, and a part of me found it charming.

"Do you have any interest in Allie?"

Iggy startled as if I had accused him of wearing off-the-rack suits. "Ms. Chaddock? I have been most careful of the widow . . . and her temper."

"Because you aren't interested or because you fear Chester

killing the people you like?" I started to gear up, adding assorted swords and other weapons, while Iggy stood glaring at me.

"The lovely revolveress is simply letting out an unused room to a gentleman in need of shelter," Iggy protested. "I hired a room at Ms. Chaddock's manse because I needed a home."

His faux posh wording didn't work on me the way it had initially.

"Bull bullocks. You only stay at Allie's the nights I am securely in Eli's care, and don't think I didn't notice that Tres texts you updates on her or me almost every time I see you."

"Texts? What is *texts*?" Iggy stared at me with a whatever-do-you-mean look that was as transparent as his excuses about needing a room here. No man needed three addresses, and Iggy had at least that. He was trying to guard us, and I knew it.

"Liar, liar, witch on fire," I sing-songed at him. "You are trying to protect me *and* Allie."

"If she'd stay in *Elphame*, she'd be safe."

I snorted. "*Would* she, though?"

The king had his eye on her, and—despite the love I felt for my husband—I was still of the mindset that I'd rather face an obvious foe than emotions. I couldn't speak of that particular pickle, though. The king had bound me to silence in a faery bargain. No one other than Eli was able to hear of the Fae King's absolutely monkey-balls bad idea to marry a volatile grieving widow with a big-assed gun in her designer handbag.

I couldn't decide if she was my hero or the dangerous relative I didn't want somedays. Mostly, I leaned toward both answers. All I could say for absolute certain was that my chosen-and-blood-family was a tangled knot inside a damn escape room with a bomb ticking somewhere.

"Thank you, by the way," I told Iggy. "For watching over her. She's important to me, and I like her in this world."

He stared at me, weighing my choice of words. "My vow, Hexen, that I will protect her as best I can."

I didn't doubt it. She had that effect on people, even those she'd threatened or attempted to kill. Allie, Alice Chaddock to most people, had injected me with *draugr* venom during her pursuit of the "mastermind" who had killed her beloved husband. The woman was ruthless, but she had become both my friend and employee--although I paid her nickels in comparison to her accumulated wealth. Still, she kept the pretense that it was a "job."

"At this hour, the widow is in her estate, out of sight, out of peril," Iggy said. "I would prefer that you were secured as well. Perhaps, you all can relocate to *Elphame* for a few decades until Chester is distracted."

Decades? Decades of hiding sounded terrible. Maybe if it was necessary to keep my friends and mother safe, and there were no other choices, but I was more of a "all paths lead to conflict" person than one who hid and waited. I'd find a way, and then Chester would die.

"So make them hide and abandon those who have careers here? Lives here? Businesses here?" I added another handful of bullets to my pocket, and I slipped a long knife into a holster on my thigh.

Since I was now outed as the future queen of *Elphame*, not many people grumbled over my public display of weapons. That was an unexpected perk of marriage that I was enjoying.

"I won't patrol tonight," I agreed. "Would you like to walk me to the bar?"

I knew I was as likely to shake him as a dog was to escape determined fleas, so the offer was more of an acknowledgment than an actual invitation.

Iggy bowed his head. "It is my honor."

Luckily, there were other ways to burn my excess energy. My husband was expecting me, and despite all of my impulsivity, I was not as foolish as my friends thought. I would be armed to the teeth, not just with magic. If I were unescorted at any moment, I had fae guards who had the audacity to start popping up—so weapons and lethal friends were my de facto normal since my wedding.

"You probably ought to leave me at the door," I added. "Eli's still scowling over your last set of crude remarks."

Eli still had moments of pondering Iggy's death. I'd like to have said it was getting better, but I tried not to lie. I'd also liked to have said it was unprompted, but Iggy had the ongoing tendency to try to provoke fights.

Iggy nodded and opened the door. "As you wish."

It hit me suddenly that Iggy's provocation was not simply to be an ass.

"You would like it if Eli felt threatened by you and took me to *Elphame*." I glared at Iggy as I pulled the door shut behind us. "You're trying to provoke him!"

I felt a hex drop over the apartment like an iron cage. That, of course, was the real reason Eli didn't grumble that Iggy stayed in my old apartment. The Hexen Master kept my home safe.

After several moments, Iggy admitted, "I would have liked to hide you away in the cave, but your Eli had to rescue you so . . . yes, I would like him to relocate you to safety. Is it so wrong to prefer you alive, Geneviève?"

I kept my mouth shut as we stepped into the parking lot. I saw faces peering down at me from the upper floors of the building. I'd had every neighbor vetted, but there was a gap between safe and friend. A lot of them were nosy, and more than one of them had sold photos of me to the tabloids. The upside was that if I vanished from my building, the world would know I was missing in about ten minutes.

"Grid." Iggy ordered from my side. "I shall watch for the living."

I felt a little foolish scanning for the dead. These days, they were all wary of me for some reason, but that was not likely to be the case every night and definitely not in every city. I could feel the presence of anything dead. It was useful for killing some and resurrecting others. And for reasons that I couldn't define—Iggy was still on that list.

He had a beating heart, but my magic still marked him as dead.

"You're becoming better at this, Hexen." Iggy's voice slipped into the tone he adopted when he was cajoling me.

"Hush."

He motioned for me to pause. "Roll out your grave magic. Visualize the grid. How wide can you take it?"

"A mile."

"Better. Concentrate on the streets, the river. . . can you follow them past that?"

As he spoke, I tried. I *was* getting better, but I sometimes felt like I had a map that was only able to be seen on a zoomed-in screen. We tried to push it wider, but even after several weeks of trying, I felt like the edges of my map faded to emptiness where *There be monsters!* or some such was mentally etched at the borders.

"Come now, Hexen. Adjust your vision for one more block." Iggy's voice felt like it was magic itself, as if he were dropping the knowledge inside my head.

When I opened my eyes, as usual, I saw the traces of deaths in purple splotches over my mental grid. I looked to the left, the right, and then pivoted to take in the other two quadrants of my map. Green was moving dead, and purple was a trail of death. Gold, apparently, were my loved ones. That was a new development the last week, and I felt vaguely irritated that my magic decided to "adopt" people.

"*Draugr?*"

"Not a one." I frowned. That was weird. I knew it, and Iggy

knew it. Maybe my Grandmother Beatrice had told all the biters to behave as a wedding gift to me. They'd been quiet lately.

"Where are your people?" Iggy pushed, as if I could hold my map indefinitely. "Locate them. Follow their recent trails, like footprints in ink on the map, and *see* them. Jesse. Sera. Christy. Alice. Lauren."

As he spoke, listing names one after the other in rapid fire, I followed their trails, seeing Jesse at Tomes and Tea, the bookstore I technically had a share in, and Sera at her coffee shop. Christy was at the bar, Bill's Tavern, which she managed. The bar was owned by Eli, who was there, too. Allie was at her house. My mother was with Beatrice—safe in The Outs far beyond the . . .

"Wait . . . Iggy!" I dropped the map and stared at him with a smile wide enough to hurt.

"As I said, you *can* see beyond the mile." Iggy's tone was nonchalant, as if he hadn't tricked me into making a leap of progress. "You think yourself into walls, Miss Crowe. I simply find ways to remove them. You are a talented hex—"

His words stalled as I threw my arms around him in a hug that left us both awkward.

I stepped back just as quickly as I had stepped forward.

"You are on the grid, too, you know," was all I said. "If I had to find you, I could."

Despite the pleased look that came over Iggy's face, he said, "Is that a threat?"

"You know it, Iggypoo." I shoulder-bumped him, but there was an undeniable comfort in owning the friendship we had created.

Assuming Chester didn't murder either of us, I could learn a lot with his guidance.

❧ 3 ❧

ELI

Eli became prickly the later it grew. Perhaps, he was perpetually prickly lately. He felt . . . settled being married, bonded with the one being in all of creation who completed him. On *that* front, he was content.

On the other hand, he had fallen impossibly in love with a woman who had a metaphorical ax ever-poised over her throat, and it wore on his mind. He hated that it was true, but he felt as if there were an endless sea of monsters that periodically found the mouth of the Mississippi River and lurched into New Orleans.

And Geneviève seemed to have a magnetic allure to them. They either wanted to worship her or destroy her. There was little middle ground.

He glanced at the door again. She wasn't late. *Yet*. He poured another drink, smiled, and reminded himself that she absolutely detested his tendency to hover.

"Boss? Do you want to call backup?" Christy, the bar manager but also one of the finest pool sharks in the city, gestured to the door where a pair of visibly intoxicated women were wobbling.

"Serve them water or soda." Eli grumbled at the drunk women.

The city had become increasingly intoxicated as the fangers started minding their behavior. It was great for tourism, but Eli suspected it looped right back to the aforementioned ax. Eli had suspicions as to why they'd done so, but he wasn't yet certain.

Beatrice gave Geneviève a crown.

The queen of the *draugr* gave the co-heir to the throne of *Elphame* a crown in public. And since that day, the biting in this city had been restricted to random barely-awake dead folk. There were no *draugr* to behead here.

Now, Eli wasn't confronting the queen of the *draugr*—or mentioning it to his wife just yet. He respected the subterfuge, if he were truly honest with himself. Beatrice had broken down Geneviève's emotional walls in a fraction of the time it had taken him.

Of course, *they* were blood family, and he had simply been a man in desperate love with a woman opposed to marriage. Eli wasn't convinced Geneviève would've gracefully accept that crown, though. For a woman who oozed power, she seemed to want nothing to do with it.

He looked at the door again.

Silently, Christy took his place at the bar as the drunks approached to order again—or to cajole him to give them a drink. Eli refused to roll his eyes at the attempts at seductive looks they were sending him. Honestly, what the average person knew about faeries—even now that the fae was all over the media—was ludicrously little. He had no desire to seduce or entice or entrap them.

Only one woman would ever evoke that urge in him. Such was the nature of marriage for his kind. Yet, ignorance persists despite easy access to answers, and so it had been for centuries. Some humans simply preferred ignorance.

Softly, Christy murmured something about "public relations"

and Eli's "image," and he wondered yet again if there was a way to convince his uncle that he simply wasn't suited to royal living. Subterfuge and fae politics seemed as pointless as human politics and fame.

Unfortunately, every conversation Eli had begun on the matter resulted in Marcus, king of *Elphame*, arguing that if Eli would simply stop being a tavern-keep this would be easily resolved.

There was no middle ground.

Eli glanced at the door yet again. There had been no attempts to kidnap or kill Geneviève these last twelve or so weeks. Much like the lack of *draugr* biting in the city, the relative quiet on that front had created an illusion of safety. But it was just that: an illusion.

Monsters would come for her as long as she was both a monster-killer and his bride.

If the world were to ever learn that she was even *more* than that . . . the monsters that would come would be armed with badges and governmental authority, instead of the usual magic and weapons.

"She'll be here," Christy said, catching his eye a few moments later. "Aren't you able to feel that she's alive?"

"Yes." If Geneviève died, Eli would drop where he stood—but there was a vast gap between alive and uninjured, and with Chester out there still, Eli couldn't relax.

4
GENEVIÈVE

The lull in conflict within New Orleans had stretched so long that the tourism was unprecedented, which was saying a lot for my home city. Laughter rang out, and for a flicker, I wondered if this was what it had been like here before the *draugr* had crept out of the proverbial grave. A city that still clung to a riotous joy, New Orleans left the worrywarts of the world to their funereal moods. Better to die laughing than cringing seemed to be our motto.

And I couldn't argue.

"I appreciate the lessons, Iggy," I said, breaking my silence finally. "I even understand why you want Eli to lock me away."

Iggy was silent as we walked through the city to Bill's Tavern. The bar was at the edge of the Marigny, which had more or less merged with the quarter sometime after the *draugr* became a problem initially.

"But?" he finally asked.

"I'm like a lot of people here. I won't stay hidden away, waiting for a monster to stumble on me. If death wants me, he's going to have to come armed and ready." I glanced over at him. "Maybe

Chester moved on now that he sees I'm not gunning for some power or influence."

"You don't believe that."

I sighed.

"And you gather power the way the moon gathers the sea," Iggy pointed out.

Poetic though it was, I couldn't argue efficiently, so I pointed out, "But I don't *want* it."

We crossed the darker area between the tourist heavy French Quarter and Frenchmen Street in silence. It used to be prime biting--or mugging—territory, so the city had offered the empty space at lower rent. Now, that space was filled with shops. They did the same at the area past Canal Street where there had been mostly businesses that were closed at night. That had meant too many shadowed doorways.

By about two years after the monster came to town—when many of the world's cities tried to build walls and ban monsters— New Orleans had simply expanded the light. The safe area extended from beyond Canal, through the Quarter, and beyond the bars on Frenchmen Street. We were far from *draugr*-free, but the whole Quarter, the edge of the CBD, and the edge of the Marigny were all well-patrolled. Once a tourist was safely in the patrolled zone, they were relatively safe. And the city's tourism shifted from tours of historic spots to haunts where our visitors could be titillated by a chance to see a real, unalive monster.

"I'm not saying I am hunting him down," I assured Iggy. Again. "I'm just saying that if he comes, I won't back down. It's not who I am."

I gestured at the city, crowds and shadows, laughter and hope. New Orleans was a con-woman and a survivor. We didn't roll up the sidewalks at dusk. We adjusted—and we thrived. Magic and monsters, booze and biters, revelers and risks, we had it all.

And I had the privilege of protecting the city.

"New Orleanians don't hide. We conquer," I pronounced,

suddenly certain that I was going to figure it out. This city had figured out pestilence, poverty, and politics. It wasn't always pretty, but I was built of sterner stuff than whatever Chester was made of. I wasn't going to seek power, but if I had it, I'd use it to survive—and protect my loved ones.

"I bid you adieu." Iggy's low voice broke into my thoughts as we closed the last half block.

"Thanks, Ig." I reached out like I might hug him, but he dodged me this time.

"Boss lady," the doorman greeted. "That one is not allowed inside."

He still gave us both a once-over. I knew the search for injuries was habit, but some nights it bothered me. I'd successfully avoided any proper attempts on my life for over eight months. Sure, there was a scuffle the night before my wedding, but that was going on twelve weeks ago now.

"No stitches needed!" I called in a loud voice as I did a little twirl.

At my side, Iggy stifled a laugh. "Go inside, Hexen. I am off to visit the widow before succumbing to well-earned rest."

"Be safe."

He bowed his head and gestured me onward. I felt a bit like a child at times when I was treated like I had to be handed from guard-to-witch-to-terrifying grandmother-to spouse. I knew it was because they cared, but I had spent the majority of my life beheading monsters.

Their overprotectiveness often made me snarl.

I stepped inside what was once my home away from home. Bill's Tavern was a standard but lovely tavern: polished wooden bar, low bar lights, and a remarkable liquor collection that had been custom designed for me when I hadn't yet noticed that Eli had been wooing me.

Yet another reason to fight.

It took less than three heartbeats for my gaze to find Eli's. I didn't need a map. I felt him as surely as plants feel the sun. He stood behind the bar, mixing drinks as if he was not royalty. It was a point of pride with him that he carried on with as much normalcy as he could even though his secret was public.

Heir to the throne, future ruler of every faery, and he'd rather mix cocktails.

He slid the drink to a patron, and then he stepped back as one of the other bartenders stepped forward to address the next order. Rational thought flickered and paused as he watched me weave between patrons.

Only an awareness that my ability to *flow*—move at the speed of the dead—was still a secret I had to protect kept my feet steady and sure. Okay, maybe the fact that if I ran I'd look desperate was a factor, too.

When I reached him, I didn't vault over the bar like I wanted to. I smiled and said, "Hi."

To my left I heard a laugh that I recognized as my friend Christy's, currently manager of the bar. "Newlyweds," she teased.

I made a rude gesture in her general direction, grateful that there was a "no cameras allowed" policy here.

I didn't look away from Eli, nor did I remark on the way his gaze traced my skin. I understood it more these days. His studious gaze was not doubt in my abilities but a need to know I was uninjured.

"Bonbon," he murmured softly. Eli watched me in a way that made me feel like I was a treasure he'd defend, a cause he'd uphold, and a gift he'd cherish.

"Take me home?" I hadn't meant for it to sound like a question—hell, I hadn't even meant to say it—but it came out that way.

He held my gaze. "Now?"

"Unless you cannot . . ."

Eli called out, "Car. Front door." Then he came out from behind the bar. "What do you need? Are you well or—"

"You. I just need *you*." I stepped into his arms, angled my head so I could whisper into his ear. "Naked. Soon."

His hold on me tightened.

I pulled back, but he caught my mouth in the sort of kiss that always made me suspect every other person I'd kissed had been imitating how kisses ought to be. Eli kissed like it was an art, and he was a master.

Someone cleared their throat, loudly, and Eli stepped back enough that there was space between us.

"Your car," the doorman said, not meeting my eyes.

Maybe I'd be embarrassed if the need in me wasn't mutual, but I knew that Eli wanted me as much as I wanted him. The best response—the only response—I had was to take his hand and let him lead me to the car.

Outside, he glared at his perfectly lovely car and pronounced, "I have ordered a larger car."

"Why? It's—"

"Not comfortable for sex."

My answering laughter was not at his plans or even at the fact that my publicly reserved spouse was glaring at the car, but at the joy that I felt realizing that he was as impatient as I was.

"Hands to yourself, divinity." He opened my door before walking around to the driver's side.

When he slid into the car, I agreed, "For the moment. You'd need to restrain me to keep my hands off you once we are home."

A glimmer in his eye made me draw a deep breath.

Never taunt a faery. It was dangerous. I knew that better than most people.

I was also a fan of danger. So I said, "I used vines to trap Iggy when we were fighting. And I was thinking . . ."

"Geneviève." Eli took a shuddering breath. "I would like you to be silent while I drive."

I laughed, but I bit my lip against taunting him again.

· · ·

At the house a few minutes later, I practically dragged him inside our home. Until Eli, I'd never used the *draugr* ability to flow for anything other than a fight. I wasn't as fast as the oldest *draugr* I'd met, but it was close now. I could move between one spot and the next with a speed that made it look like I'd teleported.

For a moment, I moved away from him—only long enough to strip out of the clothes I'd worn when fighting. I wanted no scent of anything, including another man's blood, on my skin. "I can shower too, if—"

"Hush."

I watched Eli walk toward me, sighing at the predatory gleam in his eye. I refused to look away. I *liked* looking at the desire announced clearly in his gaze.

"You're still dressed," I pointed out.

"Hush," he repeated.

Before I could answer, vines had lashed out and encircled my wrists, ankles, and waist. He watched me, giving me a chance to object.

Instead, I tugged to see if there was any slack and declared, "Oh no, I appear trapped . . . I guess I'm just a helpless damsel."

He grinned—and the vines lifted me, so I was practically levitating over him as if seated in an invisible chair. "Eli?"

He parted my knees, exposing me to his hungry gaze. Anyone else who had tried to maneuver me into a vulnerable position would have been lucky to be alive by now. Of course, no one else I'd been with had possessed the ability to use fae magic.

The vines tightened, keeping me exactly where I was even as my legs opened wider.

I could feel his breath, warm on my most sensitive parts, but he said nothing.

Without a word, he set out to show me that he craved me as much as I wanted him. He made me feel like I was the sexiest woman in either world. He was everything I wanted and needed, and he was worshipping *my* body as if I was a feast.

Finally, his hands clenched on my inner thighs, holding me steady as he drove me higher and higher.

When I reached that blissful peak, he held me to his mouth and pushed me toward more.

"Eli. . . Yes. Please. Yes. *Yesssss.*" I could feel him smile as I cried out, and my body trembled with the intensity of multiple orgasms.

Still, he didn't release me.

He looked up at me. My husband might claim that his needs were met by bringing me to joy, but that wasn't enough for me today.

So I held his gaze and whispered, "Good boy."

The flash in his eyes made me whimper, although I'd swear it was simply the shock of the vines extending so I was suddenly jerked eye level with Eli. My arms were overhead now, and my legs were spread wider than was strictly comfortable.

At some point he'd obviously dropped his trousers because in a blink, he was sheathed inside me.

My body was still clenching from my last orgasm, gripping him. I tried to move, but I was suspended in the air by vines. I had no purchase. The best I could do was lean my chest against his shirt.

"Take it off."

"The shirt or the restraint? Say the word and--"

"Shirt." I trembled that even when he was in control, even though I had the same fae magic and could end these restrictions as easily as he applied them, my beloved still required my consent.

He stayed buried deep inside me as he unbuttoned his shirt and dropped it to the floor. A beautifully challenging expression on his face made me want to taunt him again, but I knew that look. He was in control. I was restrained, and his hips stayed motionless.

"Please . . ."

He chuckled, and I let out a small animal noise at the perfection. We fit like he'd been custom made for my body.

More vines grew, creating a tether line to somewhere, and with those vines, he moved me toward him, then backwards, controlling every thrust with the fae-wrought vines—which left his hands free.

"I love you, Geneviève."

5

GENEVIÈVE

For the next few months, life continued on with a remarkable normalcy. I was more satisfied by married life than I'd dreamed ever possible. My magic was steady, and I was learning new hexes from Iggy. No one at all had tried to kill me in half a year now. It was almost enough to make me think that the *draugr* had vacated the city, and that Chester no longer wished for my death. Almost. I wasn't foolish, but I was being lulled into a safety that I'd never known, and it was beginning to make me anxious.

So I began to patrol more often, and my friends stopped asking for my schedule constantly. Eli still worried, but to be honest, I worried when we were apart, too. Not practical worries, but the randomness that comes of love—what if the increased tourism meant that there were robberies, or muggings, or mass shooting, or a car jumped a curb, or the bar caught fire, or . . . panic worries. I wasn't used to the intensity of such things, but overall, I told him where I was, and he told me where he was.

And we coped.

I texted Eli: "Patrolling. Meet at bar soon?"

"Want company?" He texted back.

"After patrol." I smiled. I always wanted his company, but this was just another routine patrol. No threats. No jobs. I honestly felt a little useless of late.

I tucked my phone away and glanced around the shadowed row of mausoleums. All the cemeteries in New Orleans were closed at night, so the only beings I typically encountered were the random angry, biting, recently arisen *draugr*. Since my wedding, fewer *draugr* were rising. I secretly wondered if there were reasons for this shift, but my attempts to ask my grandmother went nowhere fast.

There were still a few strays to behead, but it was rarely more than a moment's effort with such young ones. I still made my rounds at the various cemeteries a few times a week. I used the grid I'd been mastering to check the city on the other nights, but sometimes there was a part of me that grumbled if I was too long away from the soil that housed the dead.

I couldn't decide if it was necromancy or my *draugr* side.

Being great-granddaughter of the queen, as well as wife to the heir of the fae throne, seemed to inspire obedience. At least, so far, it did. Even the over-eager tourists had backed off after the wedding—in part due to the New Orleans Police Department arresting those who were too close to my home with Eli and in part because Eli and I were, apparently, boring.

But what they thought was boring, I thought was a vacation of the sort I'd never known. Life had, dare I say it, become *peaceful*. Tonight, the moon was only half-full, but there were lights that kept the majority of the shadows at bay. Summer was here, sticky and buggy, but it meant fewer tourists. *That* part was lovely.

I was relaxed enough that I'd begun debating a week's escape in *Elphame*—well, a week New Orleans' time. That was longer over there, as the times didn't align equally. It was the equivalent of a week's absence to those who were here in this world.

But my focus for the night was on closer matters. I had a date with my husband in about two hours, so all-in-all, it was as close to the picket-fence happily-ever-after as I ever even dared to dream of reaching. I had a partner who made me feel loved, respected, and thoroughly sated. I had friends, family, a career.

If I were the skipping sort, I'd be skipping through the tulips . . . errr, *graves*.

"Geneviève Crowe?"

I looked around. The caller had said my name in a way that sounded familiar, chastising and somehow accusatory. It was a skill to say my birth name in that way that made me think I ought to apologize. As a child I'd thought only my mother could do that, but Mama Lauren was safely on the estate of my great-times-great-grandmother Beatrice—who didn't bother with nuance. No one else ought to be speaking to me in that particular disap-pointed-parent tone.

"Geneviève?" the woman said again.

I didn't reply because a) there was no one I was expecting to see in among the graves and b) anyone I bumped into here among the dead might not be a friend.

"It *is* you!" she said.

Despite her tone, the woman approaching me from the shadows of the cemetery was not a familiar face. She was in her late-sixties, possibly seventies, hair set in the sort of old-fashioned rolls that came from goodness-to-Becky hot rollers. Support hose covered remarkable calves, and her plain black dress was topped with a sensible cardigan with big wooden buttons. She appeared to be a grandmother who still did a lot of walking to have legs like that.

"Ma'am?" I eyed her warily. "Are you lost?"

She tutted at me. "Do you know how many nights I had to prowl these wretched places to find you?"

I sent out a zing of magic, not attacking her of course, simply testing her *alive*-ness. One could never be too sure of heartbeats in a city with a solid *draugr* population, and grandmothers as old as she looked rarely had such shapely legs.

She smiled. "I'm not vermin. My ticker is still beating, and it doesn't even need a pacemaker to jolt me."

"Er, if you wander around in the dark too often, it'll need a lot more than a jolt." I motioned around the cemetery. "Things around here sometimes rise."

The stranger gave me the sort of smile typically reserved for the daft or drunk. "If that were the only dangerous thing out there, life would be easier. Things worse than fangers lurk, Geneviève."

And that's when I started to get worried. I glanced around, half-expecting to see members of the local hate-group, S.A.F.A.R.I., or maybe even an angry fae soldier. The former hated me, and the latter were determined to keep me safe at any cost since I had become their future queen. We'd recently come to an understanding about when and where I needed an entourage, but they were creatures who played word games, so rules were complicated.

"Who—" I didn't get a second word out.

When the taser hit me, I felt like the biggest fool I knew. Obviously, I had been looking in the wrong direction. That's what I got for underestimating a grannie who traipsed around graves.

I should've known my streak of no attempts on my life wouldn't last.

"The nice young man said that this model was enough juice to take down a rampaging bear." She crouched over me as I was trying to stop my body from vibrating on the ground like live wire.

I glanced back at her and muttered, "Badger balls."

Then I slammed my fingers into the soil and shoved magic into the ground. The electricity was making it hard to focus, and I didn't feel entirely at ease trying to grab a sword to stab a *human* old lady—despite the fact that she was continuing to shock me with more voltage than an average human body would be able to endure.

"To me," I ordered, summoning whatever dead were near, and here in Saint Louis Number One, there were quite a few corpses to raise. I concentrated on pushing my magic into the earth rather than trying to summon *draugr.* It took them a few moments to reassemble from the moldering bones and rags in the grave.

As long as I could stay alert long enough . . .

"Ah-ah-ah." She pulled a damp, stinking cloth out of her handbag and covered my mouth and nose. "That's not fair."

"Fuuuck . . ." My magic stopped mid-summoning, and my dead army fell back into their graves as I slid into unconsciousness from whatever nastiness was over my face.

The last thing I heard was a *tsk* and, "Language, Geneviève."

❦   6   ❦

ELI

Eli watched the door with a growing anxiety. Geneviève was rarely late, and if she was going to be late, she let him know. He looked at his phone. It was an expensive thing, modified to be used by one who was unable to handle steel or iron. No new texts. No calls. Nothing.

"Christy? Any calls on the bar line?"

Christy met his gaze. "No. Were you expecting Gen to call?"

"I'm going to the house. She isn't answering. Have the guards escort you home if Jesse isn't here—or . . ."

"Got it." She gave him the sort of commiserating smile that reminded him that she'd been through as many sleepless nights worrying over Geneviève as he had. It was oddly comforting. "I'll try Allie and Sera and Jesse to see if they heard anything."

"And Iggy," he added. He might dislike the formerly-dead witch, but that didn't mean he was unaware of the fact that Iggy was dedicated to Geneviève's safety, too. "I'll call Beatrice."

"Lead with 'she's not at the bar' please," Christy asked quickly. "I don't want fangers chasing away paying patrons. They can look for Gen elsewhere, but . . ."

"Agreed," he called as he headed to the door.

If Eli had developed an over-protective tendency toward any person other than Geneviève these last years, it was Christy Zehr. He'd hired her as manager because he trusted her implicitly—and for one of his kind that was a rare thing. Christy was a towering, brilliant Black woman who still worked freelance when the mood struck, and on more than a few off-shifts still hustled pool.

Maybe he was overreacting. Maybe she was asleep or working or . . . There were plenty of possibilities that included her being perfectly fine, but a nagging feeling persisted. He pushed his car as fast as was safe, and then he pushed it a little bit faster.

She's alive.

He knew that, at least, with surety. They were bonded. If she died, he died.

Alive means I can find her.

❧ 7 ❧
GENEVIÈVE

I woke hip-deep in a vat of water, strapped onto what felt like an old-fashioned chair.

From my half-submerged seat, I tried to take in my surroundings. Stone room, circular well of stones, no light save a few steel-enclosed fixtures, and from the feel of the room when I sent out magical feelers to search for the dead, my odds of an army were terrible. I found nothing dead that could hear me other than a few random mice.

The most troubled thing in my prison was directly overhead—a structure that honestly looked like a cross between a trebuchet and a child's teeter-totter on an old playground. In essence, it was a leverage device that had a fulcrum. The basic design enabled the person not soaking in a vat of cold water to plunge the victim—*me*—into the water.

"Dunking stool," I muttered.

The graveyard grannie smiled approvingly. "Well spotted, Geneviève. Ours is modelled on the Scarborough model."

"An educated kidnapper, how lovely." I tried to convince the dead wood of the chair to respond to my will, hoping my fae magic would deliver what I wasn't able to do with necromancy.

Nothing.

I tried to push through the chains, convince metal to answer me. That was a long shot, but I was lousy at being a prisoner.

No luck there either.

I looked at my captor and said, "Why?"

Honestly, there were a lot of things I could ask, but really, they all boiled down to that one question. Maybe if I understood, it would help me figure out what to do. Word games weren't high on my skillset, but I was desperate.

"Thou shalt not suffer a witch to live," she said cheerily. "You, Geneviève Crowe, are a witch. Your unholy congress with the Lord of Flies, Satan himself, is an offense to--"

"I only have congress with my *husband*," I interjected. "My lawfully wed, triply wed spouse. We had three weddings. I mean, really, I'm extra married if you--"

"To an unholy minion of the deceiver," she said, still sounding remarkably pleasant. "Prince of the deceivers. The fae are an aberration. The *draugr* you slay bought you some grace, but . . . Witch? Fae? Protected by the walking dead? You must confess, so you can die in a state of absolution."

"Murder is fine with you, I guess?"

"Oh, Geneviève. I'm here to *save* you from the prince of deceivers!"

I blinked at her, opened my mouth to ask whether she was saying Eli was a prince of deceivers or Satan was, but she dropped the lever and I sunk into tepid water.

Mouth full of saltwater, I thrashed, not able to do much other than panic.

I sucked at panic.

Give me a target, and I was happy to go forth into battle. Being helpless was really not my gig. At all.

"*Where are you?*" Beatrice's voice slammed into my mind.

"*Drowning.*" I tried to show her, but there's not a lot of detail when you are submerged in a vat of saltwater. So I added what little I knew: *"Dunking stool. Prisoner of an old lady."*

"Geneviève . . . how?"

The stool popped above the water, and I was left dripping wet, chained to a wooden dunking chair. I was also no longer able to thought-speak with Beatrice.

"You will forsake your evil master before you die, Geneviève." The woman gave me such a piteous look, bobbing her head and revealing that her hot-roller curls had been practically shellacked. "I want you to enter Heaven, which means you must be without sin and—"

My laughter buried her words. "You have me confused with someone else, Grannie. I have no sinful congress to repent. You want me to repudiate Satan? Done. 'Get thee behind me.' That's the words, right?"

The supposed nun sighed before saying, "I fear this will be a long night. We'll get you to atone, Geneviève Crowe. The Sisters of Purity and Redemption have yet to fail. Every witch atones before her death."

With that ominous proclamation, she affixed a ring to the other end of the lever and stepped back. All I could think about was the "every witch" part. How many people died at their hands? How could a person claim religious faith and still harm others? How did she see herself as righteous, but steal the freedom and lives of other people?

And how was I going to escape before I was added to the death toll?

I studied the room around me as I was left suspended in mid-air, chained to a chair over a vat of salt water, and Sister Purity—or whatever the batty old bird's name was—turned and tugged open a heavy wooden door that glided open on silent rollers. Beyond the door was an antechamber, what looked like a mud room, and beyond that was another wooden door. That one had a grate of metal bars so the person outside could see the face of the person on this side of the door.

"Sister Agnes," a man's voice said.

There, smiling his accountant's smile, was Chester—oldest living human, alchemist, murderer of the only reanimated Hexen I knew, and hater of yours truly.

That, more than anything else, made me question the likelihood of escape. It wasn't about the corrupt nuns, or the chains, or anything so mundane. The cold truth was that even if I were unchained, I wasn't certain I stood a chance against Chester.

Trapped and chained, I was fairly sure I was facing death.

※ 8 ※

GENEVIÈVE

I had tried to summon my fae magic, my necromancy, my *draugr* strengths. Nothing seemed to enable me to break free of the chair. I didn't know enough about alchemy to say if there was a spell, binding, or whatever other esoteric knowledge Chester had gathered to nullify my own magic. Alchemy was a field that was both credited as the source of early chemistry and affiliated with magic.

And alchemists were notorious for not correctly writing down spells, recipes, or instructions. They would leave an element out or transfer a detail, create a key that was specific to them or that had to be added to the information in a book to make it work. As such, the knowledge that I had learned was a lot of "maybe this would work if I had the key" mixed with "this feels like blatant misdirection." Chester being an alchemist already explained a lot about his personality.

It also meant that I was unable to undo whatever he'd done to bind my magic here.

Am I going to die here? The cost of being born a witch shouldn't be my life. That statement, I believed, ought to be true for most every category—with obvious exceptions like predators. In *that* case, I was intolerant. But to hold me captive because of my genetics was absurd.

Eventually, I must've drifted to sleep because I woke as another woman entered my prison chamber. This one looked barely out of high school, all spindly legs and arms, as if a scarecrow had decided to don a veil that exposed only the short fringe across her forehead.

"I'm Sister Beverly," she greeted. "I'll be your confessor for this session."

Without any other words, she flicked the ring off the lever.

I gasped for air as I plummeted back under the tepid salt water. The last nun seemed to have a sense of how long a person could safely hold her breath, but drowning was a very real fear as I tried to stay calm under the water. No magic. No rescue. Each moment my body was attacked, I weakened. No food. And if I *did* get set free, there was Chester.

There was a very distinct chance that I was going to die here.

I let my muscles relax as best I could. Panic wasn't the answer.

"Geneviève!"

At some point in the last hours, I'd convinced myself that I imagined talking to Beatrice, but now that I was under the water, I could hear her again.

"Geneviève!"

I mentally exhaled in relief and began to pelt images and words at her rapid-fire, *"Chester. Sisters of Purity and Redemption. Well. Stone room. Dunking chair. No windows. At least two stories."*

"Saltwater?"

"Yes!"

"Alchemy, Geneviève. You must—"

Whatever I must was interrupted by Sister Beverly dropping a wire into the saltwater, thereby electrocuting me. The chair was starting to the surface, so at least I could breathe.

I tried to gasp, but instead I screamed, choking on the electrified water, and convulsing.

Again and again, shocks jolted me.

I have no idea how long it lasted, but when the monstrous woman pulled me entirely out of the water, she was wearing thick black gloves and the sort of sadistic smile that no *good* person would have in that moment.

"Please . . ." My teeth were grinding together, and I was pretty sure that I couldn't stand even if I had a way to get free of my restraints.

"Confess! Repent!" She was grinning as she stared at me.

I was ready to confess to a host of things if it would make a difference. Being electrocuted wasn't on my list of things I ever wanted to experience again.

"What do you want me to say?" I managed to ask.

She nudged the wire bundle closer to the edge, not into the well but threatening it.

"What?" I repeated.

"By submerging you, the water and steel chains conduct the charge without burning you." Sister Beverly peeled off her gloves. "But don't worry, witch, you all burn in the end, either here or in the fiery pits of hell. You think consorting with the devil will save you but—"

"I do not and have not consorted with the devil," I said in a voice that was still far less steady than I'd like. "I am not what you think."

"Witch," she said.

Then the cruel nun—if that was even the correct word for a member of this random witch-torturing group—walked over to the door. "Monseigneur? I have had no luck with an admission of guilt. Shall I continue?"

The door opened, and this time, Chester entered the room. He was wearing priestly garb that was as convincing as a dress on a frog. A clerical collar didn't make a man holy.

He made the sign of the cross over Sister Beverly. "You are doing God's work."

The woman practically swooned at his attention. "I am His to command, through your guidance of course!"

Chester patted her face like she was some house pet. "Perhaps she will confess to me, my dear. Maybe she's too corrupt to share her vile words with an innocent . . ."

I scoffed, and Beverly eyed the wires at the edge of the well.

Chester, however, opened the door for her, and she took his cue to leave. I watched the door slip closed with a barely audible *thunk*.

"Geneviève Crowe. You vex me." Chester stared at me, and it was as if a mask melted from his features. The gentle monseigneur guise slipped away, and before me stood the arrogant duck pizzle that thought he could willfully destroy, kill, and maim.

Words aplenty buzzed in my head, but anger wasn't going to help here. I bit back my rage and waited.

After several silent moments, he folded his hands together as if in prayer and pronounced, "I've been pondering our dilemma. There are only a few options left to me since Beatrice pronounced you as her heir."

"She did *what?*" I asked, almost against my will.

"You were wed wearing her crown. That was an announcement," he said, as if it were obvious.

And maybe it ought to have been. I thought back to the wedding. I should've known Beatrice was making a statement when she placed that circlet of gems on my hair. *"This is not a veil. It is not a fae crown. It is in place of those things."*

Leave it to Beatrice to fail to mention what she was doing. *Fucksicles.* After centuries of answering to no one, Beatrice was obviously not keen on sharing all her machinations. And honestly, I resembled that trait far too much to be truly upset with her— but right now, I was *really* wishing she'd told me.

"I do not want to appear unreasonable," Chester said. "A war with *draugr* and fae aligned would be untidy."

I swallowed. *Untidy?* Not impossible, merely untidy. What did it take to be so arrogant that you thought even the non-humans united would be merely *untidy*?

I could not imagine such a thing.

Admittedly, I'd killed a lot of *draugr*, but I'd come to realize that they weren't all bad—or maybe Beatrice simply kept them in order, so I saw that side of them now. Honestly, I wasn't sure. Slaughter on a widescale seemed *bad*, though. That part, I knew for sure.

"I could kill the prince, ending your life that way," Chester continued as if musing idly. "Again, I think *draugr* and fae would unite to attempt to strike me. It is not your death that is inconvenient, simply the consequences. . . which brings us to the dilemma that prompted our appointment here today."

He stared at me, as if I was to participate in his monologue. What was I to say, though? I wasn't exactly onboard with my death.

Several moments passed in silence, and I had to remind myself that threatening him was *not* the solution I was seeking. He was such a piss-ant of a man, though. The first time I'd seen the son-of-a-weasel in person was when he'd been at Tomes and Tea arguing with Jesse—and then, I'd thought him merely obnoxious.

The next time we'd crossed paths was when he was shredding files at the *draugr*-run spa last summer. By then, I knew he was something more than I'd realized when the king of *Elphame* objected to me striking him. Chester—a suit clad, briefcase carrying, plain-looking man—was singing a sea shanty, and his interest in me resulted in the king threatening to kill me, even if it meant killing Eli, to protect his people from Chester.

Sometimes the worst monsters hide in plain sight, dressed like regular men.

If I had any doubts as to his heinousness, Chester clarified matters when he left the queen of *draugr* bloodied and bruised.

Whatever else he was, Chester was not predictable. He'd created a persona of being harmless, an accountant-type-of-guy—

but before all of that, he'd murdered Iggy and handed Beatrice over to die in an attempt to create a hybrid.

Now he was my captor.

Nothing about this situation was looking good, and no amount of common sense was left in my mind when I grinned at him. *When all the logical paths are gone, it's time to try the illogical ones.* Chester, for all that I didn't know, was obviously fond of order, structure, control, which meant I wanted to take that away.

"Do the *good sisters* know what you are?" I asked.

Chester graced me with a chilling look. "Do *you?*"

I repressed a shudder. I didn't. I had pieces I'd spliced together, but that was the best I had. And none of those pieces left me with a lot of hope for escape. He frightened *draugr* and fae and the Hexen Master.

And I was his captive.

"What would it take to convince you to set me free?" I asked, not because I wanted to negotiate, not because I wanted to align with him in any way, but because my death would mean Eli's death. That was all the motive I needed to bite my tongue and attempt civility.

"That's better," Chester said, sounding like he was talking to a dog that learned to roll over.

I ground my teeth in irritation. *Not your bitch, Chester.* I let myself think the words I couldn't yet say out loud. I'd try to negotiate, but there were limits to how far I was able to be broken, and he was getting close to finding them.

I didn't want my spouse to die because I was careless, but there was some wiggle room between careless and surrender. I just needed to find it.

9

ELI

By the time Eli walked into the house—hoping to find Geneviève asleep or distracted—he was approaching panic.

"Geneviève? Are you here?" he called.

Instead, he found her assistant, the indominable Alice Chaddock, at the counter in the kitchen. Finding Allie there was more commonplace than not. She took her role as Geneviève's caretaker, assistant, and food source *very* seriously. What was not typical was seeing silicone trays in the shapes of penises, hearts, and skulls. Dozens of tiny phalluses were filled with blood.

"Alice?"

"Where's Geneviève?" Allie looked around as if she was with him. That answered Eli's question on whether she was here.

"Not with me, which is—"

"I need to talk to her about . . . things." Alice fluttered her hands around. She was uncommonly agitated.

"If by 'things,' you mean why you are making blood cubes, I would like that information, as well, but first—"

"Is she at the apartment?" Alice asked.

"I have no idea. I was hoping *you* knew where she was. We were to meet at the bar, and she didn't show . . ."

"She has to be fine, Eli. She *has* to. I need to . . . I need her to be fine. I have a schedule. Disaster? Not on it." Currently, Alice had a gallon jug of blood, a ladle, and her collection of silicon ice cube trays.

"Alice? I have questions." Eli gestured at the blood cubes, hoping that the blood was not because Alice knew that Geneviève was injured. In a purposely calm voice, he asked, "Has something happened that you think she'll need quite so much blood?"

"No. Yes. I mean, I'm taking a trip. I have been saving up for this." Alice pointed at the trays. "They're labeled. I gathered a few pouches from Lady Beatrice, too. I know fresh is better, and I have made arrangements to have deliveries too and—"

"That's *your* blood in a vat."

Alice sighed. "Correct. My blood. A few others. Deliveries scheduled. An itinerary updated." She glanced over to the fridge where her schedule—color-coded—was hanging. "Two weeks. I just need . . . time."

Eli cleared his throat. "Are you going to *Elphame?*"

"No. I am most definitely not, and I won't tell you where I am going either." Alice closed her eyes for several moments, and then she met Eli's gaze. "I won't have either of you telling *him.*"

"By him you mean my uncle. The king."

"Obviously. I need time to think about his lying, manipulating—"

"The fae don't lie," Eli interjected.

Alice carefully filled another tray; this one was grinning skulls. "You're the boss' guy. I like you and all. That doesn't mean *you* can lie to me either."

He opened his mouth, but she spoke over him. "Forcing Geneviève to not tell me he thinks he can just decide to marry me? That's not fine. And as much as I trust Geneviève, and *I hate going away*, I can't stay here right now."

Eli held up his hands in a non-threatening gesture. "Where *is* Geneviève? We can discuss my uncle later, but I need to locate my wife."

"Work? With friends? With Lady B? Just call her and ask where she is." Alice glanced back down and slid over an empty tray. This one was rows of tiny little penises. "This set of blood is from Tres. I thought it would be useful to let her know these are *draugr* blood . . . and he's a guy so—"

"Alice . . ."

"What? I know fresh blood is best, but I'm trying to make sure she's taken care of while I'm away!" She gestured wildly at the blood she was ladling into penis trays.

Eli reached out and turned her bodily, so she saw the clock on the wall. It was already four in the morning. "Geneviève is out of touch, and I would like your assistance in contacting her."

"Well, shit." Alice washed her hands and snatched up her phone. "No messages. Can you do that mental talk thing or something?"

"No." Eli grabbed his phone and jabbed a button. "I need to speak with Beatrice."

Alice wandered away and started making calls. Friends. Family. He heard her tell someone, "The boss is never this late without letting me know. I need all eyes on her. Find her."

Eli wasn't listening. Alice was saying things he already knew, reasons he'd come here. The next best option was Geneviève's family.

The *draugr* queen answered. Without greeting or preamble, she started, "I have little information. She is a captive, and all she said was that she was drowning."

Beatrice sounded as desperate as Eli felt.

"*Drowning?*" Eli raised his voice. The prince of *Elphame* never raised his voice this frequently until meeting Geneviève. "She can't. This is not acceptable. We have to do—"

"I am doing all I can," Beatrice snapped.

When Eli disconnected the call, he glanced at Alice. "Drowning. My wife is apparently drowning." Then he made a gesture in the air and a shimmering doorway appeared. "I will be back with guards to start a search. Beatrice has already deployed her . . . people."

Alice started shoving the tiny skulls, dicks, hearts, and other shapes into the freezer. "I'll be here while you go there, but do not tell that lying liar that I'm leaving the city."

When Eli stepped into *Elphame*, he saw his uncle's expression brighten before the passageway closed. He started to speak, calling out to Alice, but she pivoted and stomped away.

And Eli let the passage close.

"Geneviève is miss—"

"She is not. Your Death Maiden is held by Chester," the king of Elphame pronounced with a sigh that sounded far older than usual.

The confirmation of his fears did nothing to ease the panic welling in Eli's chest. He shoved it aside. *Plan now, panic later.* "Well, we need guards. You should stay here, so one member of the royal line is secure, but—"

"No." Marcus interrupted.

"Uncle, you may be a warrior, but she's my bonded mate. I can access some of her gifts."

Eli started to walk toward the armory, but his uncle caught his shoulder forcefully. A cold wash of fear joined the panic Eli was trying to ignore. It grew as he met his uncle's gaze.

"No, you may not take guards." Marcus moved to block Eli's path. "To engage with Chester is to invite violence that I cannot allow. I warned her that—"

"You warned my wife not to be kidnapped?" Eli stepped away from his uncle, his king, his supposed family. Family was not to abandon family. That was a betrayal that went beyond machinations and politics.

Marcus seemed somehow not to realize that his nephew was plotting violence in that moment. *Are there lines I would not cross for Geneviève?* Maybe not everyone loved wholly, but Eli was fae. His very soul, his history and his future, had been bonded to Geneviève.

"I understand that this is distressing, but this is more proof that marrying her was unwise. I warned her that her trio of heritages was unstable, dangerous, and I explained that Chester was a danger to you. To our people."

"You spoke to my wife about Chester," Eli clarified.

"Of course. To kill you is to kill her. I had hoped for another answer, but I must insist that you stay here, Eli. If we sever your matrimonial bond, there is a chance you might live." Marcus gave him a sad smile, as if this was all just an unfortunate situation, and then he continued, "I understand that this was not the plan you had. You outwitted me in order to wed her, but I have an idea of how to sever this. Chester offered me this answer. You can be free and alive—"

"Absolutely not." Eli turned away from him and shredded the sky, opening the gate home with such force that it made a tearing noise. He had already started to step forward when the king called out.

Eli glanced back at Marcus.

"If you leave, you are not welcome here until this threat is contained," Marcus threatened. "Chester is stronger than any one species. Every person who went against his wishes, including his wife and countless others, learned that too late."

And though it hurt to speak the possibility, to even consider his wife dying, Eli had no doubts at all about his commitment. He shook his head.

"I stand with Geneviève. If she should die, I wish to follow her. There is no life here without her. I renounce you and *Elphame* until you are willing to protect your *heirs*."

The look of shock on his uncle's face was the only victory Eli had in this moment. Let him be worried over his kingdom.

"Perhaps now is the time to father my own heir," Marcus threatened. "I have found my bride and—"

The king's words were lost as Eli gave a humorless laugh. "Good luck with that. Ms. Chaddock *adores* Geneviève. You think that *your* needs outweigh others' *rights*, uncle, but Alice—much like Geneviève—is a fully formed person with opinions. I waited on Geneviève, and she eventually chose me. You ignored Alice's wish by trying to woo her when she said she was not ready. And you sentenced Geneviève, Alice's friend, to death at an enemy's hands. You are about to reap what you've sown."

Then Eli stepped through the gateway to the home he shared with Geneviève. Nothing, no heritage, no risk was worth letting go of Geneviève. Death would be preferrable to giving her up without exhausting every option. And if she *did* die, he wanted no part of this world without her.

Eli looked around the house, not surprised that Alice had left —or that Beatrice now stood there waiting. For all he'd had his discomforts with the undead woman, Beatrice understood love.

"I assume we are in accord? I am ready to do whatever it takes to free her," Beatrice pronounced.

"Of course."

She nodded and walked toward his main room. Eli followed her without hesitation. The queen of the *draugr* was dressed in what looked like a motorcycle suit from a racetrack—except hers was black, as if she were an assassin. Oddly or not, that gave him a flash of comfort. Beatrice was already prone to violence, and now someone had threatened her granddaughter.

"How do we find her?" Eli asked, gesturing to the map of the city that she was now unrolling.

"I will rip every door from every building if I must. I have servants aplenty." She pointed to the edge of the city. "Few buildings have structures that are deep enough to submerge her vertically. We start here, and go street-by-street until—"

"Are you trying to have the militia deployed to our city?" Eli shook his head. There had to be a plan other than brute force. If they learned of what she was, the government had the ability to steal her away, too.

Beatrice gave him the sort of look angry gods gave the least of creatures, and he was glad that such a being wanted to protect Geneviève.

Carefully, he put his hand over his grandmother-in-law's hand where it rested on the city map. "We'll find her."

"Blueprints!" Mama Lauren called as she came through the door. Her arms were filled, as were Jesse and Christy's arms.

Surprisingly, Roisin and Sera followed, with Iggy trailing behind them.

"I can think of six places that had stone walls and weren't torn down, Bea." Iggy glanced at Eli as if to ask if he was allowed to stay.

"Anyone who can help us find her is welcome," Eli said, answering that silent question.

"She mentioned *Sisters of Purity and Redemption* and at least two levels to the building. Her prison has no windows, saltwater well, stone, and a dunking chair," Beatrice said.

"No basements, though," Iggy reminded them. "Something like a Creole townhouse with a courtyard converted to a create the illusion of an ancient structure."

"So one with a courtyard we can't see on the outside? That could be anywhere," Sera interjected.

"Agreed. It would be faster if we tore down doors," Beatrice grumbled even as she starting to scour blueprints. "We give this one hour before we do it my way."

Better the threat we can try to overcome than do nothing now in fear of the threat that might come.

Eli nodded. "So be it."

And so they began sorting through architectural plans, historical buildings, and potential other lairs.

No one, even Chester, would separate Eli from Geneviève, and this odd collection of people felt the same way. They would die before abandoning her, and he just hoped there was a plan that didn't include that fate.

10

GENEVIÈVE

"Once your marriage is dissolved," Chester pronounced smugly, "you will be less of a problem. Being the heir to the *draugr* throne and a witch is not enough to be a true bother to me."

An image of Beatrice flashed from my memory. Her eyes had been swollen and blackened. Her lips were bruised and cracked, and he'd attacked her brutally enough that the powerful *draugr's* arm had dangled at an angle that was far from natural. Witch and *draugr*, ancient and clever, Beatrice was still overpowered by Chester.

Without the magic that came from being bound to Eli, I *would* be less of a threat. I would also be dead—because there was no doubt in my mind that Eli wouldn't choose life over love. If he was that sort of person, I wouldn't be his wife. Foolish man that he was, he chose me despite knowing that I was besties with danger and destruction.

I stared at Chester, trying to fully process his suggested solution. It made as much sense as asking a lion to become vegetarian.

Carefully, I asked, "So you think that my spouse, that *Eli*, is going to forsake me?"

"Women overestimate their importance." Chester smirked, looking like every skeezy businessman I'd ever met. So sure of his misogyny and arrogance. So sure that his attitude was universal. How sad it must be to hate women so much!

But the logic that said it was pitiful did nothing to quell my rage. I wanted to throat-punch him, which was just one more motivation to escape the damn witches' chair.

"You're all interchangeable," Chester continued. "A warm nothing on chilly nights. Some thinner or older or more talkative, but in the end, a man will choose life over a woman every time. He may lie and say otherwise, but your Eli? He's in *Elphame* with the ritual I gave his uncle to sever your tie."

I felt tears build in my eyes—not because I thought Eli would agree to end our marriage but that he would be faced with an awful situation. I had no doubt that Eli was now aware of who held me prisoner, and that he was furious.

I'd feel the same.

People were not interchangeable.

The arrogant ball sack in front of me said, "There. There. The good news is that as only two heritages, you are no longer as likely to require my attention. You might even survive. If you're lucky, I could potentially never see you again."

My mind was still rolling over the horrible things he'd said and revealed. I needed to focus on the *now*, but worries filled me about what came next. Once I was free of Chester, was I going to need to rescue Eli from his former home? I had doubts that the king would send Eli back here to die if he had a way to save him— and I understood that impulse. Saving Eli mattered more to me than surviving, but the truth was that I no longer thought I could agree to such a ritual. The thought of losing that part of me, the part that was *us*, was fundamentally abhorrent.

"Why can't I go free then?" I smiled, attempting to seem harmless. I had a lot of practice at that. I still sucked at it if the expression on Chester's face was any indication.

"No rage that he has forsaken you?" Chester eyed me suspiciously. "I expected more."

I shrugged, hoping I could lie well enough to trick him, and as I'd learned from the fae, a truth made the lie sound more believable. "Do you know *why* I ended up married?"

Chester stared at me.

"He made a faery bargain," I said, truthfully. "I promised him a kiss, and then suddenly I'm choosing between weddings and freedom. I never wanted to get married. I *like* sex, but the idea of just one partner . . .? Forever? That wasn't my plan."

I was skirting a line that was near enough to truth that I could see Chester buying it. I pushed back the rest of the truth—the part that admitted my plan wasn't as good as reality—and smiled at the man in front of me. *Convincing. Believe the lie, Gen.*

I thought about the person I was before marriage, terrified of commitment even though I could not stay away from Eli. That person, that version of me, was good at self-deception.

"I'm a *witch*," I said. "We aren't known for fidelity, you know."

"True."

I watched his eyes narrow. "If I recall, you met my ancestor? Beatrice. Not really a monogamous woman, was she?"

"She was far from the first witch I met," Chester muttered.

I nodded, filing that detail away to ponder if I survived the next hour. His hatred of magical women spanned back a while.

"So you can set me free," I said with a shrug. "Easy peasy. I go back to my real life. I certainly had no interest in being a faery queen. Protocol, rules, *yawn*."

With a gesture the chains around me loosened. I stifled a gasp of surprise. *Was it really going to be this easy?* For the oldest human, he was certainly carrying a few centuries of misogyny in his pocket. Not so different from a lot of middle-aged men who thought they ought to have all the power!

The easiest way to deal with them was to feed their fears, pretend you agreed with their nonsense. More than a few bigots and misogynists were pliable if a person simply let them think they were *validated*. Entire political parties were built on fear. A few years ago, members of one political group even pretended that they were subject to "witchhunts," as if *being* the haters was the same as being the victims.

It felt good to play him. It felt like I might—

"Wait." Chester froze the saltwater with a hex whispered so silently I couldn't hear it. Then he gestured me forward.

Once I was standing in reach of him, I took a step toward the door. "Right, well, glad we got that settled. I'll be go—"

"A vow." Chester withdrew a knife from his pocket. It looked like a child's toy, a pocketknife with a dark handle. "You cannot leave without it."

I paused. I wasn't interested in a vow with *him*. Maybe I could entice him into a faery bargain instead. If a bargain is begun, the fae making the bargain knows what the bargainer most desperately wants.

In an intentionally nonchalant voice, I suggested, "Before the ability is gone from me, why not enter into a faery bargain?"

Chester looked at me, curious in that way that said this was new to him. "What terms?"

I held my breath as his greatest desires flooded me. He wanted to be the most powerful being in the world, and to do that, he had to eliminate me. Mostly, though, he wanted to be sure no one ever found what he had hidden. He wouldn't be safe if they did.

But then he said, "No. Faery bargains may hold or not after you are unbound. We shall make a blood vow instead. I will not strike you, and you will not strike me. I'm not so green as to trust the word of a witch—*or* a woman."

I blinked at him. None of the terms he proposed were his greatest desire.

As he rejected the idea of a bargain, I couldn't see more details. I only knew that there was a ruined building on an island. There, the whatever-it-was had been hidden. I thought about the details, committing them to memory. The sign was weathered. Last he'd visited, the site was marked by a Historic Scotland sign.

Damn.

Everyone knew that Scotland was one of those places where historic sites were ubiquitous. Throw a bone; hit archaeology. What I needed was to find that place, that hidden thing. Weapon to stop Chester? Yes, please.

First, I needed to get out of this prison. Could I flee without getting caught? I looked toward the door. It was *so* close. If I could get it open, I could *flow*.

That was it. My magic was low, trapped and stifled in this place, and my stomach was yowling for food. Fighting when I'd been electrocuted, starved, and imprisoned—and oh yeah, partially drowned—was not ideal.

But *flowing* was no different than walking because I was *draugr*-born. It was magic but not in the hex throwing way. I should still be able to do that.

I glanced at the door, weighing my odds. He'd frozen the water with a word, removed my restraints with a word. He was powerful in ways no other creature I knew of had been.

If I couldn't escape this place, there was no chance of surviving.

"Miss Crowe."

I glanced back at him, still trying to decide if I could make a run for it.

"It was not a request." Chester slid the knife across his forearm, as he said lightly, "Hands are an unwise place to carve upon an alchemist. You may use yours or your arm, as you are only a witch."

"If I was only a witch, why are we here?" I asked quietly.

When I didn't move, he gave me a look that was colder than the worst *draugr*. His innocuous businessman guise slipped.

Whatever he'd tried to be, he was still a monster in a way that even the monsters I knew couldn't touch.

He killed Beatrice.

He killed Iggy.

He would kill Eli.

I eyed Chester. *Would anyone be safe from him?* Then I affixed a smile. "Women's lib! I do my own cuts. Thanks ever so."

Chester stepped closer, and my fangs dropped.

Not the time. Not the damn time, teeth!

I pressed my lips together tightly, hoping he didn't see. My necromancy was not secret; neither was my importance to Beatrice. He didn't need to know I was already fanged. That was to only happen to dead *draugr.*

Of course, as far as anyone knew, all *draugr* were dead.

My stomach growled again. His blood smelled rich, like magic and violence. A part of me that I tried to suppress roared to life, and my gaze was fixed on the blood welling up so slowly on his skin. I could try to run, but a wicked voice, my own voice, reminded me, "He's human."

Humans were excellent snacks.

"I thought you were a necromancer," Chester scoffed, reaching for my arm and stepping closer to me. "Let me."

But the scent of his blood was like a feast in front of me. *Why the hell not?* I gave over to that darker impulse, and I *flowed*—not to the door, though. I *flowed* toward him. Mouth open. Teeth oozing venom like I was wholly *draugr.*

A last thought shoved into my mind: was this new hunger because Eli had severed the bond? Had this man stolen my husband? Without the fae bond, would I be more *draugr?* That fear added to rage.

I latched onto Chester's throat and tore. Meat filled my mouth, and I spat it out before biting again.

Chester couldn't speak because I'd ripped out his vocal cords. I made a mental note to thank Iggy for that lesson a few months ago, but then I launched at Chester again and again, moving like a *draugr* that had become a berserker.

I squeezed, milking his body like a rag that I was wringing out. If I hadn't got the jump on him, I'd be dead, but I had. And my sneak attack was going to either free me or kill me.

Fear of what would happen if he escaped my bloody grasp added to my berserker fit.

I swallowed, drinking down blood that was carrying memories of magic and places and things. It was a tangle in my head that threatened to choke me, but every time I tried to stop, his throat knitted back together. If he could heal this fast, he could kill me.

I cannot let him do that.

Time passed, and I had no idea how long. Finally, though, the blood I'd gorged on threatened to come up, and I could swallow no more. He was already trying to speak, opening his mouth, grabbing for me.

We were drenched in red, though, and I slipped away.

I *flowed* to the door, jerked it open, and *flowed* through the city.

My mind was a barrage of noises. Beatrice. Eli. Chester's victims. It was noise of the sort that I couldn't contain. All I knew was that I had to get home, to Eli. I had to gather my family together so they could flee—whether they agreed or not.

When I tore open the front door of my home, I *flowed* inside. Assembled there with maps and weapons were all the people I needed.

Eli.

Mama Lauren.

Jesse and Christy.

Sera and one of the fae guards, Roisin.

Iggy.

Beatrice.

"Geneviève?" Eli said, carefully reaching out toward me. He

pulled me toward a chair. "Where are you injured? Talk to me. I can grab the kit, but I need words, love."

"I was trapped," I said softly, concentrating on each letter, each word. It was easier simply because Eli was in front of me. Slowly I explained, "He . . . Chester . . . helped Marcus so you would abandon me."

"I would not. I *did not*." Eli took a glass of water and poured it onto a stack of linen napkins. He did not flinch away from my blood-soaked body. Instead, he said, "Let's see were the wound—"

"That is not her blood." Beatrice *flowed* toward me and stared down like a warrior goddess glowing with pride. "You make my heart proud, Daughter of Mine."

"Touching as this is," Iggy pronounced loudly. "Our enemy is not dead, and none of us want to be in his path. She"—he pointed at me—"needs to get the hell out of Dodge. You and me, Bea? He'll come for us next." Then he made a sweeping gesture. "Friends. Family. Chester will slaughter everyone you love. All of the dead."

"Run," I whispered. "We're going to run."

"Together? And make ourselves into a big target? *Great* idea." Iggy paced. He pointed at my family. "They're defenseless. We need to *hide* them somewhere."

Roisin spoke up, "My vow, prince and princess, that I will take these to safety. I will not abandon you." The last was said to Sera. "My home is yours."

Silently, Sera reached out. "I would be happy to have more time with you."

Jesse and Christy looked at me, and the weight of keeping them safe was daunting. "Go with them. Take Mama Lauren."

"Why can't we all just go there?" my mother asked. "Or I stay with your grandmother and—"

"Queens do not run," Beatrice said. "I stay to fight."

"Please, I need you safe, Mama Lauren," I said louder. "Grandmother would be an asset in a fight that I would appreciate. You . . . I cannot risk you."

"Those who *can* go to *Elphame,* do go. Those who cannot . . ." Eli interjected, cutting off what was about to be an emotional outburst.

I shot him a grateful look.

He continued, "Your safety matters, and you will be safe over there. Chester has no grounds to pursue any of you there. Only Geneviève, Beatrice, Iggy, or me. We stay here."

Tears tracked through the blood that was all over my face, turning the salty sorrow pink. I understood the fear that they were abandoning me to a dire fate. It wasn't unfounded.

"There is a weapon that can contain him," I told my mother. "But I cannot protect you and go find it. Please. Go where you are safe while I deal with this."

My mother hugged me, coming away with blood on her arms and dress but not hesitating or flinching from it. "I'll be at your home over there. Waiting for you to come to us." Her voice sounded like an order, but there was a catch in it, all the same.

She hugged Eli and Beatrice, next, trailing blood between us as if it were nothing of note. Witches and mothers, they were made of stern stuff.

Finally, Mama Lauren gestured to Roisin. "Well, let's get going."

The fae guard looked at my mother with a bemused smile, but she still led them toward a wider space and in a blink, they were all gone. Safe in *Elphame.*

Then it was only Beatrice, Iggy, Eli, and me. I'd realized that Eli's words answered my questions about his conversion with his uncle.

That's when it hit me. "Allie! Did she already go to *Elphame?*"

"No." Beatrice exhaled. "She left. I cannot tell you where she is, but . . ." Then she paused. "We will go to her once we secure our weapon and kill Chester, though." Beatrice glanced at Eli and asked, "That is not me lying to her, yes?"

"Correct," Eli said.

My grandmother stared at me, seeming less terrifying and more upset. "Bathed in the blood of your enemy. It is a fearsome look, but humans . . . they will be alarmed. I have learned this. Bathe. Then we will depart. We have a few hours to make our escape. I have a vehicle all ready for this plan."

Iggy sighed. "I have hesitations, Bea."

She shot him an angry look.

He held up his hands and added, "But I have no better plan."

I wanted to ask questions, and I wanted to go immediately. I hated to waste time, but a few minutes would remove the gore and allow me to try to clear my mind. That seemed necessary.

Ultimately, it was not my decision. Eli took my hand and led me to our bathroom, so I could wash away Chester's blood.

❧ 11 ❧

GENEVIÈVE

Within our bathroom, plants bloomed, and light filtered in through skylights. The ground was covered in grass. Behind the plants was a marble rainfall shower to rinse off anything nasty before climbing into the tub. I'd made use of this bathroom even before this had become my home. A number of the plants were fae-origin, so they were sensitive to blood and any outside contaminant.

The shower was my first stop: wash away Chester's blood.

"I can pack a few things if you want privacy." Eli gestured to the marble rainfall shower behind plants as if to encourage me to go into it, but I needed a moment.

I stripped out of the blood-stained things and shoved them into a contaminates bag. Yes, we had those here at home. There were small practicalities in both this and my original apartment because my life included violence. Violence often meant blood.

"Do you need any stitches?" Eli asked, peering at me. "Are there *other* injuries? Bones broken? Anything . . . internal? Or that you didn't want to mention in front of your family?"

I realized then that our usual connection was tamped down. I often felt Eli, and our shared bond, like a buzz in my brain. "No. Nothing. I was dunked, shocked, and that's . . . it."

"Shocked?"

The memory of live wires in the saltwater was enough to make me flinch. "A lot. Shocked a lot."

"My love . . ." Eli took a long silent look at me. "I wish I could've been there, taken the pain or something."

"Honestly, the worst thing was that he said you were breaking our bond," I said in a shaky voice. "I was afraid, not that you actually would but that Marcus would trap you or try to force y—"

"I told my uncle I'd rather die than lose you," Eli said, staring at me like I was the loveliest thing in the world even though I was dressed in blood.

I stepped into the shower, letting the water wash away some of the nastiness.

In the far end of the room was an enormous tub. It was cut of one stone, and a small waterfall poured down the wall as if nature had been captured inside. It seemed more like an indoor pond. I admitted to myself, though, that I didn't really want to be in a tub after being dunked in one.

I glanced at Eli, thinking about him joining me. "I would like you near me."

As I turned, he grimaced. "You have a burn . . ." He gestured at my now blood-free chest where the chain links had charred my skin.

"Restraints. Electricity. Water." I sighed. "I wish I could've killed him."

"We'll find a way," Eli pronounced.

Honestly, I appreciated the way Eli looked and acted, but his clarity and strength were equally treasured. He didn't ask me to be anything other than what I was. He didn't find my dangerous life off-putting enough to abandon me. He was the steadiness I cherished, the strength that completed me, the calm that let me rage.

"Join me?" I asked as the water sluicing over me started to run almost clear. It wasn't sexual. I think we both needed the simple assurance of skin-to-skin reminders. We were here. We were together. We were alive.

My husband stripped and stepped into the shower. Without saying a word, he took a bottle of shampoo and began to wash my hair. One of the parts of marriage that not enough people address is that these rituals of caretaking, these basic acts of cherishing one another, were just as important as the grand gestures or explosive sex. I liked the other parts, too, but there was something amazing about all the tiny gestures. Grand gestures were easier, flashier, but true love included reminders every day that said "you are treasured" or "let me show you that I care."

Afterward, Eli smoothed ointment of some sort on my burns. It smelled like earth, but it slid on like crushed pearls. Iridescent and cooling, the paste seemed to sink into my skin and erase pain I hadn't quite admitted to feeling.

I hadn't thought to get clothes, but there was a wooden cabinet filled with clean clothes for both of us—practical utilitarian items for when time was short. Most of our clothes were in the bedroom, but it was nice to have a quick set of the essentials: a set of underthings, pants, and top.

As we dressed, I told him what I'd learned, and we pondered the dilemma of going to Scotland. There was an airline that specialized in fae-safe travel, but they were only accessible for chartered flights. The reality was that most faeries simply used the doorways to and from *Elphame*. Unfortunately, Iggy and Beatrice were unable to go into Eli's home world—which was likely why Beatrice already made travel plans. My great-times-great grandmother wasn't going to risk being left behind.

I went into the bedroom to pack a bag while Eli updated Beatrice and Iggy that we were going overseas.

Then he packed while I called and made travel arrangements.

"I need a flight for the heirs of *Elphame,* the *draugr* queen, and a witch."

The agent on the end of the line was quiet for a long moment. Then he said, "Cash or charge?"

"Either. We are going to Scotland, from New Orleans, tonight." I figured those details were factors that would matter in sorting the cost.

Again the silence.

"Of course, your highness." The agent cleared his throat. "Will you need secure transport to the airfield? Security is included. Likewise, will you need it on . . . which part of Scotland will you be visiting?"

"No ground transport here. We will need a secure, armored vehicle on the other side. Not obvious, but hex-proof and fae-friendly. Dark tinted windows." I looked around as my grandmother sorted through my weapons like a houseguest investigating our bookshelves. It was odd to see her here, odder still to see her toying with a poleax and then a curved sword in a way that was familiar to me.

My own coping with stress often involved weaponry.

Once our travel was in order, we went to the garage at the ground level of our home. While we typically used Eli's convertible, we now also had a car that was larger. It was a boxy SUV with everything a faery prince needed—and, in my opinion, a few things he probably didn't.

Weapons and bags in the back, we headed to the air strip.

I felt lighter as we headed toward the flight, as if the mere fact of going to find this mysterious weapon was an adventure, not a way to avoid certain death.

Sure, the oldest living man wanted to kill all four of us.

Sure, he *had* killed two of us, but Beatrice was existing as a non-living being and Iggy had "gotten over" being dead.

Add to that the fact that he'd had me kidnapped and tortured, and that his machinations created a harsh rift between Eli and his uncle . . . and I think even the sliver of hope that we might be able to defeat him was giddy-making.

As we walked toward the plane, I started grinning. I had no idea what the weapon was, but I pushed the image of the place to both Eli and Beatrice. "It's here. That was what he most fervently desired when I proposed a faery bargain. He desperately wanted no one to ever find what he had hidden. He thought clearly that he wouldn't be safe if they did."

Beatrice flashed a beautiful, vicious smile. "Wouldn't *that* be a shame . . ."

And in that moment, in that smile, with these people, I felt like there was a chance of victory. It was a heady feeling.

❧ 12 ❧

ELI

After years of hoping to be exactly where he now was with Geneviève, and even longer wondering if the person for him was out there, Eli felt a wave of relief at her return to his side. He realized he was looking at her in the sort of awe that maybe ought to embarrass him to admit. He felt no shame though.

Centuries. He'd been alone for centuries, aware that the one who was destined to be his beloved was yet to be born.

When she had been born, he'd felt it, like a spark in his chest that was burning. The last years of waiting, knowing that she was in the world but too young to meet, were a challenge.

Then she was an adult. A warrior. A vicious creature the likes of which he'd never seen.

How was he to spend literal centuries waiting, only to have their time cut short by either this repugnant man or Eli's own family? Love wasn't a thing to be easily dismissed or denied.

At his side, Geneviève's hand tightened on his.

"Are you okay?" She gestured around the plane. "They said it was fae-friendly, but is it bothering you or . . ."

"I am well." He smiled at her.

Vicious though she could be, Geneviève was also the kindest-hearted person he knew. She simply expressed it in ways not everyone understood.

"I am grateful to be here. Alive. With you," he said.

"Maybe we can pretend it's another honeymoon," Geneviève teased. "I've never been to Scotland."

He had. He'd been to a lot of places in the years he was waiting to find her. Scotland was lovely, and the people were kind. "We will be traveling to sites of interest in search of this place where the weapon might be found."

"How droll!" Iggy interjected as he entered the plane and looked around. "Are we your chaperones for this honeymoon of yours?"

The formerly dead man tried to link arms with Beatrice, who quirked her brow and softly said, "Piggy."

Iggy withdrew with an apologetic word. "No insult meant."

At his side, Geneviève giggled and told Eli, "She turned him into a pig at our wedding."

The fact that his wife could laugh after having been tortured was remarkable, and Eli had the sudden urge to make her laughter last longer.

He glanced at Iggy. "Is she planning on removing the hex at some point? Or will he always resemble swine?"

Geneviève laughed again, and this time Beatrice smiled, too. It didn't undo anything, but Eli was certain that he'd raze nations for the lightness glimmering now in his wife's eyes. Anyone or anything that threatened her was his enemy, and the fae—for all their taciturn reputation—were exceptional at grudge-holding and at meting justice.

The man who had burned his wife's skin would suffer before death.

Eli motioned Geneviève forward. As the airplane had only a few seats, they were all able to recline flat. And though Geneviève rarely needed much sleep, right now she looked weary. Not in a way that she'd admit, but in a way that said that she needed to shut down to make sense of the situation. She wasn't keen on running from a fight, and even though they were running toward a weapon, it undoubtedly still felt like running to her.

"Rest." He opened the overhead and withdrew a warm blanket. "We'll fly through the night, and you might as well recharge."

Geneviève gave him a look that said she knew what he was really saying—that she was drained, and he was offering her logical reasons to relax—but she didn't argue. The trick to life with a woman like her was to offer answers so she was able to feel no slight to her warrior-side.

"We are safe in the air, bonbon," he added. "But I will take first shift awake."

She didn't ask if he'd wake her, and that was proof enough that she needed more repose even than he'd known. Geneviève had spoken briefly of her ordeal, but both the mental and physical cost of torture were hard to quantify.

"I'll be alert to any dangers," he promised her.

Geneviève nodded.

By the time she was curled up, blankets piled over her, and drifting to sleep, the plane had reached cruising altitude. Eli tucked the blankets around her, and then he went to the front of the cabin where the Hexen-Master and the *draugr* queen were searching images of historic sites in Scotland.

Eli poured himself a drink, took a seat, and said, "Progress?"

"The likeliest sites are Highlands, Hebridean Islands, and Orkney Islands." Beatrice pressed her lips together in a thinking expression that was very similar to Geneviève's. "The archaeology is Neolithic, not recent."

"The oldest site there is likely Skara Brae, older than Stonehenge, but not visited as often." Eli thought back to the last time he was in Orkney. "A storm exposed it in the nineteenth century. The earth was ripped away from a knoll . . . and under that was the Neolithic village."

Beatrice looked pensive, but she searched for information.

Iggy, still not as at ease with the world of technology, simply watched. Calmly, the Hexen Master said, "Chester killed me not long after that time. He was drunk on rage during those years."

"There!" Beatrice said, sounding more like she was about to direct a battle than discovering an image online. "Right *there!*"

She jabbed at the screen.

An archival history of the discovery, early exploration, later looting, and eventual preservation of Skara Brae was detailed. Part of the exhibit was a series of photographs, and in one was a familiar face.

One of the early archaeologists on the site was, without a doubt, Chester.

"He was here in 1865," Beatrice pronounced. "The weapon is *there*. It must be."

It was not a guarantee, but a lead was more than they'd had before now. The start of that lead came via his wife being tortured, and so they'd already paid dearly for this clue.

They crouched around the laptop to see the proof of their suspicions.

Chester, who looked more suited to that era than this one, was wearing nondescript clothing in the black-and-white newsprint photo. He had on short pants that came to his bony knees, a shirt that hung loose on his frame, and a sunhat. He looked harmless—unless, of course, a person looked at the calculating expression on his face.

He was pretending to be a sheep, but *that* was a predator's gaze.

"The site was looted in 1913," Iggy read. He paused then, scowling, before adding, "I was dead by then, so I don't know much about where Chester was. However, we know that the site was disturbed by a group with shovels. Obvious assumption is that they were looting, but what if that theft was also a cover to leave something behind?"

It was as logical an answer as anything else. The images on the screen weren't a perfect match to the image Geneviève had drawn from Chester's mind. However, there was proof that he had been there over a century and a half previously.

And Skara Brae *was* a site monitored by Historic Scotland. Geneviève had seen that sign.

"We shall go there, rip open the earth, and locate this weapon." Beatrice nodded and closed the laptop. "Then we shall use the sword or ax or whatever it is to dismember him."

"He's an alchemist, Bea. Likely it's potion or rock or scroll," Iggy countered.

"Then I shall pummel his brains with this rock."

From behind him, Eli heard a voice say, "So we're basically doing rock, paper, scissors, potion?"

Eli turned as Geneviève grinned at them. She'd barely slept, but she already looked calmer. Rest could be brief with her peculiar biology.

"What do you mean?" Beatrice asked, frowning in a way that made her seem older than her ease with technology would claim. "There are no scissors."

"Rock, paper, scissors. It's a child's game." Geneviève clarified gently. "Except we're adding sharp things in place of scissors, as well as a random potion, so rock, paper, scissors, potion."

Beatrice nodded, though it was clear she was not sure what precisely Geneviève was saying. "I shall kill him with anything I find. Chester must die."

"Agreed," Geneviève murmured.

Beatrice turned her gaze on Eli. "And your uncle will atone for his willingness to sacrifice my granddaughter. I do not forgive his insult to my heir."

Eli tensed, but he couldn't defend his uncle. Instead, he said, "You might want to speak to the widow Chaddock. She is also rather angry with him."

Beatrice frowned. "She had not mentioned it."

Iggy stretched. "Fae King wants to make an honest woman of her. Marry her properly."

At that Beatrice laughed, a sound as cold as the slithering things that crept into ruins, and said, "As if marriage makes anyone honest."

Her obvious disdain of the very thing that Eli held most sacred stung, but Geneviève came to sit on his lap and whispered, "I don't know that it makes me honest, but I am *happy* to have married you."

And that was enough for Eli to dismiss Beatrice, Ignatius, and his own thoughts about Chester and about his uncle. The world's opinions mattered little.

Everything he had ever needed was right here in his arms.

13

GENEVIÈVE

I was glad to hear the hope in the voices of those here with me. I'd seen my great-times-great grandmother broken after Chester had attacked her, and I'd seen the fear in her eyes. I'd heard Iggy say over and over that I must not confront Chester. That had rankled. I was not easy about fear. Confrontation and damn-the-risks had always been my way. It was, in brief, a lot of why I had resisted the mere thought of one day having a child. How did anyone bring a child into this world of hate and violence? How could I protect a child from murderers and bigots?

I make the world safer. That was my best answer. I had to make the world a safer place, and not just for this possible future child. I had to make it better for those who were here already.

No hiding. No breaking.

Eventually Eli and I returned to the nest of blankets where I'd cat-napped earlier. I was still tired, but the fear of losing him that Chester had triggered—or maybe that my imprisonment had triggered—meant that I had only been able to doze earlier. I wasn't clingy, but I think that the fear of separation made me feel that way today.

Now that he was at my side, I was able to start to drift back to sleep in more comfort. His very presence made me feel stronger, braver, more capable. That, I'd learned, was the true nature of love. When you are loved, you are better for it, and when you love, you are braver to protect it. My eyes fell closed with my love at my side.

By the time the flight landed in Scotland, I was better suited for coherent thoughts that weren't about my marriage or my family. Perhaps, I had been a bit more shaken by my captivity than I'd realized.

No matter. I was alert now, and I was ready to find the mystery weapon.

Orkney—at least the island we'd landed on—was a stark contrast from New Orleans. It was neither akin to the Outs where I'd spent my childhood nor *Elphame*. Everything was green like those places, but somehow there were no trees at all as far as I could see.

A lack of trees seemed peculiar.

"The story goes that the Vikings and early inhabitants all chopped the trees down," Iggy said mildly.

"Men." Beatrice made a noise of irritation. "Human or other, your sort ruin things."

I wanted to "not all men" her, but that expression was pointless. Obviously, she knew that not every man was monstrous, but she'd been murdered by men. Men sought to steal her power. A man—the dead one who impregnated my mother—had manipulated her family. Now we were facing threats from the very man responsible for her death.

Softly, I reminded her, "There are good men."

We both glanced at Eli and then at Iggy.

"A few. A rare few. Most of them . . ." Beatrice made that same scoffing noise, and I didn't know how to address this topic. I had male friends *and* a husband, but Beatrice had watched centuries of men fail her, try to control her, and back when she was alive, steal her life. It was a lot to overcome.

Impulsively, I hugged her.

Beatrice smiled. "I will not slaughter those you cherish even if they are male."

That, at least, was comforting to hear. "I am grateful that you can overlook that detail of them."

My grandmother gave me a curious look. Then she added, "The king may not be on that list."

I sighed. I was upset with the fae king, but it was not the crisis in front of me. "Perhaps we can deal with the alligator nearest the boat first?"

"I like alligators better than men." Beatrice stepped forward, as if to give me space, but I knew her stance well. She was placing her body between me and any threat that might step forward.

I noticed that Iggy stood at an angle behind me, and Eli was on the side of me. No words, but they were at my side—literally—and that made me feel valued.

I took a moment to study my surroundings. The air tasted of sea, and even though it was the edge of summer, the wind seemed to invite itself under every stitch of clothing I wore. There were a few people at the edge of the tarmac, either employees or other travelers. A few were surreptitiously looking our way.

"Iggy?"

"Watching." He stared at them. If anyone started taking photos or videos, he'd melt the circuitry in the cameras or phones. He was rather adept at that hex.

Beatrice, being dead, seemed to be unaware of the chill. She was, however, quite aware of the strange looks she was getting. At first, I thought it was because of what she was, but that wasn't obvious to a casual observer. Cold skin? That could be explained away easily in this weather. Reptilian eyes? Hidden behind dark sunglasses.

"They think you must be famous," I said as it dawned on me.

Her attire was rather unusual. She still had on the motorcycle pants. Crash armor outlined her shape, which looked like a woman quite a few centuries younger than she had existed in this world. Her top, however, was a soft cashmere sweater that looked like a cloud. And her eyes were hidden behind designer glasses.

Beatrice quirked her lips. "Daughter of Mine, you *are* famous."

Iggy—decked out in designer trousers, suit jacket, and silk t-shirt—looked equally elegant. And of course, Eli could not "dress down" even when he tried. He was a faery prince, but it wasn't just that. Even the least of the fae drew gazes the way flowers drew bees.

And, inevitably, my vibrant blue hair stood out no matter what I wore. I'd pulled on a pair of comfortable jeans, heavy black boots, and one of my spell-wrought jackets. I wasn't as good as Iggy with that skill, but I'd been steadily learning how to weave magic into fiber. It meant that my clothes—probably all of ours, actually, since Iggy had taught me, and I'd spelled all of Eli's closet —were resistant to fire and projectiles. No magic was perfect, but it was a layer of protection to buy precious time to react to attacks.

Being recognized was inevitable, and I had no doubt that Chester had spies aplenty.

"Stonecroft?" a man said, stepping up and motioning toward a car. "I'll be your driver."

Beatrice glanced at Iggy whose mouth moved silently for several moments as we loaded a few essentials—mostly weapons —into the trunk. When we were done, I slammed it shut.

No one had yet entered the vehicle.

"I'll just hand you the keys," the driver suddenly said. "It looks like a fine day for a leisurely hike."

Eli gave him a thick wad of cash, enough to cover the inconvenience of probably losing his job, and then he slid into the driver's seat. Heads to sever? I stepped forward. Cars to drive? That was Eli's domain. We all had our strengths.

I glanced in the rear-view mirror. "Do we need to make a meal plan?"

Beatrice's diet was more particular than mine, but both of us required blood. Eli was fairly normal, although he was not keen on anything preservative or chemical-laden. Iggy . . . honestly, I had no idea what formerly-dead Hexen ate.

"Ignatius has volunteered to nourish me." Beatrice frowned so quickly that I was unsure if anyone else in the car would notice.

"But . . . side effects?" I gaped at her.

Iggy's blood was entrapping. He might be human, but he was a witch. I'd had a few sips and was ready to rip the throat out of most anyone who threatened him. It was not an ideal complication.

"Blackwood and I have an accord," was all she said.

Iggy studiously stared out the window, though he was smiling as if he'd achieved some great victory.

"In your bag," Eli motioned.

I opened it and found a giant vat of . . . frozen red dicks floating in what I was presuming was vodka. And though I knew that Eli could be a little raunchy, this was obviously the work of only one possible person.

"Allie!" I exclaimed.

"She was making you meals before she left," Eli said.

"Of course, she was!" I grinned and opened my blood-and-vodka. I would have offered a slug to Beatrice, but she didn't ask, and I wasn't entirely clear on the requirements for liquor in actual dead *draugr* like her. At some point, I suppose we'd have a heart-to-heart in case my death heralded a transition, but for now, I had enough to sort out.

Alongside the jug was a bright twisty straw, the sort one found in boozy drinks sold to tourists in the French Quarter, so I gleefully slid it into the blood and booze. A few sips later, I said, "Marcus has to know Allie will be furious at him."

"For trying to marry her?" Beatrice asked.

"And for leaving me to die. That woman is loyal." I slurped my meal and stared out the window.

"Not the alligator nearest," Beatrice said, parroting my words back at me.

She was right. We needed to survive long enough to deal with that—which meant finding a weapon, slaughtering the oldest living man, and then sorting out the troubles with the king of *Elphame*.

"First, we explore Orkney. . ." I agreed.

Orkney *was* beautiful. Green, inviting, and best of all, there was a secret weapon somewhere here that we could use to stop Chester.

We just had to find it.

ACCORDING TO THE MAP, THE ROUTE TO SKARA BRAE FROM THE airport had only two options—cut through the middle or skirt the Southern curl of the island. The Neolithic site was in the mouth of the Bay of Skaill on the west of Orkney's mainland, but as we drove over the next thirty minutes, I realized that the timeline hadn't included a faery at the wheel or the fact that he was kind enough to slow down as we drove over a section of road that quite literally looked likely to vanish any day now.

A sliver of road connected two segments of the island, but it was akin to a rope bridge for those of us not used to such narrow paths.

"We are going to end up in the sea . . ." I muttered.

"Loch. Bay." Eli gestured to his left and to his right. "No sea, bonbon."

He did, however, also slow down. On the one side the Loch of

Stenness—and I was pleased to learn that loch merely meant "lake"—and on the other a bay.

What I was realizing as we drove was that the distinctions were immaterial. The island was carved by lochs and bays, and the roads here were even worse than in New Orleans.

Maybe if my spouse drove at a human pace, I'd feel calmer.

Or maybe I was simply anxious.

His driving didn't typically bother me, and I'd been raised partly in a bayou. Land and water mingled. I ought to feel at ease here.

"We should turn back," I pronounced. "Leave here entirely."

My hand clutched the door. My skin felt like it was itching from some pressure I couldn't define. Clearly, this was a terrible idea. I toyed with the thought of opening the door. I could throw myself into the sea. That was better. Safer. Wiser.

"Stop!" I yelled.

In a split second, Eli pulled the car over. Luckily, there was little to no traffic on the remote island, and he had a sliver of earth to stop the car in.

"Bonbon?" He turned toward me and took my hand in his. "Talk to me."

I concentrated on taking deep breaths. "Back up some. Go back the way we came. Please?"

As soon as we started to drive back away from Skara Brae, the tightness in my chest loosened. It felt like a corset that had been bound tighter than any ought to be was slowly loosening, letting me inhale freely.

It hit me suddenly that this was magic, a magic that I had caused.

"Chester had begun a bond with me," I explained to them. "To keep me from harming him. I didn't take it, but I expressed that I *would*."

"How desperate did you feel?" Iggy asked from over my left shoulder.

I glanced back. His face was twisted into an expression that was a mix between fascination and worry. For all that he was an irritation, Ignatius Blackwood did care for me. That was often obvious. He *also* was a knowledge junkie, and this situation had his eyes glassy as an alcoholic watching a drink.

"I considered throwing myself into the sea just now."

At my side Eli swore in a language I was just beginning to learn. I couldn't swear to it, but I was fairly certain that it was something about feeding a dick-weasel its own testicles. I reached out and squeezed Eli's arm. Somehow the fact that he was adopting my own odd cussing patterns felt sweet to me.

"We cannot refuse to stop him." Beatrice pointed out. "I will *flow* and uproot the place until we find this rock, paper, scissor weapon."

"Or," I started, glancing at my husband as I said it, "Iggy can bind me or knock me out."

Eli pressed his lips together in an expression that wasn't hard to interpret.

"Atta girl," Iggy said in an artificially cheerful voice.

An odd noise filled the vehicle.

Iggy glanced at Beatrice, who was growling at him. *No, seriously.* My grandmother was growling like a Rottweiler spotting an intruder.

"Bea . . ." Iggy scooted toward the door, putting as much distance between them as he could. "Tossing me to wolves, Hexen. Help?"

Beatrice followed him as he retreated, crawling toward him and growling louder. I was half-convinced she was about to turn him into a pig.

"Grandmother of Mine?" I said.

No answer.

I exited the car, *flowed* around it, jerked Iggy's door open, and stepped between him and my sometimes creeptastic grandmother. "Beatrice!"

She blinked up at me.

"I need to get to that site, and if I throw myself out of a moving car, it will *hurt*." Obviously hurt was an understatement, but I think that we all knew that.

"I would enter a faery bargain with you, Geneviève of Crowe," Iggy said from behind me. "What terms?"

I was unsure whether or not Iggy knew that I would see his greatest desire if we did so. I didn't truly care either. If he would make himself vulnerable to me, more power wasn't bad. If he thought to trick me . . . well, no one actually tricked the fae who made the vow.

Eli said, "I will—"

"No." Iggy interrupted. "Geneviève. It will give *her* the power over me since she'll know what I most want. That balanced the power she is offering to give *me* by entering into our binding."

No one spoke for several moments. He was right. That didn't make the situation any less awkward.

"I accept your offer, Ignatius David Blackwood." I felt as if I had fallen into Iggy's mind as I spoke. It wasn't the tangle that Chester's had been, but it was crowded. So much knowledge, so many things he wanted to teach me, so many things he was certain I could master better than anyone other than Beatrice.

A stray thought that he had wanted me both for my power and for my resemblance to Beatrice drifted to the top, but I ignore that.

"I will accept an apprentice bond with you, Ignatius David Blackwood, if you agree in return to only protect me in ways that I agree to after *clear discussion* and do nothing to impinge upon my vow with my husband." I stared at Iggy, not at my grandmother or my spouse, as I marveled at the fact that what he wanted most was a worthy pupil, a student who would become a receptacle of the knowledge he had amassed.

"I accept your bargain, Geneviève of Crowe." Iggy smiled. "My apprentice."

"So mote it be," I said.

And that was that. Ignatius David Blackwood was my teacher officially and traditionally. All that was left was sealing that bond with a blood offering from him to me. With that blood, I would be safe from the urge to hurl myself to death—because he would be able to stop me at his word.

❧ 14 ❧

ELI

Eli watched his wife weigh and measure another man's greatest desires. It wasn't the single most difficult thing he'd done, but it wasn't anywhere in the vicinity of easy. Geneviève's fidelity was not a worry. He trusted her, but he trusted Ignatius Blackwood very little.

As every faery knew, a faery bargain was wrought of a knowledge of the human's greatest desire and a clever twist of words. Eli was certain that Iggy had the arrogance that most people did. He thought he would outwit the faery. That hubris was as inevitable as anything could be. No one entered into a bargain that was not advantageous unless it was out of love.

So far Blackwood—who had died in the 1800s—had managed to be summoned from the grave and brought to life. Both events were achieved by manipulating Geneviève. For all that she was a capable fighter, she forgave easily.

"I am not bound by any vows or bargains other than the ones I have made to Geneviève." Eli stared at Iggy, not quite threatening him, but not taking it off the table either.

The group stood alongside a soggy, green patch of road not far from the spot where there was no "side of the road." What needed to happen next was going to be awkward, and they needed no human witnesses to it.

Orkney wasn't bustling with traffic yet. It would be soon. Even for a low-population series of islands, Orkney got busy, especially in the summer. By end of summer, there was a musical festival—a global music gathering where opera, symphony, and more could be enjoyed. There would be no lodging left anywhere on the island by then. Even though Eli hadn't been there in years, he remembered that detail. He'd popped over to hear the music, and then opened a passageway to *Elphame* to leave.

"Shall we?" Iggy asked Geneviève.

She frowned. "That's all there is to a vow, Iggy. No handshakes or contracts to sign. It's magic."

Iggy laughed. "Miss Crowe, your lack of knowledge is going to land you into more trouble that anyone needs. Impulsivity and ignorance are a dangerous set of twins."

Geneviève looked at Eli in confusion.

He wasn't the one to answer, though. Beatrice's voice cut into the tense silence: "You need to drink his blood for a blood vow, and he'll take a swallow of yours."

Iggy stepped forward, tilted his head to offer Geneviève his throat, and Eli had to intervene. "No."

"Vow," Iggy said.

"Wrist." Eli pointed at the man's arm. "Roll up your sleeve."

"And get blood on my suit coat . . .?" His tone was light, but he shed his jacket and rolled up his sleeves. "Fine."

Geneviève looked at Eli, a question in her eyes. He caught Iggy's hand and lifted his arm so that the wrist was held toward her mouth. She wasn't completely at ease with her fangs, but if she was going to do this, a wrist bite was easier for her than the intimacy of a throat.

Iggy visibly flinched as Geneviève latched onto his wrist, piercing his skin, and drawing a long swallow of the Hexen

Master's blood. She drank more than she technically needed, but no one there was going to argue.

When Geneviève stepped back, she pulled a blade and dashed it over her wrist. She held out her arm, exposing a small cut, but Beatrice shoved an empty travel mug forward. "Use this."

"Bea, *really?*" Iggy flashed eyes at her, though, as if he was flattered by what looked like possessiveness.

Geneviève milked blood from her arm into the cup, saying nothing. The tilt of her head told Eli that she was anxious, but there were a limited number of ways to keep her from the compulsion to hurl herself out of the moving vehicle.

Maybe he was sensing that the time for being difficult was not now because Iggy drank the blood in unusual silence.

Then he gestured to the car. "Come, my apprentice and her family. We have a monster to defeat."

He paused and opened the door for Beatrice, who made a show of glaring at him. "Your Majesty."

She growled again, but this time Iggy just laughed.

Eli wasn't certain what to think of their dynamic other than that they were friends, or something. At least Beatrice glaring at him was superior to Beatrice turning Iggy into a pig.

Maybe.

ONCE THEY WERE BACK ON THE ROAD, GENEVIÈVE HAD HER hands clutched tightly in her lap. Eli knew it pained all of them to see her so upset, but there was a limit to what she was able to endure—and she was, as a creature of three heritages, the only threat to Chester that existed other than this weapon.

"You will need to start thinking about what areas of magic interest you," Iggy said mildly, drawing her gaze to him. "I will also need your input on plants at the site we visit. Glyphs. Some old parchment that I came across . . . you have tasks, Geneviève, so please try to sit still."

His attempt at distraction was obvious, but it still worked. Geneviève flashed him a wide smile. She also reached over and took Eli's hand as the car traveled over the narrow slip of land.

Behind her, Beatrice was poised as if to grab her.

Eli's hand tightened over Geneviève's, but she didn't reach for her door or try to flee. She was still there, still safe, and a weight slid from Eli's shoulders. He glanced at Iggy in the rear-view mirror.

Iggy gave a slight nod.

They were in this together—at least as far as protecting Geneviève. After that? Who knew?

GENEVIÈVE

I was embarrassed that I needed the bond with Iggy to overcome the interrupted vow with Chester, but I was also grateful for the aid. If not for the things I'd learned from him, or the gifts I gained from my grandmother's line or my husband's magic, I'd be defenseless . . . likely dead by now.

Part of my mind whispered that those gifts were also *why* Chester had targeted me, but the truth was that had I been only a witch—a hexen—I'd still want to stop Chester if I knew he existed. Faith, heritage, or upbringing, I wasn't sure of the cause, but I disliked those who preyed on the weak.

And to Chester, we were all weak.

Eli pulled into a car park, as they were called here, and for a moment, the weight of Chester's interrupted vow pressed down on me.

Does he know we're here?

Does he suspect?

Did we take too long?

I had little knowledge of the depth of his skills. Humans weren't typically the greatest threat I faced.

"Geneviève?" Iggy barked my name. "A worthy assistant must be at my side."

My grandmother flashed him a strange look.

"Bonbon?" Eli said, taking my hand and tugging slightly.

I shook my head to clear away the lingering doubts that the partial vow had created.

But even in my addled state, I wasn't so foolish as to travel without any weapons. I couldn't load up as I liked, but I still grabbed the pair of magic-imbued daggers from Beatrice, one handgun that I slid into a discreet holster and a sword that slid at an angle across my spine. I added an oversized scarf. That and my hair hid the short hilt.

Beatrice flashed fangs. "Always armed."

But I still shoved a German single-handed Messer at her. It was for closer fighting than a longsword—think pirate's saber— but Beatrice was more of an up-close kind of person, monster . . . whatever she was.

Eli said nothing, simply took a sword in hand. *His* sword. Not steel like mine.

More mundane issues were the next obstacle. The Neolithic site was on the far side of a visitors' centre and museum, and even though tourist season wasn't fully upon the island, there were people milling about the site.

"They're only open for a few hours," Eli said, scanning information.

"Why can't we send them all away?" Iggy asked. "Bea could terrify them, or I could hex—"

"No. What are we looking for?" I asked. "How will we know? We can start there."

I wandered toward the visitor center, and they trailed beside me like they were all wary that I would bolt. I couldn't blame them. I wasn't completely convinced of my own stability. I felt steadier with Iggy's bargain in place, but I was acutely aware that I had started to promise not to injure Chester.

Eli slipped his arm around my waist. He said nothing, but I didn't need words to know that he was there to help me stay steady, too.

"I suppose it would be wrong to summon a storm?" Iggy said lightly.

"Could you?" I glanced at him.

"With your aid." He shrugged. "I have knowledge. You have more power, though."

Eli scoffed. "Scotland. They barely blink at downpours here, unless things have changed drastically. Rain won't chase away a Scot, and I don't relish a storm."

"What if the weapon is *in* the artefact displays?" Beatrice said, gesturing to an informational placard. She read: "Gaming dice, hand tools, pottery, necklaces, beads, pendants, and pins."

I pictured trying to fight Chester with a necklace or gaming dice. It was not the sort of fight I imagined going very well. What would I do? Jab him with a rusty pin? Pelt him with dice?

"I hope not," I muttered.

"You'd rather dig?" Beatrice asked. "A magical trinket would be an easy answer. Perhaps, it imparts strength or knowledge or a spell that can defeat him."

I looked away, feeling foolish, and admitted, "I wasn't thinking of magic. More . . . weapon-shaped thing, what with it being a *weapon*."

"That, my dear apprentice, is exactly the mental block we must remove. Not all weapons are brute force," Iggy said lightly.

Then he offered an arm to Beatrice.

No one remarked when she accepted, but I suspected we were all shocked. Together, we entered the visitors' centre and started to study the items there. There was a lot of information, and a few items that looked decidedly weapon-ish to me.

A neolithic figure, about five *thousand* years old, was easily something that I could visualize bashing into Chester's smarmy face.

A necklace with what looked like fangs on it seemed like I could find a use for it—jabbed into his jugular, maybe.

What appeared to be a stone Thor's hammer and something that looked like a wee cannonball with thorns caught my eye. Honestly, I wasn't particular. Anything would do.

"Nothing here has power," Beatrice grumbled as she and Iggy rejoined Eli at my side. "I feel no magic in . . ." She gestured at the cases.

I sighed. I hated to say she was right, but I didn't see anything that jumped out as a defeat-the-jerk weapon. In a pinch, I'd try all of the items, but there was no way my heart could agree to destroying archeological artefacts without reason.

I let my gravesight slide out over the cases, and again, nothing zinged for me. "No grave notes."

I glanced at Eli hopefully.

"Nothing," Eli said quietly, undoubtedly letting the magic that he held as one of the fae dance over the items, too.

"Time to remove the humans and dig," Beatrice said. "Come."

I had a flicker of fear that she was about to start flashing fang and followed close behind as she walked outside and toward the Neolithic village.

"Give me your hand." She stared toward the sea, and as I watched the waves began to roil like something vast was surging there.

"Let go," Iggy whispered from somewhere behind me. "Trust."

Those two acts weren't high on my skill set, but I needed to know that there was a chance to defeat Chester. I needed to locate this weapon. The alternative was my death. Eli's death. Beatrice's death. Iggy's death.

I let my gravesight roll out, and when I saw that the dead had been summoned from the sea, I paused. "What are they here for . . .?"

"Truly?" Beatrice murmured at my side. "I certainly don't *shovel.*"

"The people are leaving, bonbon." Eli held my gaze. "Foolish mortals, afraid of the beautiful witches at the edge of the sea . . ."

I glanced back and saw the rest of the visitors leaving early. "Aren't they going to kick us out?"

"This is Scotland, Geneviève," Eli said lightly. "They were aware of the fae before the rest of the world even knew our kind existed, and undoubtedly, they recognize us. The *heirs* on their site? Blessing their soil with protection, they—"

"But we aren't doing that," I objected.

"We are." Eli assured me. "After we retrieve the weapon, we are going to bless this site and ask the sea to let this site remain intact even during storms."

My panic receded at his words, and resolute now, I returned my gaze to the sea. We had summoned drowned sailors and pirates, Vikings and Picts, explorers and innocents.

I joined my magic to Beatrice's.

Wake for us, I beckoned. *Come to shore.*

And it was a heady feeling, one I wish I had time to explore more leisurely. First, though, I needed to find a weapon.

Eli had known magic since his oldest recollection. In fact, until he'd left *Elphame,* he'd not known any person without it. Knowing didn't change his response to seeing Geneviève summon the dead. His magic, fae magic, was the stuff of life—of summoning plants and connecting to soil. It was nurturing of those things already breathing, be it plant or creature, but Geneviève brought faux life to the dead.

Perhaps, in some way, it was not so different. To him, though, it was a marvelous thing to witness. Seeing her ancestor, not breathing but animate and sentient as if alive, at her side doing the same magic only added to the fascination he felt.

The sea was frothing, as if a great storm was coming. Waves curled in on themselves as if kelpies rose from the depths, but it was not water horses that came. It was the reanimated dead.

The first man ashore was clad in modern garb, a recent death of some sort. His gashes and tattered clothing vanished as the witches' magic reknitted skin and cloth. Then several others like him stepped out of the sea. Next came fishermen, pirates, and finally several Vikings.

This terrifying army of the dead waited for Geneviève's

command—because although it was Beatrice's idea, Geneviève was the one they watched attentively. She was the necromancer.

"Could such an army destroy Chester?" Eli asked, gaze sliding over the soaked assembly.

Bodies remade themselves as he watched, and for a flicker of a second, Eli understood why Chester feared Geneviève. What she was capable of was terrifying, and should she decide to subjugate the world, she could.

What a glorious queen she would be . . .

"Chester cannot die." Iggy watched the warriors without a flicker of emotion. "She could have them rip him limb from limb, but he heals from every wound."

"You know this how?" Eli asked.

Geneviève glanced at Iggy, not replying but the question was clear in her expression.

With a wry smile, Iggy looked at Geneviève and then turned to meet Eli's gaze briefly. "I tried many a plan to overcome him. I don't have Geneviève's raw power, but I am not without experience in fighting him. Quite a few plans met with disaster before my death. Do you think I would suggest hiding if there was a way to kill him? Without this weapon, we are lost."

Eli repressed a shudder at the thought of the consequences of not finding the missing weapon.

On the beach, Geneviève's army of the dead, a few with ancient swords that were regaining a glimmer, waited. If they were fully sentient, perhaps some would mutiny. They weren't though. They were shells of themselves, clarity present to varying degrees depending on how long ago they'd died.

"The Norsemen are unexpected," Eli said, his words half-questioning.

Iggy nodded. "She only has limits when she thinks about it. Geneviève remains her own worst limit."

Then with a nod to the sandy ground, Beatrice ordered. "Dig. Find me a weapon."

Whatever was going on with the combining of power had shifted something inside Geneviève. He couldn't explain it, but her eyes—reptilian in shape, glowing as they sometimes did—weren't seeing this world. Something had drawn her attention.

"A heart without a body." Geneviève scanned the area, clearly seeking something. "I have to find it."

"What?" Iggy asked.

"The *heart*."

"Geneviève?" Beatrice put a hand toward her, as if to stop her, but Geneviève shook it off.

"A heart isn't a weapon," Iggy pointed out.

"It's trying to reach the water" was all Geneviève said. "It's trapped in glass. It'll batter itself against the glass . . ."

She stared back to the visitor's centre.

Eli wasn't sure of what exactly was happening, and it felt like an odd time to go out collecting hearts. A heart was not much of a weapon, but he trusted Geneviève.

"So be it," he agreed, gesturing her forward.

Then she started walking away from the beach, the ruins, the dead. Something dead beckoned her forward.

"We will return." He glanced at the others, as if expecting an argument that they were wise enough not to utter.

And in that sliver of a moment, she was gone, *flowing* toward the visitor's centre.

With barely a thought, he *flowed* toward her—not as fast or as gracefully as a true *draugr*. It was her magic, not his, so it still felt strange to use. Stranger still would be letting her out of his sight. Eli stayed at her side, while the others stayed with the dead army.

They had to collect a heart under glass.

❦ 17 ❦

GENEVIÈVE

"Geneviève?" Eli's voice followed me, and I wanted to answer, but a heart was beating against glass—a dead heart I had woken. I needed a lot of things, but in this instant, I had to retrieve that heart.

It was the only thing I could think about.

I jerked the door open, and for a moment, I paused. Listening. Waiting. Then the heart started thumping again. It was like a drum, thundering in the room. The song called me forward.

A heart without a body, it wanted to answer my summons, to come toward me like the dead had done, but it *couldn't*. And it was imperative that I found it, that I protected the heart. I had a strange certainty that this was the single-most important thing in this life that I would do.

It's not, my logical mind whispered.

But my gravesight led me forward. Like the grid of the city, this was a strange overlap, as if a map were drawn on the sand and soil. I had to follow it to the building where we had already weighed and measured the artefacts.

No magic here, I'd thought.

No magic here, Iggy and Beatrice had said.

Everything said there was no magic within that building, but something had changed when Beatrice and I summoned the dead. I heard the heart begin to beat. *Thumpthump-thumpthump* It drummed steadily as if alive.

I wasn't in the habit of summoning hearts. I was a necromancer. I summoned the dead. So why was *this* heart summoned by the necromancy? Why had it not joined its body?

"Inside a glass box," I said. "There is a heart in a box."

"Could you release it from your necromancy? Let that one be released from the call of your magic?" Eli asked, pulling my gaze to him and temporarily away from the trail.

"It's coated in grave dirt." I felt that oddity as surely as the dead in the earth—and more recently, the dead in the sea. "The heart belongs to my necromancy. I have to hold it, Eli. I must carry the heart with us."

Eli shot me a look that made me doubly sure that something was wrong here. I knew it in my bones, but the compulsion to hold that suddenly beating heart overwhelmed me again.

"Of the earth," I said, needing to feel that grave dirt wrapped around the stone heart of someone who needed that heart back.

My fist smashed through a glass case as if my body was no longer in my control. My entire body felt off, as if were a marionette whose strings were tugged and steered by someone else.

I paused with my hand curled around what looked like stone but felt like soft wet flesh with granules of dirt coating it. I could already feel it thumping against my fingers like a wild thing trying to escape.

I tightened my hand on what looked like a rock.

"Bonbon? That's a . . . stone," he touched my arm.

I glanced at Eli. "I don't know whose idea it was to grab this. Maybe mine? Maybe not. The heart wants to escape."

"The rock . . .?"

"Heart." I pulled it out, my blood rolling along my wrist and coating the rock-that-was-a-heart. "This is a heart, Eli."

And in that moment, whatever control I still had over my necromancy flickered. I could see the body that needed the heart. It was not on the beach. It was inside one of the neolithic structures.

"The weapon . . . the heart is part of the weapon," I whispered.

"A heart that looks like a rock?" Eli asked. "Is it Chester's heart? Can you stab it?"

I wasn't sure. Sometimes my various magical threads worked separately, but in this moment, it felt as they were a giant three-part braid twisting together in the marrow of my bones. I didn't quite know what to do with the stone-looking, heart-feeling thing in my hand. I was only certain that I needed to hold it tightly, protect it, shelter it.

"Eli?" I whispered, as panic filled me. The heartbeat in my hand raced louder. Terror from the heart slid into my body.

The air shifted, and whatever danger was building was one I didn't want to face. *He'll destroy me.* The thought—I realized with an uncomfortable pang—was the heart's thought, not mine.

Before I could puzzle out how I was communicating with the heart, I felt the insistence of the heart's terror, and I realized the cause of the fear.

"Run. *Flow* with me," I urged. "*Now.*"

Eli, used to the weird that was my life, caught my free hand in his, and we ran toward the beach. My grandmother was directing the dead, but as one they all paused and nodded toward me, like a zombie army welcoming their mistress.

I nodded once, greeting them. What else was I to do? It felt like the right thing to do in that moment, and as much as I argued with Iggy, I still was a witch who ultimately ran on a mix of instinct and sheer bravado.

"Bless it. The site," I urged Eli as we stepped into the ruins of Skara Brae. "Bless this soil. Hurry."

"Granddaughter?" Beatrice looked away from our army of the

dead. The Vikings watched over the living like sentinels, but the pirates dug in search of some mythical treasure. They all looked strangely cheerful, as if the act of digging holes in the beach was a treat.

"Did you find something?" Beatrice asked, staring at the bleeding stone in my hand.

But before I could answer I heard a voice that sent chills over my body. "You are becoming bothersome, Ms. Crowe."

Chester's voice was scratchier than normal. He'd shed his priestly garb, but his chilling expression was somehow worse coming from such an innocuous looking man, dressed as he was in his bland khakis and button up. And honest to frogs, he'd donned an olive sweater vest.

"Sore throat?" I asked with a smart-assed tone that I couldn't entirely contain.

"You can't help yourself, can you?" Iggy muttered from my side.

Chester paused, gaze switching from me to Iggy. "I killed you. I do not recall suggesting you should come back to life. We shall correct that, too."

Iggy shrugged. "Never did care much for your suggestions."

Beatrice was silent, and as soon as I looked at her, I understood why. She'd been directing our piratical army to a more military position. Men with tattered clothes—not because the magic hadn't healed them but because they were in that state when they'd died—surged forward, a wall of newly re-fleshed bodies.

My ancestor had obviously read about military formations, and she was arranging our forces for battle.

Behind me, Eli began to bless the site, asking the sea and earth to protect it. I wasn't sure that blessings, my smart mouth, or an army of corpses would help. The memory of Iggy saying Chester couldn't be killed didn't do a whole lot to add to my optimism.

And the weapon, so far, appeared to be a heart pretending to be a rock.

I debated stabbing it, shredding it, stomping it. The body and voice that my mind said were connected to the stone heart weren't Chester's. I'd seen the body. I knew it was buried here.

Put it back where it must be, a voice not my own urged. I looked around. I'd had Eli, Beatrice, and Iggy in my head enough times to know it wasn't them.

Stone hearts ought not speak, I told it.

The weapon, apparently, was a person whose heart was in my hand.

Putting that heart back wasn't a useful order, though. And it didn't exactly come with instructions.

"Sanctify," Eli asked again, whispering the words in that language I only understood in small measures still.

"Why are *you* here?" Chester asked Eli with the first genuine interest I'd seen. "I gave you the option to end this, to be safe."

My husband said nothing, merely continued to weave whatever magic he could over the ruins, and I felt like the lack of sufficient weapons was a measure of idiocy that I shouldn't have fallen prey to.

After ignoring Chester, Eli earned a look from the old alchemist that was akin to what I suspected many people gave dung beetles.

"Give us a vow to not hurt us and our loved ones," I suggested, knowing with absolute surety that Chester would refuse my invitation, but rather desperately wanting to keep his gaze off Eli— although *my* death would also be Eli's.

The wrongness of that particular detail made my default tactics useless. I stifled the growl of frustration that rose up. I was rather used to making myself a target if it would protect my loved ones. That was not an option here.

"I'm no longer willing to negotiate for *everything*." Chester eyed the heart in my hand. "I'll let *them* go free in exchange for your life and the heart."

"Eli would not be free if you took my life," I pointed out. "This deal is—"

"Geneviève?" Eli interrupted. He sounded as if he were only mildly irritated.

When I glanced at him, he extended a hand, and I went to his side. So far the barriers we had were keeping Chester out, but I knew from the wince that Eli barely flashed that Chester was trying to knock down the invisible walls Eli had erected around the ruins.

Eventually, Chester will overcome the walls.

The heart was dripping on the ground as I moved. My blood? The heart's blood? I wasn't sure anymore. There was blood from my injured wrist, and there was a stone heart. Neither ought to be sprinkling blood droplets so quickly.

"Friends," Eli added, louder now. "Join me, Beatrice and Iggy."

Beatrice *flowed,* half-dragging Iggy in her wake.

As I'd moved into the ruins of the Neolithic village, a veritable gush of blood had begun to pour around my fingers. It seemed like it was trying to roll toward one particular stone, as if the stone were beckoning the blood.

I stepped toward the stone, following the blood that was flinging from my hand to the stone like a red line on a map. The earth over there felt like it was calling me closer.

Surreptitiously, I hoped, I glanced at Eli. "Love?" I whispered.

He nodded once, but he rather looked like I felt: exhausted beyond reason but still unflinching as we were facing our foe.

"Sanctuary," Eli order-asked whatever force or deity faeries implored. "Grant us sanctuary now."

I felt the shimmer of fae magic rise around the Neolithic village, a cage that extended into the sky. It felt like blown sugar had taken shape, millions of interlocking magical hexagons and polygons tethering together. I could *see* the wall of magic. I hoped it was sturdy.

Beyond that wall was a veritable wave of the summoned dead, a second barrier, as if we were within a fortress under siege. They encircled the faery-wrought barrier, bodies between Chester and our magical cage. It wasn't a guarantee of safety, but it was better than nothing.

We were caged inside, and he was left glaring at us.

"You all choose your death," Chester announced. "Even if you can outwait me here, do you think I won't find you? Destroy you?"

"Maybe." I looked down at the heart that was acting a bit like a dowsing rod, hopefully leading us somewhere other than fresh water. "But we choose not to give you *this*. I sort of figure that if you want it, I *don't* want you to have it."

Chester stood on the other side of a wall of corpses. As he started ranting about "women and their uppity self-important disobedient" something or other, he began steadily dismembering and tossing our army of the dead into the surf.

I winced.

The reassembled dead felt no pain, and maybe it would burn through his temper. At the least, we had two layers of protection. That bought us time. I still hated Chester even more for his excessive violence.

"Plan?" Iggy prompted.

"There." I pointed. The tiny red droplets were practically flying toward one particular stone slab now, soaking into earth. I felt each one zing through me.

Beatrice removed the stone I'd indicated, and we all entered some sort of labyrinth under the ground. I had no idea if this used to be above ground or if there were tunnels from archeologists— or if this was Chester's doing.

Eli began to bless the stone that was now over our heads as he'd blessed the site, asking the sea and earth to protect it.

"Can we head toward the car park?" I asked. "Follow these to there and escape?"

"No." Beatrice pulled the stone over our heads, sealing us in darkness.

I felt panic. Suffocating in the dank air wasn't *worse* than death by Chester's hand, but I wasn't keen on it either. "Then what are we to do? Stay here in the dark and—"

"You need to relax, Hexen." Iggy pulled out a surprisingly modern handheld light. "Let there be light."

I could still feel the dead above us, and I could feel the threat approaching, but more than anything I felt the heart beating in my hand. It was panicking, more so than I was—and that was saying something.

We took several steps into the darkness, and there at my feet was the owner of the heart. I couldn't tell you *how* I knew with certainly that it was her heart, but I felt the heart racing faster and faster.

I crouched down.

The dead woman's blouse, top, whatever it was called, was reddened with blood, although after however many years she's been in the earth it looked more like a rust color.

"The weapon," Beatrice said from over my shoulder. "A woman. He's afraid of a woman."

Iggy shoved forward, knocking me aside with a surprising roughness.

"Gunnora," Iggy whispered the name in obvious shock. He reached down and brushed the woman's hair back from where the loose tendrils fell on her cheeks. "*Nora.*"

"Who is Gunnora?" Eli asked, giving voice to the question I hadn't managed yet to ask.

"His wife." Beatrice shook her head.

"Iggy's?" I asked, feeling like the reason for our trip had just become muddled. "I'm glad he found his wife's grave but how does that help—"

"Chester's wife," Iggy corrected as he swept the woman into his arms and kissed her cheek gently. "She's in stasis. Once we restore her heart—"

His words were lost under a small avalanche. Earth and rocks fell on us, as overhead Chester roared. Maybe he knew we'd found her, or maybe he simply was frustrated that we weren't as easy to catch as he'd expected.

"Hexen," Iggy barked. "Tunnel."

Beatrice gave him a raised brows look. "Pardon?"

But he spoke a hex I'd not heard before, and Beatrice nodded. "I see," she whispered. "It is our best chance."

I rolled the strange word in my mouth, repeating it carefully a few times before letting my magic slip into the hex.

"Roots to keep walls from collapsing?" Iggy asked Eli. "Could you do that?"

Eli nodded.

"Why aren't you doing anything?" I asked, more curious than accusatory.

Iggy answered, "Because you will need me to speak the hexes we require to let all of us breathe when we reach the sea."

"I do not need to breathe," Beatrice pointed out. "Neither does"—she gestured at the seemingly dead woman in Iggy's arms—"she."

"Your granddaughter does, and her spouse's death would kill her, so . . ." Iggy shrugged, as if the plan weren't both terrifying and desperate.

Our best option—our only option—was that we were to tunnel into the sea, breathe underwater, and then what?

"This is a terrible plan," Eli said.

I silently agreed.

"There are no better options. We cannot wait here," Iggy argued. "And if we go to the surface, Geneviève will die."

"No." Beatrice glared at the seemingly impenetrable wall of

earth. Then she began to cast the hex, carving away the soil with magic.

There was no other answer I could think of in that moment, at least not any that wouldn't include going back to face the angry alchemist on the beach, and so I added my voice to hers.

One after the other, we spoke the awkward intonations of the hex.

And together, we carved a tunnel into the sea while the monster raged above us.

18

GENEVIÈVE

I felt the bodies of the corpse army dismembered and returned to the waves. Even then, I could rebuild them. Necromancy was not so easily overcome, but I needed my energy for other things. So little by little, my magic let others of the dead fall to lifelessness before they were ripped apart. I was glad that they were distracting Chester, but the energy it took to hold the hexes as we tunneled toward the sea meant I had to either risk being buried alive in the tunnel or shift magic away from the dead army that Chester was shredding.

I chose not to be buried alive.

There was a chance Chester would notice that the sea took back bodies we'd reanimated, but I hoped that the arrogant piece of vermin vomit thought that his rage had simply overpowered our necromancy.

Dissembling the dead shouldn't make them crumble into bone dust that the tide swallowed back into itself, but for all that Chester knew—and it obviously was a vast store of knowledge he held—he had not noticed in any obvious way. My hope was that the rage he'd fallen prey to was clouding logic.

Behind me, Iggy cradled the apparently neither-dead-nor-alive woman in his arms, and my suspicion that I finally understood the cause of his death grew. He looked at her the way Eli looked at me. Iggy loved the woman he carried—a woman married to the man who murdered Iggy.

Chester's murder of Iggy wasn't about knowledge after all.

"You loved her," I said finally.

"Yes."

"And that's why Chester murdered you?" It wasn't a great time to chat, but I felt myself stumbling as we reached the last few steps before the sea. I wanted a distraction. My feet were unsteady from exhaustion, and I felt vaguely as if each hex to create this tunnel was somehow using my own muscles to shovel the soil, sand, and rock.

Beatrice had not begun to stumble, but her stride had slowed.

"Pause." Eli stopped. "The sea begins here."

He placed a hand on the earth, as if he could touch the water there. Maybe he could. My understanding of fae magic was still new.

"We have no other choice," I whispered, even as I shuddered in fear. The thought of being in cold saltwater after my near-drowning was not much more appealing than going back to face Chester.

"Run when we touch water," Iggy said. "Beatrice? If you would hold my arm . . . Hexen, grab hold of the faery. *Flow.*"

I felt like I did when I was under a spell, and I realized that I'd made an apprentice vow to him. He was using that to ease my fears.

I couldn't say if he was compelling me or not, but either way, I was obeying his wishes. Drowning was high on my "been there, done that, not interested in round two" list, so if his compulsion helped me push past that, it wasn't a bad thing.

"Yes," I agreed, taking Eli's hand in mine.

Then Iggy nodded, and the last of the earth between us and the sea was scooped away.

The sea poured into the tunnel with a roar, filling it, surrounding us.

The churning water was impossible to see through, but I ran. I *flowed* into the sea as if it was flat ground atop the earth.

My body was slower, sluggish, and the cold cut at me as if it was stealing the last of my reserves.

"Do not pause." Beatrice's voice was imperious in my mind,

I wasn't entirely sure how to obey, but Eli's hand in mine tightened. I took another step, moving as quickly as I could under the water. My other hand still held the stone-but-beating heart.

I couldn't tell how many minutes, meters, or miles passed, but eventually, my energy finally vanished—or perhaps the hex that Iggy had drawn wasn't enough.

I went surging to the surface, mouth open like a gasping fish on the edge of death. For a flicker of a moment, I thought I would not stay afloat, that I would sink and drown, but Eli caught my hand as unconsciousness threatened.

A darkness waited at the edge of my eyes.

"Can he see us?" I managed between deep breaths. "Chester?"

"No." Eli looked across the sea. We were far from any land, and while I was grateful to not be facing Chester, I wasn't entirely sure that drowning or being eaten by some great creature under the sea was ideal either. Honestly, the last couple days had more than erased the calm I'd found the last few months.

In front of us, several field-lengths away, Iggy surfaced, treading water, holding the not-dead-or-alive woman. Beatrice, looking far from amused, was at his side. She motioned us forward.

"I can't go back under there," I confessed.

Eli nodded, and without another word, he began to swim, dragging my exhausted body—and the weight of the weapons I still wasn't willing to surrender—behind him.

We alternated between swimming and floating for what felt like hours.

Eventually, Iggy glanced at the sky. "Hoy is nearby."

"Hoy?"

"Island. Not crowded." Iggy was panting too, now. "Perhaps three hundred souls in all . . ."

No one spoke again, but I felt like I was the only person who had no idea what or where Hoy was. All things considered, it wasn't shocking. I'd only lived a couple decades. Beatrice was centuries old. Iggy . . . honestly, I had no idea. Eli . . . we didn't discuss it.

I took a steadying breath and said, "Are we faster under or over the water?"

No one answered.

So we carried on, swimming and resting until we reached Hoy.

Eventually, we dragged our soggy selves to shore at what Iggy called "Braebister Mound." Honestly, it looked like what the largest structure area at Skara Brae might've been if the tops of the buildings were not ripped open by humans or sea.

"It's a mound." I stared at it. "Not exactly the luxury digs one dreams of after escaping underground and running under the waves into the sea."

"There's a passageway," Iggy pronounced, earning a quirked brow from Eli.

No one asked how Iggy knew, but I was fairly sure that asking would've been met by silence anyhow. No one here was eager to spill secrets, and I could respect that.

My Hexen Master was still clutching the dead-ish woman like a bride on a particularly macabre wedding night. Whatever else was going on, I was certain that he wasn't going to let the woman go.

"Why don't we go inside, and I'll see if can put this heart back in her chest?" I walked toward the mound that Iggy had pointed out.

Apparently, some of these little hill-like structures in Scotland were hollow and others were not. Nothing indicated that *this* one was anything other than rock and dirt, but then again, nothing indicated that the bleeding heart in my hand was something other than stone when I'd first seen it. Not everything in this world was as simple as appearances might indicate.

"There aren't any visitors centres or doors or—"

Iggy whispered a hex that he obviously wasn't trusting me to learn, and a doorway opened. It was not much more than a stone archway, but my Hexen Master had a thing for underground lairs. I'd been held captive in a well-appointed pirate lair not too long ago.

This reminded me of that lair, but it also looked like an alchemical workshop: a kiln, stone jugs, and glass jars of some sort of things in viscous fluid. I reassessed. This made the pirate lair where he'd imprisoned me last year look downright posh.

A word, whispered again, from Iggy and whatever stasis charm was holding the materials here vanished. A loaf of bread, supposedly fresh because of the stasis, and jugs of indeterminate contents sat on a stone shelf as if they were new.

Interestingly, there were animal pelts that looked rather like furniture—a bed shaped one and a few that looked like someone had stitched and stuffed them into crude chairs.

Iggy carried the woman to the bed, even though the rest of us could probably appreciate the comfort more than the un-animated corpse could.

"We should eat before we do anything else." Eli motioned toward Iggy. "What do you need to—"

Eli's words died at a frustrated sound from Beatrice. She stalked forward and met Iggy's eyes only long enough to warn him of her intent before she was sinking fangs into his throat.

I felt rude watching her drink, so I glanced away.

"I hope Nora there has some shiny power or something because I'm not sure a mostly dead woman is much of a weapon," I admitted to Eli in a low voice.

"Someone"—he glanced at Iggy—"*obviously* hid Gunnora here

before Chester do *that* to her. If hiding is our only option, we will do the same. I will not let Chester kill you."

Beatrice released Iggy, who leaned back against a giant stone. "Next," she said, shoving him toward me. Then she gathered a woven basket that looked new. "I'll catch fish."

When she stepped outside, moving quickly enough that I felt a chill in the air, I backed away from Iggy. I was steady enough, and he didn't look like he was up for another bite.

"Liquor," Eli said, sniffing a bottle. "Whisky from the smell."

Iggy nodded.

I needed two things for nourishment, and that was one. The other was in Iggy's veins, but I thought perhaps waiting until he'd eaten was best, considering how drawn he looked after feeding Beatrice.

Eli handed me the jug after wiping the mouth of it. Then he glanced at Iggy. "I have questions, Blackwood, and if you are smarter than I think you are, you will answer them."

19

ELI

Eli wasn't convinced that he could trust Iggy, but right now, the Hexen Master had answers—and there was no reason to let him keep them to himself. Secrets weren't the ideal when they had a powerful enemy.

"You love her." Eli nodded toward the dead-ish woman.

"Maybe...? Once upon a time." Iggy shrugged, but he gave the lifeless woman a look that Eli recognized. Words weren't always as true as actions.

"And you need Geneviève to put that heart back," Eli surmised.

"I could do it."

Eli grinned at that. "Somehow, I doubt that. You need a necromancer. The heart was rolled in graveyard earth. I'm not the only one paying attention, Blackwood."

Iggy sighed and sat down on the earth floor. "I was already dead when she died, but he still made sure I couldn't save her. I can do many a thing, but this . . . even though I was vowed to the loa of the dead, I could not stop him. I expected her to die before me. Instead, she watched my murder."

Geneviève was cradling the heart in her cupped hands like a child who held a secret treasure there. "I want to put this back."

"Is she an enemy?" Eli asked, glancing at his wife. "You know I will use everything I know to protect Geneviève, and if this woman is going to hurt my wife. . ." He didn't finish the threat, but it was clear enough.

Iggy nodded. "Understood." He sighed deeply. "Honestly, I'm not sure what to think. I . . . cared for her. She betrayed me, but if she is Chester's greatest fear, there is reason to think she can help us."

"And?" Geneviève asked.

"Her husband killed me. Slowly. It took months. The beauty of alchemy. He healed me just enough to make my pain last . . ." Iggy rubbed his chest, as if there were wounds there now. "And the whole time, he told me how she laughed at me, how she mocked me for my words to her, how . . . I don't know what was true. I never thought I'd get to ask her."

Eli folded his arms over his chest. "So she may be the only weapon that can destroy Chester—who wants us dead—but she may also have been complicit in your murder."

"Summed up tidily." Iggy looked up and met Geneviève's gaze. "Will you restore her heart? I am not ordering you, Geneviève. I am not compelling you. As your friend, I implore you."

But Geneviève shook her head. "I am halfway into a bond with Chester, and my bond says I cannot."

Geneviève looked at Eli, gaze pleading and pained. He realized then that she needed help. That she was resisting the half-made vow so she could ask for aid.

"Order her." Eli held his wife's gaze as he told Iggy, "If Geneviève is resistant to it, that means your betrayer actually *is* a threat to him. Do it."

"You are my assistant, Geneviève Crowe. Put the heart in her chest. Summon her to life." Iggy's hands curled into fists as he spoke.

Moving like she was afraid, Geneviève stepped toward the life-less woman. She stopped just beside her, and then she dropped to her knees. Whatever magic she used was not fae, Eli was certain of that. The air smelled of the grave, and Geneviève's eyes were fully reptilian.

The heart looked like stone still, but as Iggy moved the clothing away from the woman's chest, the heart started thumping loudly. It looked like a fresh, still-beating, blood-dripping heart.

Geneviève's hand pierced the woman's flesh, tearing a hole in the skin.

Iggy blanched, but Geneviève wasn't connected to the *now* anymore. Whatever was going on with her magic, she was far beyond niceties that reminded people not to tear holes in other women's chests.

Geneviève shoved the heart into the still-dead woman's chest.

And in the next moment, it grew roots, stretching out and tying itself to the withered vines that were arteries and veins. It was somehow horrible and beautiful simultaneously to watch that stone heart take life, connect to the body around it.

Then the woman opened her mouth and released the most agonized scream that Eli had ever heard. Over and over, she screamed.

Iggy pulled her into his arms. "Shhhh! You're safe now, Nora. You're safe." He repeated some version of that over and over.

And yet the woman still screamed as if hell itself was clawing her back to her grave.

20

GENEVIÈVE

The screaming slowed toward a gasping-squeaking-sobbing sound, and I watched as the woman started backing up in a sort of crab walk. I felt a flutter of guilt that she was terrified of me, and I wanted to reassure her. That was difficult with her blood literally coating my hands.

"Don't hurt me!" she looked at each of us with no awareness of who we were—including Iggy.

"Nora . . ." Iggy held his hands up, indicating that he was harmless.

But Nora was scanning the room, as if she was seeking an exit or maybe an ally. Her already unstable state was only worsened when the doorway slammed open as if a storm had torn down the barrier.

I had a weapon raised in the next blink, my body positioned between Eli and the threat. The threat, however, was an irate *draugr.* Beatrice flashed a fangy smile at me before slapping a hand over the crying woman's mouth.

"Stop it!" Beatrice glared at the sobbing, seemingly human, woman. "This caterwauling will draw every predator within miles. *Cease this instant.*"

Nora blinked and visibly swallowed.

"Now, what use is that?" Iggy tried to grab Beatrice's wrist, but he was a mortal. A Hexen Master has plenty of resources, but still, Beatrice was ancient, a Hexen *and* a *draugr*, and she was stronger than many of her own kind.

Beatrice made a sound that managed to be imperious even though it sounded a lot like a snort. "What use is this creature? Weak. Whining. No weapon here. Chester will kill us all and—"

"Chester?" Nora interrupted, backing away from my grandmother's hand, which had obviously relaxed. "You are acquainted with my husband?"

It was the first seemingly logical thing she'd said, but now Iggy was glaring at her. I wondered if she had betrayed him.

"Are you his servants?" Nora straightened herself, smoothing her hair anxiously. "We were only just wed, so I admit to not knowing the *entire* staff here."

"I am no man's servant," Beatrice seethed. She pivoted and jabbed a finger into Iggy's shoulder. "What are we to do with this insipid creature? She seems *fond* of that monster. I doubt she's going to be a useful weapon to kill Ch—"

"You are our enemies!" Nora was suddenly on her feet, hands crackling with a blue spark that was both intriguing and slightly worrisome.

Apparently, Chester was not the only ancient alchemist anymore. This could go very poorly . . . or be the asset we needed. With the way Nora was glaring at us, I was starting to suspect we had summoned a second enemy.

Iggy turned away from Beatrice and took a step toward the lady Lazarus. "Now, Nora—"

"Enemy!" Nora slapped her hand toward Iggy, not quite touching him but simply stirring the air in his direction.

Suddenly, he was writhing on the floor with blue sparks jumping all over him.

I wasn't sure how to handle this. So far, our sought-after

weapon had screamed, attacked Iggy, and was now looking at us as if she was weighing which person to attack next.

Out of one frying pan into another.

"We are *not* your enemies," Eli said, his voice pitched low in a placating tone I had heard often enough when I needed stitches that I wasn't interested in getting. "Before death, that man was your lover. Stop this."

"Lies!" Nora raised that hand again as if to attack my husband.

"Fae." Eli shrugged, but he still sounded calming. "We do not lie. You know that, don't you, Gunnora? My kind cannot lie outright. Surely, you recall that. Things are unclear, though, are they not?"

She nodded, and then her hand folded into a fist that was still sending blue arcs over the knuckles.

"I do not know any of you." Nora looked at each of us, as if reading our faces. "There is blood on my gown. What am I to think?"

Beatrice made a sound that was the verbal equivalent of an eye roll.

"What month is this?" Nora asked.

"The year might be more interesting," Beatrice said carefully. "Possibly the century."

"1630?" Nora asked.

"Add a few centuries," I muttered, feeling immediately stricken when the woman stared at me.

Her eyes widened, and she looked around at us. I held out my phone—not turned on as it was still too recently submerged no matter what my case claimed it would protect.

The phone was curious enough in appearance that Nora sat backwards, collapsing into the bed of furs. She looked at Eli.

"Truth. She spoke truth. You died well over one hundred years ago. Murdered." Eli still sounded soothing, but it was no longer working. His agitation slipped into his voice. Undoubtedly, I was not the only one here exhausted from our run-swim in the frigid, battering sea. Every one of us had expended magic and muscles, and yet another enemy stood glaring at us.

"And so you are telling me that there are memories after these now in my mind." Nora tapped her head as if she could summon her recollections. Her lips pursed briefly, and her gaze narrowed. "I remember this. There was a book in my father's laboratory. Stasis of the living."

She placed her hand flat over her bloodied gown and bowed her head. "He killed me then. My spouse?"

"He does that to a lot of people," I offered, but her expression was no less darkened.

In that moment, I had a glimpse of the terrifying woman that Nora might be if enraged. There was a glint in her eyes that promised violence. I glanced at Beatrice, who nodded at me. She saw that same promise.

"I need to speak to him." Nora nodded, as if that was *that*.

"You cannot." Iggy pushed to his feet. "And though I have feelings for you, Gunnora, if you strike me again magically or otherwise, I will not forgive it."

She looked down her nose at him, even though he was taller. "Oh? I've no proof that you are *significant* to me."

Iggy sighed. "Do those not significant know about the double cherry birthmark on your—"

"Cad!" She raised her hand as if to slap him, and Iggy caught her wrist.

"You are alive at the will of my associates, Gunnora. You are here safely, as you are *useful* to us." The Master Hexen was anything but gentle in his words. "I died because you were untrustworthy, so until—or *if* —your memory returns such that you might explain yourself, I shall treat you as a hostile entity."

Nora's mouth opened and closed.

"He'll find us eventually. With her in"--Iggy made a sweeping gesture with his hand toward his former beloved--"this useless state, I recommend we exit."

"And how do you propose we do that?" Beatrice rolled her eyes. "You are too depleted for us to traverse the sea, but even if we did that . . ."

"Not a lot of options here." Iggy pointedly stared at me. "If there were a way to travel that was . . . magical."

"Donkey nuts." I reached over for Eli's hand. "Is it the worst idea ever?"

"Quite possibly," Eli murmured, but without another word, Eli opened a doorway to *Elphame*.

Nora whispered, "Avalon!"

"Not quite. Daughter of mine?" Beatrice met my gaze and then looked at my spouse. "Eli? Shall I?"

He nodded.

"In you go." I stepped through the portal, leading the way. I wasn't sure that we'd receive a kind welcome by bringing the exiled prince, the queen of the *draugr*, and Chester's resurrected wife.

Or me.

Or Iggy.

I had a sword up and a hex at the ready as soon as my feet touched fae soil. A heartbeat later, the rest of our motley crew was at my back.

"Judas," Beatrice hissed in greeting as the king stepped forward.

"Dungeons." Marcus pivoted to leave, and we were at the mercy of the same guards who had once fought at our sides, protected us, called us heirs. He was as much an enemy as Chester now.

"Uncle," I called.

The king of *Elphame* paused but did not look back.

"Do not be so foolish," Eli said, though I wasn't sure if he was speaking to me or to Marcus.

"You threatened my *vows*," I said, calmly, lightly, not hexing him. "You would sacrifice us both?"

While I was speaking, I ripped open another tear and shoved Eli and Beatrice through it. They landed in the kitchen of our home in New Orleans, a place Chester couldn't enter, a place Marcus wouldn't.

That left me, the woman who was to be a weapon, and a Master Hexen. Neither of them was strictly banned from *Elphame* —nor were they people Marcus would refuse to let out when the time came. I was the only person here that was not allowed, but I wasn't leaving the weapon here undefended.

"You have the common sense of a viper, Death Maiden," one of the guards whispered.

It felt like praise.

"Dungeons," Marcus repeated before vanishing to wherever he went to pout and rage.

We might be captured, but I wasn't as daunted as maybe I ought to be. The weapon Chester sought—and the man who apparently loved her—were imprisoned in *Elphame*, while Chester was in Scotland hunting us.

It wasn't exactly perfect, but honestly, I'd faced worse odds earlier in the day. Progress, however slight, was still a reason to smile.

⚜ 21 ⚜

ELI

"Absurd woman!" Eli lifted his hand as if to tear a rip in the air, to go after her, but Beatrice spoke, "Wait!"

He paused.

"Think, Eli." She had the cajoling tone that *he* was used to adopting when dealing with his irate spouse, and he wondered briefly if Geneviève found it as grating as he currently did. "Marcus has the might to imprison us all, possibly to hand us all over to Chester."

"If this is a pep talk, you're not doing very well." Eli lowered his hand to his side, nonetheless. She might take her time getting to her point—seemingly assuming what was obvious to *her* was obvious to everyone—but Beatrice was an elder *draugr.* She knew warfare in a way that made her a clever adversary.

And she likely knew warfare as well as his uncle did.

"Everyone has a weakness," Beatrice continued. "Geneviève is yours."

Eli nodded, not quite following. "That's not exactly a secret."

"What is Marcus' weakness?" Beatrice stared at him, her lips curving in the sort of smile that reminded him that his grandmother-in-law was a predator—one who was currently furious with his uncle.

Before Eli could reply, she continued, "Alice adores Geneviève. Rightly so. And I am not so patient as to think that we ought to wait to explore exactly how much that man ought to grovel."

"You know where Allie is." He stared at the *draugr* queen in a kind of admiration that nearly made him speechless.

Beatrice said nothing. She simply picked up a mobile and made a call. "Unfortunately, my dear, your time to think about what you want is at an end."

Eli watched as she caught Alice Chaddock up on the events that necessitated her actions. Even without fae hearing, he'd have heard her response: "Well that badger-buggering, pencil-dicked, fool!"

"Yes, dear." Beatrice looked at Eli and smiled, flashing extended fangs. "I knew you'd want to help."

"That's my *boss*. That's Geneviève," Allie exclaimed. "She's the *princess*."

"He's rescinded that," Beatrice murmured. "He offered to end their marriage. To--" She paused. "Yes, dear. We can wait right here at the house. Yes, Geneviève and Eli's house while you—"

Beatrice held the phone away from her then. "She disconnected."

"Can she enter *Elphame* without aid?" Eli wasn't sure where she was or how long it would take to get there, but he was willing to risk anything for Geneviève.

"Oh, there are always guards on Ms. Chaddock," Beatrice said. "I've had my people look after her, but *his* kind are nearby."

"My kind," Eli reminded her.

And for a strange moment, Beatrice looked almost pitying. "Eli, you bonded with Geneviève. You've notice the *draugr* gifts you now have, yes?"

"Yes."

"You and Geneviève are your *own* kind now," Beatrice continued. "She is more than me. More than fae. And so . . . by your bond, you became something more. As much as I would like to shove your uncle in a woodchipper inch by traitorous inch, he is not wrong to remove you from his throne."

Eli blinked at her. "But you made Geneviève your heir."

"In this world, she will be magnificent, but surely, you know that she is not meant for *Elphame*." The *draugr* queen stepped forward and patted his cheek. "You would both be bored there."

He stared, realizing that she was, in truth, playing a game several steps ahead of them all, and Eli was grateful that she was not their enemy.

"You knew she'd draw Chester's attention," he finally managed to say.

She had the grace to admit, "Not quite so soon, but it was inevitable after you bonded. I have made plans."

"You knew he'd come after her, and you simply allowed him to nearly k—"

Beatrice *flowed* so she was chest-to-chest with him. "Do not think for a moment that I want her to die. I thought she'd have enough sense to learn more before drawing his attention, but there are contingency plans. Always. I will not let him destroy my legacy."

Eli turned away from her, saying only, "One hour. Then I go after my wife, and damn the consequences."

22

ALLIE

Allie wasn't ready to deal with that sidewinder of a man, but she disconnected the call and sighed. "Got to go, Aunt Glory. Geneviève needs me."

"You just got here! You tell that boss of yours that you'll be there five minutes before the pope starts wearing frilly knickers." Glory finished her sentence with a slap on the kitchen table.

Luckily the coffee was down to the dregs, so nothing spilled.

"She's been taken hostage," Allie clarified.

"Well, that's different." Glory pushed back from the table with a screech of chair in the visible grooves from prior outrages. She was an expert in temper, drama, and ass whuppings. "You need to get anything from the closet?"

Glory Nichols was somewhere between forty and sixty-five. No one really knew, but the woman had smoked so many packs of menthol cigarettes that she had that vaguely mummified look going on. The smokes and the tanning salon made her expressions always seem over-exaggerated, as if she needed to verbalize what her muscles no longer revealed.

"Grab your purse, girlie." Glory marched out to the Closet of Surprises, which—though the name remained—had grown and evolved into an entire spare room these days. Glory claimed that it was "on account of these neck biters," but the truth was that Glory had always had an experimental streak in her. It's why no one thought it was particularly odd when her second husband had walked into the grocery, started shoving packages of discount burgers into his trousers, and waited until someone called the sheriff. He'd had to stop and restart his theft a few times before he was finally arrested. Jail was better than facing his wife when she was in a vengeful spirit.

"What about a varmint trap?" Glory pointed at what looked like a bear trap with an external battery wired onto it. "Stopped more than a few of those biters with that one."

"New invention?" Allie studied it, not touching the contraption.

"Last year." Glory held up what looked like bear spray containers. "This one is a holy water base with a salt and cayenne juice."

"Holy water doesn't work on *draugr*," Allie pointed out.

"So *they* said, but they don't always tell the truth, do they?" Glory snorted. "Raised you better than this, girlie. Can't trust the government."

Allie nodded.

"I have a fae one I was working on, too. Not perfect, but it's a salt and iron one. Miss Billie? You remember her? She has that little herbal store, selling tinctures and tonics, though if you ask me they're mostly moonshine with some things floating in it, but she gets around those liquor laws by adding herbs, so who am I to argue? Anyhow, she had this iron supplement one, and so I bought it up and dehydrated it to lower the liquid, you know?" Glory paused, obviously waiting for a response.

"Clever," Allie dutifully supplied.

"Isn't it? So I evaporated a bunch of the 'shine. Now it's more iron but in a purse size." Glory held it out to Allie. "Go on. Take it. You can be my field tester."

Allie took it, a few tiny smoke bombs, a stick or three of dynamite, and she dropped them into her purse.

Glory must've seen something on Allie's face, though, because she paused and patted Allie's cheek. Then she said, "You need me to call up some of your cousins? Nothing they got over there will stop the boys from coming back home if they go with you for back-up."

Allie felt like the weight of a mountain slid off her shoulders. "Would they mind?"

"Not if I tell them not to," Glory announced with the surety of a woman who never saw a river too deep, a rock too heavy, or a person too stubborn. Glory did what she wanted, and damn the fool who tried to stop her.

"You know you're my idol," Allie called after her.

Her aunt's laughter was a thing of joy. This, of course, was the part that most folks didn't understand about Alice Chaddock. She was a Nichols' girl first. She was a backwoods, mountain bred, sass slinging, country music singing, take no guff kind of woman. She'd figured out poise and polish—layered it on like the foundations and powders, designer labels and expensive jewelry—but under it all, her roots were fed on a rather liberal understanding of the law.

Not an hour later, Allie and five of her cousins stood in the yard outside Glory's house.

Not thirty minutes later, they were at a doorway, a place where Allie herself could open a passage to *Elphame*. She knew it was because of the bracelet that Marcus had given her—which she clutched in her hand now—but she also understood that it was because he was trying to trick her. Woo her. Court her. And do it without admitting that he wasn't *really* her friend.

She slid open the passageway, motioned her cousins in, and then she stepped inside.

Guards, of course, greeted her. They had orders not to harm her, and she was hoping that was enough to keep her family safe, too, but then again, the dirty snake had tried to ruin the boss' marriage—and agreed to let Geneviève get murdered.

Allie flipped her shotgun from her side up to rest in her arm like she was cradling a baby. With a big smile, she announced, "I am here to rescue Geneviève, and the first one of you who tries to take me to his royal ass-pimple before I do so will discover how much spare rage I have tucked inside my handbag." She looked around at them. "Questions?"

23

GENEVIÈVE

I sat on the floor of my cell. It wasn't exactly posh digs. For all the fae did beauty, they apparently decided to really lean into the whole dungeon idea. Earth cell, steel bars, and tight space. The cells were damp, and they smelled vaguely of mold. Iggy and Gunnora were in other cells. Iggy was pacing, and Nora was sitting on her cot glaring at him.

Considering recent events, though, I was fairly calm. I had been debating a nap, but when I'd stretched out on the earth, Nora shrieked. "Is she dead? The witch. Is she dying? *Do* something!"

Her panic wasn't restful—but in fairness, if I was awakened from a magical slumber, told my spouse had basically killed me, and surrounded by strangers, I wouldn't be too chipper either.

"It will be fine," I said yet again as Nora started to rock like a frightened child. "These sorts of things happen."

Iggy shot me a look, but I shrugged. All things considered it was better than I could have hoped. Now I just had to hope that Chester wasn't going to appear here and take away both my Hexen Master and my weapon.

Or my life.

A clanging sound echoed, and Nora jumped up, poised to fight. "Maybe it's just a guard," I whispered.

Then, I heard footsteps. A lot of footsteps.

Iggy met my gaze. He looked as tired as I felt. "Into the breach once more . . ."

I nodded.

"Geneviève? Boss?"

"Thank goodness." I felt the tension release. Though I can't say I was genuinely shocked when I heard the angry tones of my assistant, I was relieved in a way that I hadn't expected.

"Our calvary approaches," Iggy murmured.

The part that I wasn't prepared for the last few years: friends who were willing to raze castles or face monsters. I'd kept my life-long friends—Jesse, Christy, and Sera—as sheltered as much as I could manage. For most of my life, I'd kept the whole "oh hi, I behead monsters" thing as separate from my social circle as I could, but then people regularly started trying to kill me.

I mean, sure, *draugr* had tried when I was beheading them, but that wasn't personal. It was simple survival instinct, which apparently didn't die even when people did. The moment they started an unlife, *draugr* were in full possession of that urge—despite the lack of a pulse.

But it wasn't just the undead anymore, political assassination attempts or hate groups. Lately everyone seemed to be trying to end my life. Honestly, I wasn't even sure they could. Being the only living *draugr* made that question difficult. Still, they could—and did—bring the pain. And my friends, old and new, were still here.

Case in point: Alice Chaddock.

I looked through the bars of the dungeon, which was fash-ioned after some sort of Wild West jail with steel bars and hard beds. At least it had a partition to allow for bathroom privacy. For that, I was inordinately grateful.

"Allie?" I called out. "Down here. I'm so glad you . . ."

Whatever else I was thinking vanished as she marched toward me, leading what looked like a squadron of fae guards and hillbilly mafia.

Allie was wearing a combination of hillbilly and designer, and her purse was bulging—as were the pockets of the vest she had over her t-shirt. From the back of her purse, the hilt of a knife jutted out. Her entourage was, well, as *un*expected as I'd come to expect from her, to be honest.

"Allie?"

"Hi boss! Lady B said you needed a key," she chirped. Quieter still, she added, "You might want to step back. *Way* back."

I had known her long enough to realize that my assistant-friend-almost-murderer was mild in her words, especially when she was at her deadliest. So I walked to the far back corner, braced myself, and was pleased when I looked up to see Iggy and Nora following my lead in their cells.

Then my sweet, designer boot-clad assistant pulled a stick of what looked like dynamite from one of her vest pockets and jabbed it in the lock. Gleefully, she lit it with one of those bright pink plastic lighters that every gas station used to keep at the front counter.

"Fire in the hole," she whispered, sounding a bit more like a pyromaniac than I'd heard since our ill-fated "girls' weekend" at a spa where the menu was more murder and mayhem.

A moment or two later, the *pop* of the lock exploding almost covered Allie's gleeful giggle. The guards watched her the way children watched fireworks on the rare occasion that we still had any.

Allie was like that right now, a light show in motion. Clad in designer boots and a pair of elegant trousers, she might look like her usual self, but that was topped with a bright red bandana tied around her throat like she was going to tug it up and rob a bank. She finished her uniform with an armory vest, and under it, a sequined t-shirt that announced "I warned you. Now you get the horns." The bull's eyes—on either side of the word "you"—were big red stones. On anyone else, I'd think they were fake. With Allie, you never really knew.

I didn't even try to smother my grin. "I missed you."

I stepped out and accepted the weapon she handed me.

"Sorry you were kidnapped and imprisoned," she said lightly. "Oh! Do you need a snack?"

Two of the hillbilly mafia with her—wearing forest camouflage despite our setting—jerked open doors of cells once Allie had blown the locks.

I mutely accepted what looked like a homemade popsicle out of a freezer bag. Blood ice cubes weren't as silly looking, but I wasn't going to turn it down. "I wonder if you can make a jello shot sort of thing," I asked.

She handed me a couple airplane bottles. Vodka. I awkwardly stuffed the popsicle in my mouth long enough to twist them open.

"I had a hard lemonade, but Ike was nervous, so . . ." Allie shrugged. "I gave it to him."

The refrigerator-sized man in flannel who looked sheepish was obviously Ike. "Must be cool to live on booze, right?"

"Tiny already does," another man said. "Ain't that right, Tiny?"

I slid the hunting knife into a holster. It was a terrible fit, but it was just for a moment while I drained the vodka bottles.

"I like popsicles too," the tallest of the men, Tiny, said, eying up my blood-pop. "What kind of juice is that? Looks like you used food coloring. Strawberries?"

Apparently, breaking and entering or jailbreaks weren't enough to rattle them. I wasn't sure that the contents of my meal would be, but I didn't feel like checking. Knife back in one hand, popsicle in the other, I looked at Iggy and Nora who were having a heated conversation in whispers.

"I'm okay with Iggy and Nora staying here and—"

"Nope." Allie popped the word. "Lady B says they need to go

home." She started to direct the troops, checking the other cells and marching toward a wall.

It looked like we were headed deeper into the dungeon, though, which was exactly the wrong direction.

"Revolveress?" Iggy called.

"What kind of pissant weasel makes cells of *iron* in a fae world?" Allie gestured at the jail cells. Then she motioned to the fae guards at her side. "Look at them. It would make them all sorts of sick to be trapped here."

"Allie!"

She looked at me.

"That's a dead end." I pointed with the knife.

And she gave me another of those ridiculous, beautiful, mad grins. "It's a door." Then she stepped around me and opened a passageway to my house. "Take the boys, please."

One of the guards bowed to me. "We go where you go."

"I need to see a man about his lies," Allie said, as at least three of her cousins flinched. One covered his balls with a hand. Allie ignored that and glared at each of them before saying, "She's family to me, you hear? Don't be a bother."

The chorus of "yes, Cousin Al" and "on it, cuz" and "you sound like Glory" must've been appeasing because she shooed them forward—Iggy went first to avoid any stabbings on the other side--and then I was back home with guests.

24

GENEVIÈVE

"Where is Alice?" Beatrice asked as we stepped into my house.

"She's fine," I offered—because that was what Beatrice really wanted to know.

Her gaze scoured me like she was an anxious mother and I'd blown curfew, so I knew she was already certain of my safety. Still, she paused, "I am pleased no one is dead."

"How's she know that?" Ike asked.

"I cannot smell any blood," Beatrice said with a flash of fang.

All five men stepped in front of me, forming a wall of camo and shotguns. Honestly, I was touched. . . if not for the fact that my grandmother could rip all their throats out without warning.

"She's a *fanger.*" Tiny pulled out a stun gun that was buzzing with enough voltage to make me wince. "Harlow? Get the holy grenade."

"Primed," a very feminine voice said, and I realized awkwardly that the fifth person wasn't a man after all.

"Bonbon?" Eli prompted, asking what we were to do.

I threw a hex that caused the *draugr* to be behind a wall. "*Draugr.*"

Then I pointed at Iggy, "Witch."

Then at Eli. "Faery."

Then at myself. I stumbled briefly on what to say and settled for "All the above."

I didn't know what to call Nora. *Dead until recently? Lazarus? Alchemist? Amnesiac? Weapon, hopefully?* So, I ignored her briefly and looked back at the five humans and four faeries.

"This is my home," I said plainly. "Anyone who threatens *anyone else* who is present right now will answer to me, and honestly, I make all of you look like paper dolls."

Iggy scoffed. "Only if you stop hamstringing yourself."

Beatrice raised a brow at me, but she didn't argue. I wasn't as sure if I could actually best her, but I also had no desire to do so. For all of our awkwardness, she was family now, as my wall of protection made more or less clear.

Suddenly, the tension dropped as Allie's cousin Ike said, "Heeeey!" With a low whistle, he pointed. "That's a *bar* in your house, man."

"Help yourself," Eli said genially. "You have rescued my wife. I will not begrudge you a drink."

❦

"I HATE THAT WE HAD TO LEAVE ALLIE THERE," I GRUMBLED AS I finished filling in Beatrice and Eli.

"Lady Alice will make the king rue the day he deceived her," one of the guards said sagely.

The camo-clad person with the high voice said, "Cousin Al will make his guts into garters if he thinks he can treat her like a child."

"Cousin Al?" I asked.

"Alice."

The other members of Allie's family all lifted their glasses.

Tiny lifted a bottle of vodka in a toast. "To Cousin Al, long may she reign!"

Beatrice looked at them with a strange glint in her eye, but unless she was plotting a murder, I wasn't sure I had the bandwidth to ask what thoughts she was mulling over. Honestly, I was more interested in Nora, who was remembering more apparently.

"You!" She crossed her arms. "You were . . . we . . . He'll *kill* you if he hears what you said to me." She slapped Iggy. "I am not that sort of woman."

Iggy just stared at her for several moments. Then he said, "Liar."

Nora backed away from him, tears in her eyes. "How dare y—"

"Wait till the next century comes to you, doll." He scowled. "He did kill me. It was worth it, though. Having you under m—"

She muttered something, tossed what looked like a handful of grass at him, and Iggy froze completely.

Beatrice *flowed* toward Nora, but Nora pulled something out of another pocket and again, she attempted to freeze someone.

I *flowed* not at Nora but to Eli's side, just as he moved toward me. I wasn't going to leave him vulnerable, and he obviously felt the same. The faeries who had come through with us moved toward me, and the cousins looked to me for instruction.

"Stand down," I ordered. Everyone but Nora obeyed.

Honestly, the fae and the cousins were better trained than some military members.

I caught Nora's gaze, realizing that she looked like a feral thing that had been cornered. Whatever I didn't know about her —and that was a *lot*—I was certain that she was dangerous when corned.

"Look I don't know what you're going through, Nora, but maybe don't attack the people who brought you back to life." I had my hands out, palm facing her, in a placating gesture. It also would make hexing her faster if I needed to do so. "We aren't your enemies."

That, obviously, was the wrong word. Nora glared at Iggy. "He stole me away, like I was . . . chattel."

"Iggy cares for you," I said.

She gave me a look that could burn buildings down. "So he says. Has he lied to you? Misdirected you? Do men still do such things in this time?"

"Everyone does such things, I suspect," I allowed.

"I do not." Nora crossed her arms. "I remember him stealing me. My husband was distraught, destroyed the manor. Then I remember being back there without Ignatius. My door was barred, and I could hear . . ."

"I wasn't there, and *your* memory is still wobbly. If he was the one who left you in stasis, do you suppose he is truly your ally?" I stared at her, trying to direct her toward the obvious conclusion: Chester was her enemy.

The recently dead woman nodded slightly, acknowledging my statement as valid. I think she must have been formidable in her time—which begs a question.

"How did you meet your husband?"

Silently I added, *the rat gnawing bastard.* Somehow, I don't think she'd appreciate hearing my opinion of Chester spoken aloud. Yet. I wished her remaining memories would return, but I suspected it was a complicated process after decades of death.

"He was a student of my father, and over time, he won my hand." Nora sounded less sure of herself now. "I was lucky to have such a talented man interested in me."

"You chose him then?" I pushed.

"My father wanted a successor, a worthy student. I was the . . . incentive to accompany the knowledge. I was trained, but as a woman"—Nora gave me a rue smile—"I was thought to be less capable, so the knowledge was not solely mine. If we had created a son, perhaps, but . . . I was not worthy. Not to my husband or father. There were rules for women."

"That, unfortunately, still remains your husband's stance on women, Nora."

I felt like we were connecting, making progress, but she stared at me. Silent. Thinking.

"Let Iggy go, please. Then we—"

But everything went dark suddenly, and my words were lost in sudden chaos. I couldn't say what had happened.

All I knew for certain was that I was on the ground, and Lady Lazarus was done listening to me.

25

GENEVIÈVE

Whatever Nora had done left me on my knees, unable to rise. I felt as if a hand had reached into my chest, squeezed all the air from my lungs, and rolled those thin membranes into a crumpled ball.

I wasn't sure if I was dying or not—and I wasn't sure if dying would *matter*. That was the trick of my heritage. *Draugr* were, by definition, dead. I was . . . not dead, but still *draugr*. So if I died, would I wake? Would it kill Eli, as we were bound together? I had more questions than answers, so I was typically a solid member of the "death bad" camp.

But in that moment, I didn't think it mattered. Whatever Nora had done meant that I was crouched on the floor as chaos erupted around me. The hillbilly mafia was alternately trying to attack Nora and trying to protect Eli, Beatrice, and me. At my side was Harlow, the one I'd thought was a man like the rest of the humans but whose voice made me re-assess.

Since I couldn't move, I studied Harlow. Clean face, not a speck of stubble. Features and dress and voice all combined to say that "nonbinary" was probably the right category. Labels were weird—as

I realized when I was classifying Eli as fae, Iggy as Hexen, Beatrice as *draugr,* and unable to figure out what word there was for what *I* am. I am those, but not just any one of those. Perhaps labels weren't always as hard as I thought, even though some people acted like they were.

"Can you blink?" Harlow asked.

I tried.

"So that's progress," they said. "Once for yes. Twice for no."

I blinked once.

"Can I shoot her? The one who froze you? Gunner? Nora?"

I blinked twice.

"Damn it." Harlow crouched as a chair flew past us. She looked down at me. "Your husband is raging."

I tried to turn my head to see him, to see anything, but it wasn't working.

"Stop her. No bullets," Harlow yelled.

"Aw, man," a voice grumbled. "Ask the boss about stabbing."

I blinked once. *Stab away,* I thought to myself. Hopefully, they all had the sense not to stab anything vital.

Harlow reached down and brushed powder off my face. Within moments, I could turn my neck. I wasn't sure there was a connection, but I started shaking my head. Alchemy was connected to what I practiced, but it was also the sort of magic work that required herbs and tinctures more than *just* will. I suspect, like a lot of similar fields, there was overlap.

Harlow threw a knife, looked down at me, and said, "Whatever is all over you is magic, right?"

I blinked once. I wasn't *sure,* but a yes/no communication system was a bit limiting so I couldn't say "maybe" or "probably." And I was guessing Iggy was also frozen.

That left Beatrice as the only magic user. Now that I could turn my head, I could see her. She wasn't *flowing.* It was as if the ancient *draugr* was moving through a thick vat of cold molasses. Whatever alchemical mix Nora was using, it was powerful enough to slow down Beatrice—who wasn't giving up despite that sluggishness.

Nora, however, kept side-stepping the *draugr*'s punches.

"Getting the magic off you is good," Harlow prompted.

I blinked.

Harlow took in where I looked and my facial expressions as I struggled to make my mouth shape words. Finally, I managed, "Dust...witches."

"Rinse *all* the witches," they called. "Boss says so."

With that, Harlow uncapped a bottle of tequila and dowsed me with it. Later I might wince at the cost of that bottle, but in the moment, all I could say was, "Thank you."

No one seemed eager to do the same to Beatrice, but Iggy was promptly rinsed with a carafe of red wine and a bottle of milk that someone had fetched.

It felt like my muscles were slowly reactivating. I could move my hands, my arms, my legs. Iggy wasn't as agile yet.

And Beatrice was still trying to attack Nora in her slow-motion way.

Eli was in command of the fae guards, protecting the lot of us as they tried to knock down Nora's shield.

The old alchemist, however, was simply attacking everyone—like her pent-up rage bubble had found its way to her surface and she was experimenting with various herbs and sachets she'd had hidden in the myriad hidden pockets of her dress for a century or two. Every so often, she would glare at Iggy and sniffle.

"Nora, love," he said, as his head was finally free of whatever spell she'd doused him with a few minutes ago.

"You made me break my *vows*." She made a sound that was best described as a feral growl. "How could you?"

"No one made you do a damn thing, woman." Iggy took a step toward her, and her hand raised as if she was going to strike him.

Honestly, I wasn't sure what other herbs or poisons she had hidden, so I decided to remove her from the possibility of threatening anyone else. I *flowed* toward her fast enough that I knew it looked like teleportation to the humans in the room.

As I reached Nora, I wrapped my arms around her, stopping her from flinging anything else at the inhabitants of the room. Then, not slowing down, I crashed us through a window and into the yard below.

At least we didn't put in that fountain, I thought, as we crashed into the earth.

"Release me," Nora demanded.

I realized I was wrapped around her like a koala on a tree, which was obviously a little awkward for at least one of us if Nora's expression was accurate. She struggled briefly, but she had taken the brunt of the fall. So her body probably hurt more than mine, and I was decidedly achy.

"We are not your enemies," I explained carefully. "You attacked my family, destroying my sitting room, and we brought your moldy ancient carcass back to life."

She stilled.

"Your husband kills, tortures, and by the way, *hates women*." I stared down at her. "You don't have to believe me, but if he's such a great guy why did he leave you in a Neolithic tomb?"

Nora said nothing.

"I found you. *We* found you. And aside from Iggy, none of us knew you." I paused, and when she said nothing else, I added, "He was torturing me, and I saw what he considered his greatest fear. You. That's how I knew you existed, and we came to find you."

"Please, release me."

I rolled off her, wondering briefly why no one had followed me until I realized that the sensible move was to take the stairs rather than leap out a window.

"Women have more rights today, Nora. Remember that as the rest of your memories come back." I considered holding out a hand, but while I apparently forgive a lot of things, I'm not so daft as to do so within moments of attack.

"I will speak to Chester before I make any decisions," she said before pivoting and walking away.

I whispered a command to the gates, which opened to let her exit, just as Iggy came outside, yelling her name and a few sentences in French that I couldn't translate at all.

"Why did you release her?" Beatrice asked from the doorway of the house. "Not only do we have no weapon. *He* has one."

"She's not a weapon!" Iggy. "She's in peril!"

"Would you have me hold her prisoner? Force her to obey us as Chester would do? As the King of Elphame would do?" I looked from Iggy to Beatrice. "She has choices. All women should."

"He'll kill her," Iggy whispered.

Beatrice reminded him. "He is afraid of her. That is not for nothing."

I hoped Nora would survive. Hell, I hoped she'd take her rage to Chester and destroy him.

26

ALLIE

llie walked through the palace with a purpose that twisted her belly, but what she needed to do wasn't avoidable. Not now. She hated it, hated the King of *Elphame* a little for making this all happen. She'd simply say her piece and go home. It sucked, thinking that she met someone who respected her, saw her, cared for her—only to find out what he really was.

"Alice!" Marcus held out both hands as she approached. He had that same beautiful smile, the one that made it perfectly clear that her very presence brightened his day.

And damn him if he wasn't every fine thing that a man could be. The fae were always beautiful. It was simply as much a truth as water being wet. He had the sort of eyes Allie thought she might fall into, and she knew from her prior visits here, that the arms that were open in invitation were as strong as steel. Muscles corded the fae king's body, and she'd had a few damnable dreams about the body that stood before her now.

A part of her that was controlled by a more southerly set of impulses was ready to get closer. For all that he was a jerk, the king of *Elphame* was easy on the eyes, and being a widow—a high profile one—meant that Allie wasn't a huge fan of casual sex. She was still on long-term contraception because she wasn't a fool, but her options had been to either casually break her vow to too-recently departed beloved or jump into a relationship before she felt ready.

"You weasel-dicked, lying, deceitful . . . turnip head," Allie muttered.

"Alice?" His invitation didn't vanish, but he scowled now.

She stepped closer, swatted his hand away before he could touch her and slapped him hard across the face. "Do. *Not*. Touch. Me."

Guards seemingly materialized out of thin air. Hell, maybe they did materialize. She wasn't exactly well-versed in the nuances of all things fae. What she *was* far too well-versed in was lying men.

"I told you I wasn't ready to even be thinking of dating anyone." She poked a finger into his chest. Fine, *against* it. For a man several centuries older than her, Marcus was as fit as a construction worker in summer. "I said all I wanted was to be your friend. How dare you try to *marry* me? And ask my boss to hide it? What sort of deceitful--"

"Now, Alice—"

"Nuh-uh. You don't talk to me like that." She sniffled and then continued, "And then to say my boss is fine to let that Chester person just . . . *murder her*? What sort of person agrees to that? Certainly not one I'd ever call a friend. And poor Eli! Do you know what it would do to him to lose her?" Allie realized, awkwardly, that she was crying. Big tears were streaking down her face.

"There was a spell. If I severed their bond, he wouldn't die," Marcus explained.

"Die? When my husband died, I'd have rather been dead than suffer as I have." She swiped at her tears. "I'm not talking about his body. I'm talking about his heart."

"I have to think about all of my subjects and Chester—"

"Coward." Allie crossed her arms. "Do you know what I did when someone wanted to kill my husband? My stepson?" She glared at him. "I tried to *save* them."

"You have to understand—"

"I do not. I don't like you, Marcus. I will not be returning here visiting you or . . . *anything*." She turned to leave. "Anyone who thinks breaking his family's heart or trapping a woman in marriage to such a fucking *monster* . . . well, you're not the person I thought you were, Marcus."

He spoke a word in his language, and suddenly, she was faced with two armed fae guards. They didn't touch her, but they blocked her path. And while Allie was a resourceful woman, she wasn't ready to resort to violence against people who were simply doing their jobs.

"Move."

They didn't reply--or move out of her way.

Allie pivoted. "So help me, Marcus. You're crossing the wrong woman right now. . . . Tell them to get out of my way."

A *thud* sounded behind her as the door fell shut.

"They are out of your way." He stepped closer, approaching her warily but still approaching her. "It's just us here, my love."

When she looked over her shoulder, there were no guards. At least, there were none on this side of the door. "Sharing your true colors, I see."

"You are angry," Marcus started.

"You think?" She tried waving her bracelet in the air to open a doorway, but he caught her hand and slid the circlet from her arm.

Allie backed out of his touch, hating that even as he enraged her she felt like he left fire on her skin.

"I know you are upset about these things, but you cannot leave me, Alice." Marcus gave her a sad look. "There are no longer heirs to *Elphame*. And you, my love, are the woman I've waited for my entire life."

"Go to hell."

He let out a long sigh. "Let me take you to your chambers, Alice. When you are calm, we can discuss this again."

Alice was fairly sure she had never been this infuriated in her entire life, and for any woman with a speck of self-respect, there were eight hundred and thirty-seven reasons to be spitting mad on an average day.

"Your throne will turn to dust, Marcus of Stonecroft, before I let you so much as touch my foot." Allie shook her finger at him. "You might be easy on the eyes, but I will not sully my body with a liar. Now let me go home."

"Faeries don't lie," he pointed out. "And you *are* home. In time, you will calm, and then you will see what foolishness this is."

Allie hissed. It was all she could do not to scream, and the noise slipped between her teeth like a warning from something deadly.

"Call it what you want, Marcus, but hiding things from me is the same as lying to me," Allie said, voice level finally. "I want to go back to my home. My job. My things. People I *like*."

He offered her his arm, as if her rage was no more than a snit, and it took all of her self-control not to slap him again.

"You came here, and you will stay here. This is my domain, Alice, and you will remain here where I can be certain of your safety."

27

GENEVIÈVE

ack inside my home, I looked around and smothered a gasp. My home was in shambles, and Iggy was pacing like a tiger in a cage.

Eli, however, had me wrapped in his arms, and though my husband was not particularly fond of public displays of affection, his mouth covered mine and he kissed me so thoroughly that I was ready to ignore the disaster that was our current situation and pull him into a private corner.

When he pulled back, I sighed.

His hands cupped my cheeks. "You are amazing, but seeing you hurtle through our window . . ."

"Yes." And that was it, really. What else could I say?

He understood why I did the things I did, and I understood that it took a faery's kind of patience to not wrap me in cotton and hide me away.

That was the part that had made me feel so unlovable for so long. I was convinced that a relationship would mean changing myself, trying to fit into an artificial mold of what a woman ought to be. Eli proved me wrong before I even realized that was what he had been doing all the times he stitched my wounds and bandaged my bullet holes.

"I love you," I whispered.

He smiled and lowered his hands, letting me get back to work.

Then his hand slid into mine, and despite the unmitigated disaster of our weapon acquisition and loss, I still felt like maybe I could move mountains—small ones, at least—because he was with me.

"Right, then," I announced. "Weapon? Gone. Alchemist who wants me dead? Still out there. House?" I glanced around at the destruction. "Not looking too promising."

"As a matter of fact, bonbon, this house, and the land under it, are functionally a part of *Elphame*," Eli reminded me. "I am within my rights as the heir of—"

"Your uncle disinherited you," Iggy interrupted.

"Well, to put a political point on the situation, Blackwood, should I want to contest his role as king, I am within rights to do so." Eli mentioned this as casually as noting that the sky was blue or that I had *draugr* traits. His implacable calm was a beautiful thing. "I am of the royal line, and I am no longer sure that Marcus has the good of the people as his first priority."

"You'd take the throne," I asked, turning my head to stare at him in shock.

"To save my wife?" Eli's voice remained calm. "I'd burn this world to save you, but to be clear, Marcus allowed a *named heir* to be tortured. He had not unnamed you when you were taken. How then do I trust the good of my people to such a man?"

He looked away from me to the fae guards that had come with me from *Elphame*. "Tell the king that a challenge for his throne has been issued. Tell the people of his crime against the royal line."

As one, they bowed and departed into a slash in the air that had opened. Before we were the heirs, those gateways were not instant or located wherever we were. The fact that they had become so was a result of our roles as the heirs to the throne—and the fact that they continued so meant that *Elphame* itself still considered us heirs. The land recognized us, even if Marcus had thrown me to the torture chamber and tried to end my marriage.

With nothing more than a nod to Beatrice, Eli pronounced, "You are guests of my home tonight. I would ask that you stay here on this ground. If Chester were to attack you here, it would be an attack on the rightful regent of *Elphame,* and I could declare war."

Iggy shook his head. "Shouldn't one of you two be reasonable?"

Beatrice let out a peal of laughter that felt rather like music to me. "Oh, I like this man, Daughter of Mine. I don't like many of them, but this one? He will do. He will do quite well."

The remaining guests—Allie's cousins--stood awkwardly, and I decided that even dirt covered, blood and seawater soaked, and possibly not likely to see morning without war or other deadly surprises, I was going to step up as lady of the manor.

"Let me show you all to our guest rooms."

I walked away, leaving Iggy with Eli. I wasn't sure what plotting they had yet to do, but I wasn't going to let the humans stay here. If I could, I'd see them to safety, but I wasn't sure how to do that without leaving the house or cutting through *Elphame*—and both of those options seemed dangerous.

I showed Beatrice her room and gave the cousins a pair of rooms that were currently functioning as my fight studio.

Harlow smiled. "Feels like home."

And the rest of the cousins alternated between exploring my in-room armory and the attached bathroom, which was mostly standard fare, or as standard as things can be in a house designed by a faery.

WHEN I RETURNED TO THE MAIN ROOM, IGGY WAS CLEANING.

Beatrice walked back into the main room a few minutes later with a glass of what I was fairly certain was blood. She swirled it in the highball glass. "May I partake of your guests?"

"Freely given?" Eli asked.

"No magic or threats involved. I asked to milk a wound . . ." Beatrice made it sound mundane.

Still, I flinched at that description, but I wasn't in a place to cast stones. Their cousin, my assistant, fed me. A flicker of a thought as to what that would mean washed over me.

Beatrice, reading my expression, said softly, "Iggy will provide for you. That's why I milked Alice's cousins. They offered to feed you, too. It might not be a terrible idea to keep a stable as I'm not convinced that declaring war on the sitting king will entice him to return his only leverage."

"Do you need food?" Iggy asked. Without waiting for a reply, he grabbed a coffee mug with "Dangerous When Provoked" written on it. It looked relatively clean.

Then Iggy whispered a hex that made his skin part and blood poured into the mug.

"That's a hex that I wouldn't mind knowing in a fight," I said, thinking not only of Chester but how nice it would be to fight at a distance more often.

"It only works if you're alive," Beatrice said. "He likely doesn't want an answer to that question, which is why he hasn't shared it yet."

"I *am* alive."

"You're drinking blood, like the formerly-dead do." Beatrice shrugged.

"Not all formerly dead," I grumbled. "Iggy. Nora. The people we reanimate . . ."

"Do you want to learn the hex?" Beatrice asked.

"Well, not now if you're all going to watch me . . ." I pouted in an exaggerated way. Then when Beatrice looked away, I whispered loudly to Iggy, "Tomorrow?"

"I hear you," she said, but she was smiling now.

Iggy rolled his eyes. "Fine."

My ridiculousness had broken some of the tension, which was all I wanted. My great-times-great grandmother and the Hexen Master both smiled.

"We'll figure it out," Eli said calmly. "Even if it means that I must ascend the throne, we will not allow this threat to continue."

No one argued. I wasn't sure we believed him, but no one argued. Chester couldn't be killed, and our weapon had attacked us. I had arguments aplenty on why Eli's plan was not my top choice, but I was bone tired.

"We will figure it out," I agreed.

Tonight, hope would have to be enough.

⚘ 28 ⚘

ELI

Eli watched his wife, his heart, his soul-bonded partner cajole and charm the present members of her odd coterie of chosen family. For her, he would start a war, claim a throne, or burn the world. There was no doubt.

She walked into their bedroom, pulled the door shut, and in the next moment, a wall of thorned roses started to climb the walls as if they were rooted in the very floor of the room. These were not necessarily her doing—as far as he knew. It was just as likely that the house had become increasingly fae because he'd claimed the throne he'd never wanted.

Geneviève marveled at the roses, her eyes alight with wonder, as a riot of color exploded as buds grew and blossomed. She reached out, petting the petals gently, and without looking at him, asked, "So . . . king?"

"If I must."

"You don't want that."

Eli stood watching her, well aware that she did not want to rule either. Between death and ruling, he'd take the throne. "I do not, but he risked your life, Geneviève."

"And yours," she amended, glancing over her shoulder.

"So, you see? We are both upset at the same actions, but in relation to the other," Eli said.

"I was pretty pissed off that he was willing to cast me to death, too. I tried to get along with your uncle. We fought side-by-side. I accepted him as family." Geneviève finally turned to face him. "Family doesn't sacrifice you."

Eli nodded. "Ergo, challenging his throne."

In her usual way, Geneviève switched topics with a speed that made evident how many ideas were swirling in her mind at any given moment. "Do you think I can use the hex?"

"Yes."

"I'm more *draugr* than I used to be before . . ."

"Before you were injected with venom and nearly died? Yes." Eli extended a hand toward her, inviting her closer. When she stepped in, he added, "But your heart still beats, bonbon. You are alive."

"If I died . . ."

"You didn't, and even if you had, you are alive here. Now." Eli wasn't going to deny that he'd pondered what would happen if she truly died. Would the draugr part of her—a part that resisted being subsumed when they'd bonded—mean she was, as with Beatrice, animated as if alive? Would her death mean that they were unbonded?

Would her death even kill him since she likely would continue to exist after death?

The fae bonded, and so the death of one spouse meant the death of both. There was no record of a bond with a *draugr* so there was no answer as to what her peculiar ancestry meant for them. There had, as far as they knew, never been another living *draugr.* It was a sort of magical circumvention of biology that her mother had managed.

Honestly, Mama Lauren was terrifying.

Beatrice, their several generations removed ancestor, was terrifying.

It was no wonder that the King of *Elphame* found Geneviève frightening—or that Chester did. Fear of the unknown, of the *other*, was one thing that never seemed to die. And many men, Chester included, were utterly horrified by powerful women.

Eli, however, was not. He was certain that being loved by her was everything he wanted, and so he would do whatever it took to keep her safe.

"You are a gift, Geneviève. I am sorry these men do not realize that." He pulled her closer still, hands coming to rest on her hips. "I do not quake at the magic you can summon. I do not fear the tripled ancestry in you."

"I know." She tilted her head, asking for a kiss that he gladly gave.

Kissing his wife was a sort of magic that was still new and precious, and Eli suspected it always would be so. When she pulled away, she sighed. "Do you mind if I wash off the blood, booze, and alchemy dust before I climb in that bed to be ravished?"

"Ravished?" he teased.

"Yes, please." Geneviève brushed her hands over his chest and gave him the sort of innocent look that could launch the dogs of war. For that look, for this woman, there were few things Eli wouldn't do.

"Be quick about it," he grumbled, earning a laugh from her.

"Yes, sir."

He paused. "So, it's like that tonight?"

"Yes, sir," she repeated as she *flowed* toward her shower.

What only a wise person realized was that the strongest of women sometimes simply needed to have someone else make the decisions for them behind closed doors.

Not always. Not every day.

Sometimes.

There were plenty of times when Geneviève was a feral creature, but there were plenty of times when all she needed was to not be the person in control—and that, too, was a beautiful thing to know.

Eli was certain he was the luckiest of men.

※ 29 ※

GENEVIÈVE

I took a hurried shower, body free of blood and whatever else remained from our fight with Chester in Scotland . . . and our escape through the sea, imprisonment in *Elphame*, and most recently, the fight with Gunnora. Honestly, that was all on the heels of imprisonment and torture with the twisted sisters in their crackpot faux holy order.

How am I even alive?

I felt a fierce longing for the days when a beheading was the whole of my duties. Maybe there was a way back to that, but it definitely wasn't by becoming a queen. What the fairy tales all fail to mention is that ruling, that balls and banquets, that the stuff of a political life is fraught with assassination attempts and assorted nonsense. I wanted none of it.

Just Eli.

Just a life with my bar-owning faery and my weird friends.

Just the contentment I'd felt the past few months.

I wasn't sure how to reach that, though, and the weight of figuring it out was overwhelming tonight.

When I stepped out of the shower, I brusquely toweled off and walked into the bedroom where Eli had apparently lit a dozen candles around the room. He looked at the bed, and I didn't bother with words. I dropped my towel and walked past him to the bed.

"Arms."

I opened my arms, knowing that restraints would follow.

"Legs."

Again, I obeyed.

There were plenty of times I played at resisting his commands in order to make him more forceful, but tonight, I simply wanted to enjoy being taken care of. So, I watched him stare at me, as if I were a feast for his enjoyment. Honestly, that was all it took for my body to be ready.

"Touch me. Kiss me. Love me," I ask-begged.

"Always." At a word in his language, the room became completely dark. I could see nothing. My inhalation was sharp as I felt his fingers trail over me.

His mouth followed after his hands.

"More," I whispered.

And my husband laughed. "What happened to 'yes, sir'?"

"Please, sir. *Please . . .*"

The room was completed dark and silent but for my whimpering.

And then he was touching me, mouth between my legs and fingers inside my body. I lost count of everything and could only gasp and say, "yes, sir, please, sir, *yes.*"

By the time he was convinced I was boneless, he was over me, sliding into me with enough force that I knew no human could endure his lovemaking without injury.

I was not entirely human, though. We were made to be together. Of that, I was certain.

Afterwards, I could barely move. All the stress and fears of the last few days had been chased away by Eli's love and touches. That was exactly what I'd needed: being taken care of until no thoughts but him remained.

I snuggled against his chest, folded into his embrace face-to-face since we were both on our sides, and said, "I can rest now."

He looked smug at that, but honestly, he *should* be smug. The problem with my strength was that, as I'd learned before him, most people couldn't give me what I needed. Eli knew me as well as I knew him, and together, we were magic. Not just the literal sort of magic, although we had that too. We were the sort of magic that every person dreamed of finding: perfectly matched.

I drifted to sleep like that, curled against him, nestled in the shelter of his arms.

OUR ROOM WAS A VERITABLE FORTRESS. OUR HOME WAS FAE ground. And we were together. It was enough to make me think we were safe.

I should've known better.

I woke not long enough afterwards to the sound of a far-too-familiar male voice roaring "Where are they?"

The door to our room rattled like a monster was ripping it asunder.

"That badger bonking baboon needs to learn a few manners," I muttered as I crawled out of Eli's embrace.

I snatched up a sword and marched toward the door.

"Geneviève. Trousers, perhaps?" Eli gestured at my nakedness.

"Right." I tugged on jeans and one of Eli's shirts. Undergarments could wait. I had a score to settle.

Behind me, Eli made short work of his own dressing. "Could I speak to him before you stab him?"

I sighed. I wasn't *really* going to stab the king of the fae. Logic would've kicked in before I opened the door. I was *almost* certain of it.

I was also vaguely surprised that Marcus hadn't said anything else—until I remembered that we were not alone in the house.

"Pus waffles! Beatrice. She's out there, too." I waved my hand at the vines, and thankfully, the house agreed to let me out despite the angry faery king in my hallway.

Eli looked unruffled at the thought of the *draugr* queen cornering his uncle. Clearly, he was actually *angrier* than I was. Any lingering doubts of that I may have had were quashed when he stepped around me and opened the door.

"If I may?" Eli was facing Marcus in front of me but spoke as if he were addressing me: "I thought I should come out first, Geneviève, in case he's here to try to kill you again."

"Don't be absurd," Marcus said. "I have never tried to kill Geneviève."

"Outsourcing is still murder," I pointed out, leaning around my husband. "Just as deceit is still lying."

Beatrice had a long steel dagger in her hand. She was glaring at the faery standing between us, but she had neither stabbed nor strangled him. I thought it was remarkably patient of her.

"I did not injure him," she muttered. "I could though . . ."

"Not even a bit injured, grandmother?" Eli asked, sounding far too jovial for the moment. "I am impressed."

His calm was a mask. I knew that. I still wasn't sure that teasing Beatrice was a good idea. She was as angry as Eli was about Marcus' recent actions, and she had fewer reasons to resist violence.

"If it's on the menu of options for houseguests, I would be grateful . . ." Beatrice said.

When Marcus tried to side-step her, she hissed at him. Her fangs were an impressive display, but she was family, so it also made me want to toss a ball of yarn in her general direction to see if she swatted it.

"I am the offended party here," I said, drawing all gazes to me. "Shouldn't I be the one to assign his punishment?"

"Am I not offended that he would kill my wife?" Eli still

sounded jovial, and it made me shiver. Maybe I was perverse, but seeing his rage was exciting in a primal way.

"What do you want here?" I asked, ignoring my husband's rage and my grandmother's glee. Beatrice was not stabbing Marcus, but she lunged a few times as she casually flashed her fangs. I could see the *draugr* venom on them and knew that was intentional as well.

"War, Eli? For a man who has no desire to be my heir, you would declare war?" Marcus asked.

"You threatened the heirs to the throne, the *only* heirs." Eli reached out and tapped Beatrice's arm finally.

I guess we are done with the grandstanding for now.

She lowered her weapon and stepped back. It might be posturing, but she had thrown her lot in with Eli in that moment. She obeyed him and threatened the sitting king of *Elphame*. Absently, I realized that may have been the entire point in her actions—politics.

I fucking hated politics. I always felt like I was several steps behind, and sure, maybe I would become a manipulation machine in a few centuries if I lived that long, but right now, I was out of my element.

"This is *my* heir, Marcus of Stonecroft." Beatrice straightened, looking every bit the regal warrior she was. "Every *draugr* I command will come to her aid, whether Chester is her enemy, or *you* are, or any other being is."

"You stand with us against him, or I stand against you with her," Eli said. "And *then* I join my people to hers for this fight against Chester. No one will tear asunder the vows that I made before humans, fae, and *draugr.* Geneviève is my wife. Eternally. She will be made safe."

It hit me then that there was a significance to my three weddings beyond the witchy appreciation of that sacred number. I was a lousy heir to any throne, as my political machinations were absentee at every turn, but I had soldiers aplenty.

No wonder Chester hates me!

"We have found a weapon," I said, drawing all three of their gazes to me.

"If I join this fight, you will rescind your challenge?" Marcus asked.

Eli nodded once.

"And . . ." Marcus cleared his throat. "You'll speak to Alice?"

Beatrice and I exchanged a look.

I muffled a laugh and said, "I'll speak to her and tell exactly what you did here . . . and before. No lies, Marcus. I'm fae now, so I take that 'no lies' things very seriously."

"Let us ready for war, then." Marcus strode away, leaving us there to follow. He might be willing to join us, but he certainly still seemed to act like he was the one in charge.

Men, unfortunately, weren't often as amazing as Eli.

30

GENEVIÈVE

A teenager stood at the fence around our home. I was used to tourists, what with the whole being-fae-royalty thing. I doubted that there had been a declaration from Marcus that we were no longer the royal heirs, and honestly, if there had been a statement, it was likely to draw out more of the lookie-loos rather than discourage their presence.

Rubbernecking wasn't just for horrific accidents.

Being a witch as well as the fiancé and then spouse of *the* faery prince had meant that tourists were like humidity in New Orleans —always vaguely inescapable. At the best of bad situations, Iggy had simply melted the circuitry in tourists' phones. At the worst, well, I had a feeling that the worst was yet to come.

"Two days," Iggy said as he joined me.

"Trapped here?"

"Yes, but also Nora with *him* and . . . for the last twenty-two hours, that child has been pacing at our step." Iggy gestured out the window. "She is here for something."

I stared at her. She was a thin waifish girl, maybe seventeen at most. Her hair was scarlet, the rich tones that said it was recently dyed, and her clothes were nondescript. "She left a few times."

"Food and toilet breaks." Iggy turned away from me and strode toward the door. Since we'd found his lost love, he was surly. I mean, he hadn't been a barrel of funny drunken monkeys previously, but he'd had a wry sense of humor that had offset his dire proclamations.

My Hexen Master was in mourning. There was no other way to explain it. I wasn't sure whether it was simply mourning the loss of a chance with the dead lady or the expectation that she—and possibly *we*—were all doomed.

Allie's cousins were rotating in and out of the room, alternately attacking the fight dummies I'd added to the house and playing poker. Beatrice and Eli were plotting with Marcus. I'd tried to be a part of the planning process, but my desire to see peace between them meant that I'd made Beatrice have to pause to assure me she wasn't really going to rip out Marcus' throat, whereupon Eli shrugged.

Better to deal with a maudlin Iggy and semi-sober hillbillies than my complicated relatives. I weighed returning to the conversation, but then Beatrice came slamming out of the room, *flowing* as if she was going to attack someone.

"I swear to Saint Rita I will behead that man if he doesn't release Alice." Beatrice glared in the direction she'd come. "I needed to step out or rip out his vocal cords. Eli indicated that the rug in there is a priceless one, so blood was a terrible burden."

"Saint Rita?"

"Patron saint of mourning wives and abused women." Beatrice sighed. "Do you know how many of my guards were abused women? Mourning wives? Women forced into marriage? Sex workers?"

I shook my head. I actually didn't know as much about her past as I'd like. She told me this and that, but what I did know was that my great-times-great grandmother had been forced to become a *draugr* by Chester, that she was Jewish—so the patron saint thing was a bit odd—and that she had turned more than a few men into alligators and feral pigs.

I wasn't going to start waving a "*draugr* are people too" flag, but I had been learning that they weren't all inherently evil. I'd seen more than enough proof that Beatrice was sort of an unliving patron of women-in-need. Right now, she'd decided Allie was a woman-in-need. I wasn't sure if she was right, but I did agree that holding any woman against her will wasn't cool.

"You know we'll go get her if we have to," I assured Beatrice. "You aren't the only one who cares about her."

"Forced marriage is wrong."

"Here, here!" The hillbilly brigade lifted glasses in cheer.

We'd need to have a talk about exactly how scary *draugr* could be before they could be released back into the wild. They'd quickly adapted to thinking that Beatrice was their mother duckling or something—unless I was present, at which point I became the duckling-in-charge.

That, however, was a bridge we could build or burn or whatever that saying was once we survived the next few days. Chester hadn't attacked, but somehow, I was sure that we weren't going to wait weeks or months this time.

I glanced out the window. Iggy was talking to my teen stalker through the gate. He took several steps back, and the teen stepped up and shoved an envelope through the gate. She looked up, met my gaze, and pointed at the letter.

Then she was gone.

"Who sends letters?" I mused.

"Chester." Beatrice crossed her arms. "Those of us who existed before *texting* sometimes remain old-fashioned. That letter is a demand from Chester. Possibly from Chester and our runaway weapon. I will tell the others."

Once she left, I watched Iggy cross the yard.

By the time Iggy returned to the room where I was waiting, he had opened the envelope without my consent. He read it aloud, "I am not safe. Act soon or we all perish."

"Who—"

"Gunnora. This is her hand."

"A real hand?" one of the cousins asked, a bit too excitedly in my opinion. "Is it sliced up or—"

"Handwriting. He means her handwriting," I clarified because it was a flat envelope, and well, because I couldn't smell blood.

Iggy was staring at the paper as if there were other secrets on it that we couldn't see. Maybe there were. She was, after all, an accomplished alchemist. Perhaps there were clues or hints there.

He was sniffing the parchment when Marcus and Beatrice entered the room. I filled them in.

And Beatrice said, "This is clearly a trap. You cannot trust her. She *attacked* us."

Iggy scoffed. "Who here hasn't attacked one of the other of us?"

"Present!" one of the cousins called cheerily.

"Same!"

"Yeah!"

Beatrice gave them the sort of endearing look she often gave Alice, glanced at the faery king, and whispered, "I will drink you dry if you hurt Alice."

"Seconded," I added.

"The motion carries!" called Harlow from the poker game.

"Time to stop Chester?" Marcus looked at each of us, pointedly ignoring the Allie topic. "I can summon guards as needed."

We rehashed the plan of attack, but then Iggy let out a shaky sound.

"Blackwood?" Eli prompted.

"This is the spell to remove a heart," he said, shaking the parchment. He breathed over it again. "Revealed by breath. This is it—the same one used to remove her heart."

"Can you—"

"No," Iggy interrupted me. "You and me together? Maybe. Depends on if you're considered alive." He glanced at Beatrice and frowned. "Sorry, old girl. No pulse, no spell."

She glanced at her hand, buffed her nails on her chest, and shrugged. "Heads to sever. Bodies to bleed. I'm sure I'll find something to do while you do that."

"Gear up, cousins," Ike called. "Time to fight."

Beatrice closed her eyes for a flicker of a moment. Then she announced, "My forces are joining us."

"Witches, and faeries, and *draugr* . . ." I sing-songed. "He won't know what hit him."

But none of us really believed that. Chester had mopped the floor with me, with Beatrice, and Marcus had bargained to avoid fighting him. Hell, Iggy had been murdered by him. Nora had lost her heart—literally—at Chester's hand.

I was far from optimistic, but when had terrible odds ever stopped me?

31

GENEVIÈVE

"The last place he was that I know of was with the so-called *Sisters of Purity and Redemption,*" I told the assembled group. "You know, a few *days ago* when Marcus was okay with my torture...?"

The king of *Elphame* winced at my pointed barb. He did not apologize or express remorse, even now, and I made a mental note to kidnap Allie back if I survived if for no other reasons than to make sure she was safe and make Marcus suffer.

Beatrice tapped her fingernails on the wall like she was counting down the ways she'd like to murder the older faery.

The hillbilly mafia made a series of remarks that boiled down to "daaaaaamn."

And Eli smiled coldly. "I have not forgotten. The fae do not forget." After a long pause, he motioned to Beatrice. "The maps?"

She said nothing as she went somewhere and retrieved a pile of papers, blueprints, and notes. I couldn't say much. Part of me thought needling Marcus was wrong, but a larger part of me was well aware that I still had a wound from electrical burns while I was being tortured.

"We were researching where to find you," Eli explained to me as Beatrice began unrolling the documents. "Can you see if anything strikes you?"

I tried to clear my memory, to recall what was happening when I fled Chester. I was drunk on his blood, memories, and power. I shook my head. Honestly, torture, stun guns, and being blood-drunk made for spotty recall.

"What about the princess tracker?" Ike asked, drawing every gaze to him.

"The *what?*" I asked.

"The people who see you out and stuff use hashtags for spottings, and then this one site collected your whereabouts into a map." Ike had a phone in hand, as did Harlow now.

They both pulled up different social media sites with hashtags about me. There were over four thousand pictures of me.

"Cousin Al said she uses it to see if there are any 'issues'"—Ike made quotes in the air with his free hand—"that need squashed."

I gaped at the pictures.

"That's drone footage there," Harlow said. "Long range witch spotting is a growing thing in the city. It lets people get close without whatever magic thing keeps destroying phones."

My stomach turned at the realization that my notoriety since marrying the fae prince was so . . . ubiquitous. I could meltdown into a puddle of self-conscious rage later, assuming I survived. For now, I flicked through the information on Harlow's phone.

Cemetery.

Kissing Eli.

Arriving at the bar.

Getting coffee.

Staring at the river.

"This is terrifying," I whispered.

"Emotion later. Hunting Chester now," Beatrice said lightly, and it was very obvious by her tone and Eli's expression that I wasn't the only one completely dumbstruck by the massive invasion of privacy.

"Hexes to correct this later," Iggy added, from my side. "Keep turning the page to reach the date."

"Scrolling," Beatrice corrected with a prideful tone. "She's *scrolling*, Iggy, not 'turning a page.'"

I kept looking—a nice shot with light on my dagger, obviously edited because moonlight wasn't that bright; a few more stopping for coffee shots; one where I was unaware Eli was gazing at me adoringly.

Then at the bookstore.

Then . . . *there.* I was dressed in blood, looking rather grotesque. My chin was red, and my clothes were soaked.

"I look like an extra from a cheap horror film," I said, holding it up.

"That's near North Villere Street." Iggy gave me an assessing look. "You were practically flying to get from there to here that fast if the photograph's clock is accurate."

"Timestamp, Iggy." Beatrice *flowed* out of the room, returning with a pair of holsters before I'd finished realizing she was gone. "Let us go then to the field of blood, Daughter of Mine."

I was still thinking that the nuns were hiding in a fake medieval looking set-up with a house that was gorgeous and modern outside. Shouldn't monsters be in the Outs? Or in the ghost zone?

Even as I thought it, I realized that I was, actually, held in the ghost zone. "Not there. It's a trick. Look."

This photo had been altered, too, probably because someone wanted to avoid getting caught being in the ghost zone. No one was, technically, allowed to be out there overnight without entering quarantine. The ghost zone was dangerous. When the draugr came out of the shadows, people vacated entire towns. The suburbs were completely emptied in mere weeks, so every city had a ghost zone now—and *draugr* claimed whichever vacant houses they wanted. To stay out there was to almost always risk contamination.

"Where are the *draugr* who were here, Beatrice?" I looked at the queen who was pointedly not saying anything. "It ought to be filled with . . . where are they?"

"Moved to locations near me or . . . evicted." Beatrice folded her arms like a defensive toddler accused of naughtiness. "If they made a vow to you, they could stay. If not, they are gone."

"Gone *how?*" Marcus finally spoke. "Where?"

"To the earth." She shrugged, but I heard what she was saying clearly anyhow.

"You killed them? *All* of them?"

"Unless they accepted you as their future regent, yes." Beatrice held my gaze now, no shame, no flinching. "I would have told you but . . ."

She made a sweeping gesture, which I took to mean "things were chaotic."

"No more secrets," I said. "If we survive, I want your promise."

She nodded. "My word."

"Right, well, fang-free ghost zone, fam." Harlow rolled their shoulders. "Who's up for some holy whack a moly?"

"Let me get the extra *boom*." Ike scurried away with a chortle of laughter that made no sense in the circumstances.

A rational part of my brain said I ought to make them all stay here, but I wasn't entirely sure they'd listen. I still had to try. "What if you all guarded headquarters? That's useful, too . . ."

"Psh. We've been training for this since forever, boss lady." One of the other, typically quiet cousins, grinned. "Cousin Al told us about that spooky assed spa with the corpses and angry faeries and . . . shit, it's our turn to light it *up*."

Beatrice grinned at them with the sort of fondness that made me weirdly happy. She had little tolerance for men, as a rule, but I suspected their glee in violence outweighed all other traits.

"They will handle the nuns," Iggy suggested, staring again at the spell that was delivered to us. He was reading it, making notes, and reading more.

I debated whether we were rushing in, but there were only so many ways to interpret Nora's "I am not safe. Act soon or we all perish."

We solidified the rest of the plan: Beatrice and Marcus would try to distract Chester while I joined Iggy and Gunnora in spell-work. We would work a spell to remove the madman's heart. Eli would stay as guard at my side.

No worries.

"There will be fae and *draugr* aids, as well," Eli murmured, reminding me that we were many and Chester was one. His minions were not a major threat. Just him.

"Let's gear up and go hunting, then." I wasn't particularly convinced that all would go according to plan. It never did. I was as positive as can be, however, that this was our best shot. We'd pull it off, or we'd be dead.

Either way, our troubles with Chester were at their end.

🌿 32 🌿

GENEVIÈVE

I was apprehensive about the fight, despite verbal bravado, so when Iggy raised a hand to stop us, I tensed. "What?"

He read the paper silently, glanced at Beatrice, and scowled again. "You won't like it."

"How *much* won't I like it?" I looked around at the apprehension on everyone's face.

"No steel, silver, brass, bronze, or gold in the casting zone," Iggy announced, holding the paper out as if the words on it were still visible. "No magic allowed other than the spell itself."

"The fuck . . . Seriously?" I reached for the paper, as Beatrice *flowed* forward to do the same.

"We'll die," Marcus said, staring at Eli, and clutching the sword in his hand already. "One of us ought to stay back, Eli. If we both perish . . ."

Eli shook his head. "We fight. Together we are strong. . . or have you forgotten?"

I knew better than to believe that this was simply about the throne. Marcus loved a good fight. He'd merrily charged into violence at my side last summer, but it was different to fight unarmed. It was harder to fight when there was a chance of love waiting at home. And I knew that Marcus thought what he could have with Allie was the sort of love that bards spoke of and poets dreamed of.

"I get it," I said, deciding honesty was worth the fact that it looked like I was agreeing with the knob who had left me to drown and be electrocuted at Chester's word. "I feel naked without my swords or necromancy. I was submerged, electrocuted, and certain of death a few days ago. I was again faced with a certainty of death when Chester found us in Scotland. I literally had to walk under the frigid waves and ignore the memory of near downing . . . I understand your fear."

Marcus looked at me. "I do not wish you death. I cannot sacrifice *Elphame*, though. If we both go there, if we both fail . . . my people. *Ephame*. What will happen?"

"Another will rise and take the throne, Marcus. But bowing to a bully once means they know you'll bow next time, too." I shrugged. "Rather dead than subservient is pretty much my stance."

"Agreed." Beatrice preened. "That's my *descendent*. Murder us? Fine. Break us? Never."

As far as family mottos went, it could use some work. I wasn't keen on being murdered as a matter of fact, but I understood the sentiment.

I deposited my weapons on the sofa, and then I turned to the hillbilly crew. "You're coming. I need you to keep the nuns at bay and out of the spell zone."

"Night vision goggles!" a cousin called. "We have extras if you—"

"Most of us see in the dark," I interrupted.

"Predator," Beatrice said with a shrug.

I glanced at Iggy, who accepted a pair of goggles. Eli and Marcus had no need. And while I couldn't use necromancy, I was still a mix of things. I had speed, strength, and I had a living and a dead army at my back, especially since Marcus would bring fae fighters and Beatrice had sent summons to the *draugr*.

"Only *us* in the spell zone," Iggy reiterated. "No one else enters there. Weapon check. Even a tiny knife is not allowed." He nodded at the cousins. "You may arm yourself to the teeth, but do not approach any of us even if we are dying."

Ike and Harlow exchanged a look. Then they looked at the rest of their family. Finally, Harlow says, "Cousin Al won't like it if the boss lady dies."

"I dare say she wouldn't want any of us to die," Marcus grumbled.

One of the quieter cousins scoffed. "Oh, I wouldn't be so sure about that. She ranted about you for hours. We took shifts listening."

"Weapon check," Iggy said again.

It was the opposite of the sort of weapon check I liked, most everyone stripping off assorted guns, daggers, and swords. I preferred gearing up to gearing down, but I had to trust the spell. Nothing else stopped Chester, so we were gambling on ancient magic.

"This better work," I muttered.

"He's killed two of us, tortured more, and no other weapon has stopped him." Iggy stared at me. "I have taught you so you could run, hide, escape, so *my* newfound desire to confront him now without these metal things should comfort you."

Marcus cleared his throat and offered, "We can pass through *Elphame* to reach the battleground." He caught Beatrice's eye and added, "All of us."

It was an olive branch, one that was unheard of. He hadn't even allowed her into the land of the fae for my wedding. I watched my great-times-great grandmother to gauge her reaction.

Ever the imperious one, she merely made a "commence"

gesture. Apparently, it would take more than a heretofore unheard-of offer to appease her level of anger. I guessed that the fae weren't the only species capable of long grudge-holding.

Marcus opened a slice in the air, and once we were in *Elphame,* he did the same again. One-by-one our group entered the conflict. Beatrice led, with Eli behind her, Marcus next, the fae who were fighting, then the cousins and Iggy, and lastly, I stepped forward.

We walked into the eerie silence with an odd assemblage of fae, Hexen, and the *draugr* queen. Insects chirruped. Frogs croaked. It was silent in a way that I loved, nature singing and no sound of car or machine.

I miss this.

The Outs was where I grew up—a greater distance from New Orleans. This, however, was the ghost zone. Every city had one, what in the end of the 1900s, early 2000s was called "suburbs." There had always been something unnerving about areas that were all the same houses. Rows of similar roofs, driveways, shrubbery, mailboxes. It was made for horror, but the ghost zone felt worse somehow. These had been people's homes. They couldn't sell them. They simply had to abandon them and start over with what they could carry.

Some of the houses we passed were visibly empty: doors yawning open, windows shattered. Wildlife thrived here, and I had to remember that coyotes, alligators, and snakes were loose out here.

And wild dogs, cats, and who knew what else.

"Are you well, bonbon?" Eli asked quietly.

I nodded. "Thinking about the people who used to live here before . . ." I glanced at Beatrice and left the "the monsters came" silent.

"I removed my subjects," Beatrice murmured.

"Recently."

She shrugged. "I am making efforts, Daughter of Mine. Civilizing them is not so easy. It was asking them to walk to a buffet and not eat."

The old *draugr* looked at the area with a dismissive glance, and I wondered yet again what year she'd been born.

"Any sign of him?" Marcus interrupted, a voice in the dim light of the moon.

"Or recognition of the area?" Iggy added.

I shook my head. As much as I was pleased that we were taking the fight to Chester, I was also keenly aware that we might all die.

"Iggy and I are the only two here who can"--I lowered my voice further—"remove Chester's heart."

Beatrice nodded. "And so we keep you safe while you do so. If Iggy dies, can you complete it alone?"

"Not planning to die." Iggy scowled.

"Priorities," Beatrice replied blandly.

Then I saw the building. I knew for certainly that this nondescript house hid the torture chamber. "Here."

The troops of faery soldiers fanned out. No *draugr* had arrived yet, but I knew they were likely in the shadows waiting. They were fierce fighters, and goodness only knew what surprises the hillbilly mafia had in their backpacks.

But the simple fact of not leading the charge didn't feel good. My loved ones and my subjects—because for some backassward reason I *had* those now--would enter peril before me.

I *hated* it.

As Iggy drew the spell circle, I heard the combined battle cries as the corrupt nuns, assorted humans proudly proclaiming themselves members of SAFARI (our nationwide hate group) poured out of the building. Hundreds of people charged toward us

"Well, that looks like fun," Marcus said to Beatrice. "Ladies first . . ."

She flashed fangs. "With pleasure."

To the sides, I saw the cousins launch a series of homemade weapons that were both loud and nasty-smelling.

And the darkened street was awash in a mix of headlamps, torches, and night vision goggles. The goggles and torches were at odds, but I had other concerns. Strolling toward me as if the street was not a massive bloody brawl was the creature we had to defeat. Chester didn't seem to be merely a man, although I knew he was. Some people swallow so much evil that they become something else, something horrific.

"Do you realize that all you are doing is guaranteeing death?" Chester called out from where he paused. He stood in front of what looked like a homemade church. Nora was cringing at his side, looking like he'd been hitting her regularly and she was waiting for the next blow.

"Stay in the circle," Iggy ordered.

"You do realize that *I* cannot die." Chester gave us a mocking smile. "I am a saint. Human but undying. I drink of poisons and do not fall."

Around him, women and men nodded. Sometimes people were so desperate to believe in something that they clutched snake oil and swore they were healed.

In a world of monsters, darkness, and loss, who could blame them? We'd lived in a fast-food, one-hour service, one-click world for so long that the desire for simple easy answers wasn't hard to understand.

"Everyone dies eventually," I called back.

"Not everyone. I am above such things." Chester's words had a certainty, a ring of truth to them that made everything suddenly click into place.

I realized then that Chester had accomplished the two feats that alchemists dreamed of mastering: the elixir of life and the panacea. He'd mastered eternity by creating the potions that imbued him with eternal life *and* the cure-all.

The fabled panacea, the cure-to-all-ailments, was why he wasn't able to be killed.

This spell had to work because if not he would continue to cure whatever else we did to him.

33

GENEVIÈVE

After I whispered my theory to Iggy and Eli, Iggy nodded. "We need her in here."

I tried to subtly send a thought to Beatrice: *Panacea. Elixir. Need Nora to do this.*

She didn't reply, but I had no doubt that she understood. She cut a swath through the nuns to where Marcus was. Whatever she said or did was enough that the king of *Elphame* marched toward the church.

"You attacked my heirs," Marcus pronounced.

"You say that as if you are surprised." Chester glared. "You agreed—"

"You attacked her *before* I renounced them." Marcus gestured widely. "There is protocol. The laws of *Elphame* are clear. You have declared war by doing this, Chester. If you do not appease our insulted pride, I have no choice. Surely you understand?"

Beatrice *flowed*—directly at Chester. She grabbed Gunnora by both arms and kept moving.

And for all that Chester could do, he could not *flow*. In fact, to anyone present who had no *draugr* heritage, it likely looked as if Beatrice blinked from the fight to the church and then to me.

I watched her, saw her concentration, saw her struggling not to stop or falter.

All while Marcus continued, "I would accept a reparation in the form of sharing your knowledge with my colleague."

"With your—"

"Beatrice." Marcus gestured to where she had been. "I swear I left her over . . . oh, well, I don't see her."

By this point, Chester noticed that his wife was not at his side.

"You would betray me *again*?" Chester glared at Nora, who looked like the picture of a domestic violence survivor. Her eyes were bruised, one was partly swollen, and her mouth was bloodied.

She wasn't cowering. I'll give her that.

Iggy quickly closed the spell circle.

"Because boinking a monster is better? Seriously? How old was she was when you starting hitting her?" I was as offensive in tone as possible. I might not like Nora, but I *hated* Chester. "Couldn't get it up, so you hit her?"

Chester didn't reply, and behind me I heard Iggy and Gunnora whispering.

In his rage, Chester decided to ignore me and started attacking our forces. I wasn't sure what all his little sachets of nastiness were, but the air was thick with herbs.

The *draugr* arrived, *flowing* into the crowd with the silence of shadows. They were dressed in head-to-toe black, faces covered, hands covered. If not for my affinity for the dead, I wasn't certain I'd have noticed them.

The screams of the SAFARI members and the nuns were the only real proof that there were monsters ripping human throats out.

The faeries were more precise: swords and snapped necks.

And the cousins were simply having a great time. Molotov

cocktails lit the night, to the point that at least two houses were aflame.

The simple truth was that the assembled humans on Chester's side would all be dead or incapacitated shortly. That part of the battle, we were not going to lose. When your army is monstrous, blood-thirsty (literally), and trained, you don't lose.

Chester, however, looked unperturbed. He didn't care about the people who were dying, and he did seem to take a callous glee in tossing violent spells at our side—as if it were a giant experiment. *Does this work? What about this? Is it different with fae?*

And that part turned my stomach. So, I decided to draw his attention to me. "I bet Iggy was a better lover. Was that what pissed you off, Chester? Knowing that someone showed the lady how good it could be?" I paused. "I bet that was it, huh? Wee willy?"

Behind me, I heard Iggy mutter, "He killed me once for being with her, Hexen. Could we not repeat that event?"

Chester tossed something that looked like a money bag of dust. It bounced off the spell circle.

"Don't worry, Ig. I can bring you back." I grinned at Chester, and then pointed at his herbal hand grenade on the ground. "Is that why you hate me? I can resurrect people. Necromancy is finicky, and it probably takes more . . . stamina than you have."

He was silent, but he flared his nostrils like a bull about to charge.

To be fair, this wasn't my best plan ever. "Enrage the psychopath" wasn't terribly bright as far as tactics, but he'd just plowed through the *draugr* with some sort of spellwork that left a lot of them near-motionless and a few melting like soup.

Beatrice was winded, and either she or Marcus had to be agile enough to distract him when the spell finally started.

So they needed a breather. I was . . . the logical choice.

"Men like you are why I had a wealth of women in my bed,

you know?" I said cheerily. "Misogynists don't make great lovers. Too selfish. Too clueless. Maybe I should give Gunnora a---"

He charged and caught me in the gut that time, tearing through the spell circle.

Rather than come to my aid like I expected, Iggy grabbed Nora, and clasped her hands in his. It wasn't exactly the plan, but they finally started intoning the spell in what was initially two voices but effectively melded into one within moments.

Behind them, I could see Harlow give me a thumbs up as they herded another nun into a police cruiser. At some point, I might need to ask where the cruisers came from, but all I knew for sure was that my friend Gary Broussard was there at Harlow's side with a stern glare for me and a taser for another nun.

I turned my gaze back to Chester as he kneed me between the legs. Contrary to popular opinion, being kneed or punched there still hurt like a throat punch for a woman. Lady parts? *Very* sensitive to pain.

I stumbled backward, tripping on broken sidewalk as I did. Out here in the ghost zone, there were no repairs. No people, no repairs. So on top of everything else, the buildings and sidewalks were dangerous.

As the chant grew louder, Marcus and Beatrice moved to stand on either side of Nora and Iggy, guards to keep Chester from them if he got past me—and Eli joined the fight.

He smashed Chester's knee sideways. Hand-to-hand meant fighting dirty, but no steel, silver, brass, bronze, or gold in the casting zone meant that we were without many options.

Eli and I couldn't use fae magic.

I couldn't use necromancy.

It was like having both hands tied behind our backs.

As Chester pushed back to his feet, I headbutted him like I was a baby ram.

"No more than a tavern slag," he muttered, wiping the blood from his obviously broken nose.

"Bet I could still show Nora a better time than you *ever* did," I taunted.

"Bite him," Eli suggested.

I glanced at my husband—which gave Chester a chance to grab my arm and twist. There was something slimy on his hand, and I felt bones breaking. Not just in my arm, either. A rib cracked. My shoulder started to splinter.

"Old wounds," Beatrice yelled.

Eli body slammed us, and Chester lost his grip from the impact.

I rolled away.

"Bite him," Eli yelled. "Worked before."

And as much as I hated it, he was right. My fangs were ready before my mind was, and I latched on to Chester's throat.

His blood spilled into my mouth, and the energy from it started to knit my bones.

I realized that Marcus and Beatrice were there, too. Together we managed to hold onto him as I drank as much as I could swallow.

I was gagging on blood, and his throat was healing within the mere instant it took me to retch and be ready. My grandmother leaned in and bit while I was puking up blood.

Not exactly the holiday card image, but I was grateful for her willingness to let me catch my breath.

When she pulled back, Marcus jabbed his fingers in the savaged meat of Chester's throat and ripped.

Still, it was knitting back.

"Hurry up!" Eli yelled to Iggy and Nora, who were too busy chanting to reply.

Then Eli motioned to Chester's stomach and shoved the man's sweater vest aside.

My grandmother flashed bloody teeth and took a bite of his stomach.

As Eli started ripping flesh from Chester's stomach, pulling out actual organs that were healing as fast as they were severed, I leaned back into Chester's throat.

❦ 34 ❦

GENEVIÈVE

When the spell finally took hold, I felt like I was no longer tethered to the world.

Chester froze, motionless, eyes watching me. Beatrice and Marcus stepped back as of they were nothing more than puppets controlled by the magic.

Eli walked backward, as if he no longer controlled his feet.

I briefly thought Chester would topple without them holding him. He didn't.

The spell seemed to be removing everyone but me from Chester's vicinity. And once they were gone, the spell circle snapped around me.

I could see that everything around me, outside the circle, was still moving at a normal speed, and both Iggy and Nora were continuing to loop the spell in that sing-chant-whisper thing that they did. It was as if they were one terrifying voice.

I admitted briefly that I didn't like Nora, trust Nora, or particularly dig the idea that she was this powerful. My only consolation was that she was helping us remove this monster— her husband.

One crisis at a time, I whispered in my head. If I had to deal death to her, too, I would.

I felt as much as saw her look away from Iggy and give me a raised brow. Maybe being looped into the spell meant that my thoughts weren't as private as I had thought. Just in case, I grinned at her and thought, *If you hurt Iggy, I'll destroy you for that, too.*

He might be a manipulative, moody, meddling man, but he was my family now. No one but me was allowed to kill him.

Focus, Iggy's grumbling voice yelled in my head. *Hand of death, Hexen. Get on with it.*

Unlike putting Gunnora's stone heart back, I couldn't just reach into Chester's chest. I mean, Eli had been doing that to no avail, but as the spell grabbed me, my mouth started intoning the same words that Iggy and Gunnora were—as if the spell was a living thing that had taken space in my blood-stained mouth.

But all the injuries we had wrought on Chester were gone.

His clothes and skin were bloody, but his flesh was unmarred.

Apparently, heart removal was messy. I shoved his sweater vest up and ripped open his shirt, buttons flying. He was surprisingly fit for a man who wore sweater vests and accountant glasses.

There was no way to use a metal tool in this part either, which sucked. Instead, I had to go primitive.

The stone ax that Iggy had given me earlier to use was basically a vaguely pointy rock. I pulled it out of my pocket.

I scraped it over Chester's skin as he glared up at me, motionless in the thrall of the spell. A smart assed part of me wanted to point out that I found his weapon, but an exhausted part just wanted to saw faster so he didn't wake.

Saw. Slice. Bruise.

It was taking longer than a sloth stretch on a rainy day.

And my alchemical-hexen team was swaying from the exhaustion of holding him in stasis.

No metal, I thought.

Stone wasn't cutting fast enough, even though I had arrogantly assumed my strength from my fae and *draugr* heritage would make his skin slice like warm butter.

I had another tool, one I already knew would tear through his skin with ease.

I bent forward and bit a chunk out of Chester's muscles. It was worse than biting his throat. I wasn't sure how deeply Beatrice bit earlier, but I was not used to biting people at all, much less in the chest.

I tried to tell myself it was like eating steak—really undercooked stringy steak.

Never eating steak again.

I shoved the stone tool in the gap and worried it until I was closer to the heart.

Chester glared at me, not even wincing in pain. His eyes were alert. He was completely aware of what I was doing.

Again, I tore at his muscle, spitting the meat away as Nora stared at me in horror. I could finally see the glimmer of bones. I hammered at them with the stone ax, cracking them with the remains of my strength.

It shouldn't be this hard to steal a heart.

Or maybe it should be *exactly* this hard. This spell was a horrible sort of imprisonment. He would—as Gunnora had been for decades—be alert enough to know he wasn't dead but trapped in a body that was as immobile as stone.

I wanted to shatter the heart once it was petrified.

Nora looked at me with such a turmoil of emotions that the spell slipped, and I remembered that she did hear more of my thoughts than I'd like.

In that instant, Chester grabbed my wrist, squeezing, shattering bones inside my wrist this time. He wasn't free, but he was no longer motionless. I could see the wave of pain from his savaged chest and broken ribs, but even that wasn't enough to keep him still.

I switched the stone ax to my other hand, tightening my grip on it and slamming it down as hard as I could.

At the same time Chester reached up, squeezed my throat, crushing my airway.

Within minutes, my eyes were blurring from lack of air, but I had my hand around his heart—squeezing it as I jerked it toward me.

I felt it turning to stone in my hand, but I heard Eli shout my name in what sounded like despair.

I wanted to tell him I was fine, bloody but fine.

Except . . . I couldn't move. The last thing I knew, I was falling on top of Chester.

❈   35   ❈

ELI

Geneviève fell, motionless atop the seemingly dead man. Eli knew she was alive because his own heart still beat. *Would it still beat if she were in stasis?*

Honestly, he hadn't known a person could feel terror this often. Marriage was both the greatest joy and an endless source of heart-stabbing fear. He rolled her over, so she was on her back on the ground. Eyes open, staring sightlessly at the dark sky.

"Is she . . . dead?" Gunnora said from over his left shoulder. "That shouldn't happen with the spell frequently, and with three of us speaking it—"

"This was a *known* risk?" Eli asked.

Gunnora shrugged and scooped up Chester's heart. "Not if she was as powerful as she seemed."

Beatrice was growling, a sort of rumbling sound that Eli was well aware could turn into more violence. Marcus was silent as he walked off to see to the fae who were all waiting on his orders.

Eli crouched down and touched Geneviève's throat. There was no pulse. Panic washed over him.

Iggy was barely upright, but he stumble-crawled to Geneviève. His hand hovered over her skin. "Not gone."

"Which means what?" Eli lowered his mouth to her and gave her breath.

Iggy gave her chest compressions. Then he said, "Take me home after this."

Eli went to lean down to breathe for her again, just as Iggy said, "Here."

In the Master Hexen's hand was a small ball of what looked like a storm cloud filled with lightning. "Shock her."

Then Iggy collapsed, convulsing slightly.

Beatrice tugged Iggy backward, met Eli's gaze, and smiled. It was a wobbly smile, which was not encouraging, but she was still hopeful at least.

Praying to each and all possible beings, Eli pressed that ball of lightning into his wife's chest. At first, nothing happened. He felt her pulse point again. "Nothing."

Whatever it was to do, it hadn't, and Iggy was unconscious, and this wasn't Eli's sort of magic. "Could we do magic here now?"

"No," Gunnora called out. "That's why he's . . . like that."

On the ground Iggy was convulsing from violating whatever magical rule he'd broken. But pain, all pain, was a worthwhile price if there was something Eli could do to save his wife, but he wasn't sure if his magic would hurt Geneviève, too, since they were bound.

Then, Geneviève let out a scream, a hellacious sound that lasted for several full minutes.

When the horrifying sound stopped, she opened her eyes. Whatever it was that had happened, her body was awake and sitting upright.

"Did we win?" she asked, voice raspy.

Eli nodded.

"Chester is frozen," Beatrice said, pointing to the ground beside Geneviève.

Geneviève smiled. "And you're all alive?"

"Harlow has a broken leg," a faery reported. "One of the other relations of Lady Alice is dead. Twelve fae, and several dead things."

As she listened, Geneviève looked stricken.

"It could have been much worse," Eli said. "War has loss."

"The heart?" Geneviève asked, looking around.

For a moment, Eli wasn't sure. Honestly, he wasn't sure he cared either. Geneviève was safe. Chester was stopped. All he wanted was to carry his wife home, barricade the doors and hide away with her.

There was family to attend to. There were friends to reassure. There was a Hexen Master flailing intermittently as Gunnora watched over him, looking far softer now that her memories were apparently returned.

And his uncle, the king, was standing awkwardly beside the *draugr* queen.

Eli's odds of stealing his wife away and ignoring all of them weren't high, but you can't blame a man for dreaming.

"We need to let everyone know you're safe," Eli said.

"I can inform them," Marcus offered. "They can enjoy my hospitality while Geneviève recovers."

"And the heart?" Geneviève asked. "I don't want to ever have to do *that* again so . . ."

Gunnora was clutching it. "He was my spouse."

"Right," Geneviève said. "Don't care. I finished the spell. That's my rock now."

"If it's not kept safe, if someone restores him . . ." Gunnora looked like every terrified woman, afraid her abuser would return.

"If I may?" Beatrice asked, hand extended.

Shaking, Gunnora gave her the stone.

She'd no sooner done so than she smothered a gasp as Beatrice cracked it in two. "Here." She tossed half to Marcus. "Take it over there. I'll make sure this piece is securely stashed, too."

I respected her cunning. Giving part of it to my uncle meant that no *draugr*, no human, could return it to this world. Keeping part of it meant that she still had some assurances that Chester was un-animated.

"One of you can take care of that part," she said. Then Beatrice paused to give the king a glare. "Hurt Alice, and you will have an invasion of draugr in *Elphame*."

Marcus opened his mouth as if to argue, but Beatrice *flowed* away, and every remaining *draugr* followed.

"Always dramatic," Geneviève muttered.

"Runs in the family," Eli teased.

The cousins were scooping up Iggy. One of them said, "Going over to visit, Cousin Al."

Harlow was hobbling, being aided by a fae soldier, and they sent a challenging look at Marcus. "Not staying in the dungeon either."

With a sigh, the king of *Elphame* said, "My future bride's family is wel—"

"Future bride," Ike crowed. "Uh huh. Can we be there when you say that to Cousin Al?"

The cousins and the rest of the fae left, and it was only Gunnora still there in the destruction with them.

"I'll put him somewhere safe," she said softly, and then she grabbed one of Chester's arms and walked away into the darkness, tugging him along the ground like a battered child's toy.

And Geneviève smiled. "Home?"

❧ 36 ☙

GENEVIÈVE

"Geneviève . . ." Eli started before she could say anything else. "I am carrying you from here. I know you are an independent—"

"Oh thank goodness. I'm not actually convinced I *can* walk." I reached up, and he bent down to scoop me into his arms.

I wasn't entirely sure what the future held. We'd destroyed the man who was trying to kill us, and we brought his wife back from her stasis. That could be a problem—or not. I wasn't sure yet. Gunnora was, seemingly, powerful enough to be a threat, and I was not one to ignore the potential for an angry woman to spiral into violence. My own family tree made the peril of a woman with rage quite obvious, but in a world where a misogynist like Chester could gain power, who could blame us for rage?

I snuggled into Eli's arms as he lifted me up and held my exhausted body close. I hoped I'd never have to give up feeling cherished like this. For most of my life I thought I couldn't have love without sacrificing my identity. Eli proved me wrong.

"I am the luckiest person in either world," I murmured. "You are a prince among men."

My husband gave me a look, but he smiled a moment later. "Indeed."

"In a world full of men who want to hurt women . . . " I said quietly. "I never thought I'd find someone who made me *more*."

"I am sorry you have had to wade through the villains, but I'm grateful that I get to be the hero to carry you home." Eli kept his voice light, but I knew it was only partly a joke. He was the prize at the end of my quest, the cherry on top of my desserts, the man who taught me to love and be loved.

Obviously, not all men were villains. Iggy wanted knowledge. Hell, Marcus—for all his going about it the wrong way—wanted to protect his people and marry Allie. And of course, my best friend Jesse was nothing if not reliable and kind. There were plenty of good men in the world, in *Elphame* too, but the monstrous ones always seemed to harbor an unfathomable hate for women with opinions or power.

I wanted all my friends to find their own princes—or princesses—too. Embarrassingly or not, I had become that person so blissfully in love that I wanted to be a matchmaker.

Eli paused in his steps as we entered what had once been a playground before the Ghost Zone was abandoned. "Bonbon?"

"Mmm?" I snuggled closer.

"If the *draugr* are yours to command when your indomitable grandmother passes, that makes me your consort . . ."

I opened my eyes. "Hush. Beatrice will never die."

He grinned. "I rescinded my claim to the throne, but unless Alice marries my uncle and gives him an heir, we are looking at two thrones."

"Not today." I shook my head. "I'm looking at a nice quiet life with my tavern-keep husband. Maybe a quiet stroll through the graves here and there. Dinner with friends. Maybe even a big fruit bowl so I get tipsy and throw myself at you . . ."

Eli caught my mouth in a kiss when I paused.

Then he carried me toward home. I felt the dead out there in the dark, watching. I felt the dead in and atop the soil where they had fallen and been left to decay. The world wasn't perfect, but that was fine.

I didn't need perfect when I had a reasonably safe life with a loving spouse, good friends, and the weirdest family I could have imagined.

In the distance, the lights of my home flickered, and behind us, nature chirped, peeped, and howled.

"If the *draugr* are going to behave, what do you think of building a home out here?" I whispered.

"I think it's a good idea," Eli said quietly. "Not for every day but . . . if we can be in nature part of the time, I think we'd both be happier."

I paused. "You know some of them won't obey. I'll still have to patrol."

Eli gave me a look. "You wouldn't be happy without challenges, bonbon,"

Sighing, I let go of my worry and stress. My husband knew me, and he still loved me. It was the one dream I never thought I could have, and with Eli, I had it and a near eternity to enjoy it.

AFTERWORD

As I know not everyone reads the stories between the novels, I wanted to add the third novella, the wedding, as an extra at the end of this novel. The novellas are generally fun "in the middle" stories, but I thought for those of you who wanted the extra romance, I'd include it here at the end as a bonus.

It's not *required* reading. I'd structured the novels as more linear, and the three novellas as side adventures (Winter Holidays, Girls Weekend, The Wedding). It occurs to me, though, that you may enjoy having this event included.

So you are cordially invited to Eli and Gen's wedding. Should you want to attend, turn/flip the page . . .

BONUS CONTENT: CHAMPAGNE & COMMITMENTS

A Faery Bargains Novella

Set after

Daiquiris & Daggers

※   I   ※

Living in New Orleans meant that the coming of Autumn was synonymous with the coming of Halloween. It was *also* a time filled with the Jewish High Holidays, witchy holidays, and fae holidays. This year, however, was more stressful than usual because I had to plan a wedding—actually, *two weddings*. There were rules about entering the realm of the fae, and I had human guests, so I had to have a ceremony here and one in *Elphame*.

I hated ceremonies.

I hated being the center of attention.

So I was, in typical avoidance tactics, ignoring my wedding planning until I absolutely positively *had* to deal with it.

Plus, I was restless since my magic had settled and my privacy was upended by tourists with phone cameras. I'd spent my entire life trying to hide who—and what—I was. Suddenly being unable to behead a monster without a reel of my actions on social media was creating a bubble of irritation that was starting to feel like it was festering.

Worse yet, I had no one to blame for it, no enemy to slay, no mystery to solve. It was simply a side effect of public interest in the blue-haired witch marrying the crown prince of *Elphame.*

I'd finished working out. Again. Now I'd tackle the wedding plans, at least some of them.

Since my apartment was a ground floor unit with questionable air conditioning and ventilation, I was wearing one of Eli's shirts and nothing else. Not exactly workout clothes or going out clothes or--

"Bonbon?" Eli walked into the bedroom.

I was surrounded by wedding catalogues and hand-drawn illustrations from *Elphame.* Dresses. So many twice-cursed dresses. I had rejected everything from what looked like mermaid tails to cartoon princess gowns I wasn't sure I could walk in without tripping.

"Why?" I gestured, glaring at the images. "I like trousers. I mean, I can deal with leggings and a tunic but—"

"We could go naked . . ."

That caught my attention. I looked up. He was still standing in the doorway of the bedroom, out of reach.

"Tell me more?"

"*Tell* you?" Eli started to remove his shirt, offered me what I used to think of as an innocent smile. I knew better now. There was nothing innocent about the formerly exiled faery prince currently stripping in our doorway. Wiley. Charming. Clever. Gorgeous.

"Show me more," I modified, taking a moment to admire him. The bare expanse of skin he was now exposing was dusky and taut over muscles, a reminder that he was an agile fighter and a tireless lover.

With a flick of my hand, all the catalogues and drawing went flying off the bed. A bit of plaster drifted to the ground as a pen stabbed the wall. My magic was a still a bit erratic since our bonding.

"My lovely witch," he murmured before I could apologize. "My warrior wife."

I watched as his shirt hit the ground. "*More. . .*"

"More explanation?" he teased. "Well, being naked would solve the dress decision for you, too, I suppose."

I looked back up to catch his gaze. His cut glass cheeks and nose were softened by a mouth that made me think of a courtesan's lips. "I can't imagine your uncle would approve of—"

"Bonbon?" Eli's hand passed over his chest and lingered at the top of his trousers.

My brain went completely silent. I met his gaze again with effort. Looking away from bare skin and taut abs required a lot of focus.

"I'd very much like to ravish you now, Geneviève," he announced, stepping closer and unfastening that first button. "Perhaps we could *not* discuss my family now?"

"Mmmmhmmm."

"Shall I take that as a yes?" Slowly, button by button, Eli unfastened his trousers. "To the not talking or the naked? Or the ravishing?"

In the next heartbeat, I'd crossed the room without thought. "Yes, Eli. Whatever you say. Whatever you want . . . *yes.*"

"All I want is you, Geneviève."

I opened my mouth to attempt to reply, but Eli lowered his mouth to mine and saved me from the perpetual embarrassment over how much his words got to me. I'd rather kiss him than fumble at words. With my kisses, I could attempt to tell him just how much I loved him. With my touches, I could try to be eloquent.

I'd never have the constant pretty fae words to share, not like he did, so I set about telling him how I felt with my kisses and caresses.

. . .

A FEW HOURS LATER, I WASN'T ANY MORE CAPABLE OF SPEECH, especially articulate and flowery words, but Eli understood me all the same. He whispered, "I love you too, Geneviève."

I sighed out loud this time. "No one else has ever . . . known me so easily."

He chuckled. "Easily? Oh, come now, divinity! I have dedicated literal *years* to the Study of Geneviève. Your silences, your expressions, your temper . . ." Eli pulled me closer into his embrace. "I surely have earned degrees in the tilt of your head or the curve of your lips, and I am not done. You are my enigma, my lifetime pursuit."

I flinched guiltily. "I didn't set out to be perplexing to you."

"You didn't set out with a single plan about me," Eli corrected. "But now, you are mine. Unto eternity. My prey caught in a snare . . ."

"Not prey," I muttered.

"And yet, you are captured, are you not?" Eli's words were light —but I heard the question he was truly asking. While I hadn't studied him for quite as long, I had begun to learn to listen to the silences in his statements and the questions he lobbed gently my way.

"I'm happily ensnared," I agreed. Despite being anti-relationship, I'd been stealthily courted and bonded to *the* prince, but as he had reminded me regularly, he'd never *said* he was merely a bar owner. He'd *also* never said he had chosen an exile from his people to stay in New Orleans as my friend while plotting to wear down my resistance to the romance he'd wanted from me.

The fae might not lie, but they weren't always forthright.

Now Eli and I were fae-bonded. It was more permanent, none of this "until death" business. Our lives were connected on a heartbeat-by-heartbeat level. If I died, he died. If he died, I died.

Don't even get me started on how much panic *that* responsibility caused me. It was right though. We were right. And as sappy as it felt, I admitted, "Being bonded to you is the most natural thing I've ever done. I'd rather be with you in a grave than here without you. My pulse is yours, and I wouldn't want it any other way."

"And she says she has no pretty words for me," he murmured, lifting one of my hands to his lips and kissing my wrist at the pulse point.

I cleared my throat, determined to have this conversation. "So you *know* that avoiding wedding planning isn't cold feet, right?"

"I do." Eli watched me in a way that made me feel like I was a treasure he'd defend, a cause he'd uphold, and a gift he'd cherish.

"I just hate being the center of attention in a crowd," I tried to explain. "And in my defense, I had planned to go over some details with you tonight. Honestly. But then you came home and . . ."

"Bonbon, you were already half-naked when I came home," he pointed out. "It seemed foolish not to join you."

"It's hot, and the apartment was humid."

"Getting naked was simply practical then," he agreed with a laugh.

"*Exactly*. That's me. Practical. And maybe I was hoping you'd be home soon. I feel like any minutes without you are too long lately." I looked up at him, and he answered with another kiss.

"Bonbon? I *adore* your appetite," he reassured me when he pulled away.

Lately, I was fairly sure the only reason we hadn't been arrested for public indecency was that people were too stunned to react when we'd been caught in public. Well, that and the fact that I was witch enough to baffle them with a quick spell long enough to get away, typically with our clothes in hand, although I'd lost at least two pairs of boots this past month.

Tonight, we were inside. *See? I could be practical.* Meeting at my apartment tended to mean we were less likely to get caught naked in public, and the tourists were flooding the city as they did every year in October. Nowhere celebrated as often or as vigorously as New Orleanians did.

"What's your plan for the rest of the night?" Eli stretched as if he were some great cat.

I couldn't tear my eyes away from the fae man who'd plagued my dreams for years. He stared at me as I watched him. Like every faery, he was not shy. He definitely had no reason to be. His lips curved into a smile that said he was well aware of how he looked sprawled out in our sea-blue sheets. His hair—currently coming unbound--could pass for the dark strands of plenty of middle eastern men, but it fell longer than most human men wore theirs.

"Wedding stuff . . .?" I sighed as I caught his gaze. I could see stars, eternity, a universe hidden in the dark braid that twisted across the pillow. *Mine. All mine.* I still had moments of panic that someone or something would tear us apart. I'd never really dared to believe that I could be this happy, that I'd find a person who accepted me as I was—fangs and all.

"You're far away from me, Geneviève."

I slid closer, so I was half draped over him. "Better?"

"Yes, but I meant inside your thoughts, love." He kissed the inside of my wrist. "Trouble with the 'wedding stuff'? I could help."

"No, I was thinking about you."

"Mmmm, tell me more." Eli's eyes glittered in a different sort of interest, a seemingly impossible trait, but I realized it was simply another way to communicate for the fae. My own vision had shifted when we bonded. There were layers to sights, sounds, tastes, and scents that I hadn't know existed, even with my heritage. And touch . . . Eli's skin against mine was a pleasure that I would've called impossible before our bonding.

"Marriage. How it changes everything . . ." I trailed my hand over his stomach. "I'm sorry I wasted all that time running."

"Eh. I like a chase." He pulled me on top of him for a kiss that left me straddling him. Again. He stared up at me and added, "And I have won the prize I desperately wanted. . ."

When I straightened and sat upright, I was breathless at the love in his expression. It wasn't an overstatement to say that I was certain that I was the luckiest woman—of any species, dead or living—in either world. Love is always a gift, and compatibility is precious.

"Faery struck," I whispered as his hands gripped my hips.

"Likewise."

"You can't be! I'm—"

"Fae-bound? As am I, Geneviève. So, whatever could this be? Am I bewitched? Bespelled? Ensorcelled? Addicted?" His teasing laughter made me start to giggle.

A part of me was mortified that I was even *capable* of giggling. I was a witch, a necromancer, and the last sight before the death of many a monster. A half-witch half-*draugr* with spells and weapons ought not giggle!

But the rest of me reveled in feeling safe enough to laugh. Eli was my haven, and I'd do anything in my power to keep this feeling, this man, this love.

"I love you," I murmured, holding his gaze.

"Likewise."

"Show me, *bonbon*." I grinned as his hands tightened on my hips, leaving marks that I'd remember for the next few days.

Both my words and my giggles faded into moans and demands as my beloved did just that.

$\qquad\qquad \text{❧} \quad 2 \quad \text{❧}$

Later, as Eli drifted toward sleep, he gave me a drowsy smile before his eyes closed. "Good night."

I brushed one last kiss across his lips before I slid out of bed. My nocturnal schedule wasn't ideal for him, as his daylight one had been a struggle for me. Now that we were bonded, I was equally alert at sunlight and sunset, noon and midnight, and everywhere in between.

It had been three days since I last slept.

For most of my life, I'd barely slept at the best of times, but I somehow slept even *less* since my magic had returned. I felt like I was washing down Ritalin with coffee chasers every hour. I could either try to be quiet while Eli slept or I could go find something to do.

Eli was good for my stress. He understood me fundamentally, but since he required sleep and I didn't these days, I had to find things to keep me occupied at night. Patrolling for *draugr* or training were my default options, but maybe I could see if Allie, my assistant, was awake and work on wedding plans.

Patrol my way to her house. Plan. Patrol more. Wake Eli for mid-morning sex. Train. I needed to find a hobby or something if there were no new jobs coming in. I'd accumulated more enemies than I needed of late. The peril of power is that having it meant that there were always people trying to kill me for one reason or another, and it had put a dent in my jobs.

Maybe that could be my cookie for getting the weddings planned—start a new hobby or side job. I had too much downtime.

I grabbed a jacket and pulled the bedroom door shut.

As I walked into the main open space of the apartment, I looked for the jeans and boots I'd left in the training area earlier. My apartment didn't scream fae royalty. When I bought it, I had no dream of becoming royal. Hell, I hadn't even known Eli was royalty when I bought this place.

The listing had been a bad area, filled with *draugr,* so I got the first apartment—the one Eli slept in currently—for a steal. Over time, I bought the rest of the apartments on this floor.

I looked around at the mess. Definitely far from royal fae living, but it was still mine. I shimmied into jeans, shoved my feet in a pair of combat boots, and put on holsters. There were things worse than the monsters I had been beheading my teen and adult life, and I didn't leave the house unarmed.

"Ready . . ." I held my hand out, bracing myself before touching the forearm-long dagger on the settee. It was half of the pair of magic imbued daggers the *draugr* queen had given me.

I concentrated on grounding myself.

The sizzle of magic in the dagger had me gasping as if I'd jumped naked into a snowbank. I wasn't sure I could carry both blades, so the other was on the nightstand beside my sleeping husband.

With the dagger, a sword on the other hip, and a pistol in my underarm holster, I slipped out the heavy door into the building's lobby and then stepped onto the sidewalk.

I paced the perimeter of the well-lit lot. My neighbors were tolerant now that I was a princess, and agreed to extra lights, but that didn't mean I wanted to be illuminated like a target.

An engine turned on as I walked toward the sidewalk. Someone had been waiting inside the car because I sure as sugar hadn't seen anyone walk toward it.

I drew my pistol. Not nearly as comforting as a sword, but I wasn't going to get close enough to stab a tire. I stood at the edge of the parking lot outside my building, eyeing the dark-blue SUV.

Engine running.

Lights bright.

Between the glare of the lights and the tint of the windows, I couldn't identify anything about the driver. I tried to think of non-threatening options. Was this a ride for one of the residents on the top floors of the building? Were they simply pulled over to check maps? There were plenty of logical answers, but I still had a welcome flicker of fear.

I stalked toward the SUV, hoping that whoever was inside was not packing venom-filled rounds or something else inconvenient and painful. My bouts of insomnia and extra energy meant that a fight sounded lovely, just a little sparring with a new partner.

But the driver shifted the car out of park and drove toward the exit of the parking lot.

"Weirdo," I grumbled, hoping it wasn't another camera-mad "influencer" determined to catalogue my life for clicks. Honestly, I'd rather have a fight than be in anyone's lens.

I looked away—just as the SUV sped up and swerved toward me.

The grind of tires on pavement was low enough that without my enhanced hearing, I'd be roadkill right about now, but I heard the tires crackling and crunching, and I'd turned at the revving of the engine with a slice of a second to spare.

The mass of blue metal was trying to hit me.

Fortunately, SUVs aren't exactly bullet-speed. I launched myself into the grassy strip alongside the parking lot and landed with a *thunk* as my feet tangled in the tree roots that didn't have the good sense to stay under the sod.

"You badger-bonking jerk!"

The driver backed up and paused. Not departing. Not charging. I was cornered.

The urge to *flow* warred with the logic that my ability to move as fast as the dead was still a secret to most everyone. If the driver had a camera, I'd be exposed if I did that. The mere thought of such hate terrified me.

Being a witch meant I had the occasional death threat or murder attempt. Being a Jewish witch meant that some of those attempts were fueled by the hostility every Jew encountered in their lives. But being a half-living half-*draugr*? That was the sort of thing that landed a person in laboratories. Nightmares of vivisection had plagued me for years.

No *flowing*.

So I stood there, playing chicken with an SUV and debating the options. If I *did* decide to *flow*, I could go over, jerk the door open and ask Mr. Badger Bonker what his issue was.

And he'd report me . . . unless I kill him.

His word against mine.

Unless he has one of those dashboard cameras...

More and more I had to remind myself that a viral video of a living *draugar*, especially one who was also the future queen of *Elphame*, would be deadly.

So my choices were to try to walk away or wait him out. On the upside, unless he planned to ram the oak tree beside me, he wasn't likely to smoosh me even with however-many-pounds of steel.

My phone chimed.

A text from Allie popped up: "Tourists. Gate. Help?"

Decision made, I turned toward the oak and asked permission, "Aid?"

The lowest branches quivered, and a thicker branch slightly

above them crackled and stretched toward me. When it was in reach, I wrapped my arms around it, hugging the tree, and held tight as it returned to its position in the leafy boughs.

I looked toward the SUV and gave them a jaunty one-fingered salute.

Then I dropped a big smacking kiss on the oak branch, not feeling the least bit silly despite hugging and kissing a tree.

I hopped over the fence beside the tree. I might still be new to this faery princess gig, but I was a born witch. I already knew nature was the sort of magic that mere mortals—or near-immortals like the fae and *draugr*—couldn't match.

❦   3   ❦

Safely out of reach of the SUV, I looked again at the text from my assistant. The text was classic Allie in that it included emojis for emphasis: a dagger, a baseball bat, one that was for swearing, and a wine glass. The last image I understood, though. She'd added a castle, which was her way of saying she was at the house I co-owned with Eli.

The rest was a mystery. Honestly, I couldn't tell if Alice thought that I would be swearing and need a drink or if *she* was swearing and drinking. It didn't matter, though: Alice Chaddock was my right-hand-woman: somewhere between a Renfeld and a teenager on her bad days, and somewhere between psychic and best friend on her good days.

"Inbound" was my whole reply.

I flagged down a police cruiser on St. Charles.

"Crowe." The officer, a man I'd met a handful of times, had a name. I was certain of it. That didn't mean I could recall it.

"Distress call from my assistant," I said as I dutifully put on my seatbelt. "Garden District."

I rattled off the address, as if anyone in the city needed to hear it. Eli being outed as the future ruler of *Elphame* had meant that our home was now on every tour and tabloid.

"The prince?" Officer Whatshisname was already reaching for his radio.

"Blissfully unaware at my other home, and I'd like to keep it that way. I just need a lift."

I thought about Eli's reaction to the crowds outside his house. It happened more and more, and Eli was on the verge of agreeing to fae guards—although neither of us wanted that. Any guard was likely also going to report to the king, and while Eli and his uncle were on good terms, I had reason to prefer that the king wasn't in my business more than absolutely necessary.

"I'm hoping they'll go away quietly," I added.

The officer nodded, not quite saying the "are-you-daft" aloud, but his expression covered that part.

What he didn't realize was that now that my magic was back, the city as a whole felt like it was as much my "kingdom" as Elphame did. Eli felt protective of our homes, our friends, me—and I felt like my fae traits had only enhanced my need to keep New Orleans safe. The residents of my city had no idea that I felt like they were my *own* citizens or the lengths I'd go to keep them safe. Of course, I wasn't sure how far I could go. Honestly, I was a little afraid of how easily I now accomplished the same things that used to require concentration.

Sooner or later, I'd have to test the parameters of the new energy that came from being bonded to a faery prince. His energy was life-affirming, and mine . . . well, I was a necromantic witch and the sperm donor who impregnated my mother was already dead when I was conceived. I was complicated.

Neither wholly dead nor alive.

Neither wholly *draugr* nor human.

And that was before a murder attempt when I was injected with *draugr* venom and before adding a bit of fae to my genetic goulash. I wasn't entirely sure what I even was these days.

Tonight, though, I was trying to be considerate and patient. That transcended species. Right?

We stayed silent as Officer Probably-Has-A-Name navigated us through the streets of New Orleans. A few human stragglers were out, but fortunately, I saw no *draugr*.

Or faeries.

Just humans, mostly tipsy and laughing.

"Safe?" I texted Allie.

"So far. They're trying to climb the gate. Lots of cameras."

I paused at that. Tourists could definitely be intense, but that was a shade too far.

"Attempted break-in," I told the officer. "Can you get me there faster?"

He sped up but, eyes still on the road, said, "Ma'am, I know you've instructed NOPD not to use your title, but this is a royal residence. You put us in a bad place if I can't call it in and there's trouble."

I grabbed his radio. "Dispatch. This is Crowe. I need Gary Broussard at the castle if he's on duty."

"Blood? Fangers?" was all dispatch asked.

"Tourists." Frustration laced my voice.

The dispatch officer's laughter was muffled, but I caught the edge of it under the cough she tried to use to hide it. "Units en route, Ms. Crowe."

I let out an audible sigh as we stopped half a block from my home. The officer was still fumbling with his seatbelt as I marched toward a building in the Garden District that looked like it could have been one of the first in the city.

Home.

As much as my apartment was mine, this house had become my haven—and not just because it was where Eli had lived before we were bonded *or* because it was where we resided most nights. It was magic in a way that felt revitalizing to me.

A fence, stone not iron, surrounded an almost plain house, but as both a witch and the bonded mate of a faery, I could see the shimmer of old magic. My home practically glowed.

The tourists were snapping pictures, even though all they could see was a plain, old house. It had no balcony or gallery, no porch or Ionic columns. It was almost so plain as to be unnoticed —which required a great deal of magic in this area.

Gary Broussard, my "liaison" these days for New Orleans Police Department, stepped out of his car just as we walked up to the back edge of the crowd. Either he was driving like a teenager at curfew, or he'd been in the area.

"Officer Broussard," my ride started to say as he practically ran up beside me.

Gary held up a hand to him. "Crowe. Could you maybe wait in my car?"

I grinned and said, "Nope."

"No beheading tourists." Gary gave me a look that was mostly joking. "Davis, you handle crowd control on the street. We don't need tourist pancakes."

Davis nodded. "Yes, sir."

Gary looked at me. "Can't ever take a back seat can you, kid?"

"My house. My assistant. My city." I shrugged. "Doesn't seem like I need to sit this out."

Gary sighed. He was a sort of father-stand-in for me, and my fondness for him was why I'd done a few weeks of crowd control and monster-mashing earlier in the year. And I suspect it was why I tried to play nice with the city mayor, who oozed political charm but lacked ethical everything.

"Let's get you inside before anyone decides to come make a political moment out of this." Gary motioned me forward. "What do you need?"

I let my magic curl out like a wave that any dead or *draugr* would feel. It used to be a simple thing, but now it felt like a medical assessment of nature, too.

I stumbled as my magic touched the fence that separated my home from the street. It was sturdy, stone with living wood and vine coiled around it currently. That was my magic, not just Eli's. I'd added a layer of natural deterrent that was only triggered by someone attempting to scale it.

Frowning, I reached a hand out toward the vines, feeling the places where someone had tried to cut them. They'd been hacked at, assaulted, and trampled.

"They cut my wood roses," I said, staring at the vine, willing it to expand into the street like a fast-growing hedge.

"That assistant of yours said you got your juice back," Gary half-asked, half-declared as he watched my hedge shove tourists backward into the street. "That's you . . .?"

"Yep."

People—*intruders,* my mind whispered—were yelling and crying out as they swatted at my vines.

Silly mortals, an increasingly apathetic voice murmured. *Treading on our territory.*

I shoved that thought back in the box. It was an unwelcome side-effect of my newly fae side cozying up with the witch and *draugr* parts of my genetic soup. Apparently too many supernatural genes in a bowl made for an internal voice leaning toward sociopathic when I used any magic while upset.

My phone buzzed again, drawing me closer to the moment and away from that inner voice.

"Boss! I feel like Briar Rose!" Allie's text had emojis, of course —neon roses and cartoon swords—and then the words, "Rescue me, princess!"

I rolled my eyes, but her Allie-ness made me focus. The wood roses were spreading over the whole of the fence, crawling up the house, and had at least three tourists held aloft as if they were bugs caught by a giant spiderweb.

"Crowe?" Gary said, his voice tilting into a cajoling tone. "Could you put them back down on the ground? Bad press and all that . . ."

I noticed the phones, the recordings, and thought about my vivisection nightmares. With a whisper of a panicked thought, I sent a surge of electricity into every phone within a half block—including my own.

There was a clatter as everyone dropped their phones, which were hot to the touch. My aim was still more akin to an antique Tommy Gun than precision sniper rifle.

"Well then." Gary looked over at his car, which was now smoking. I guess I'd caught more than phones in my surge.

Then the tourists saw me, realizing what had just happened was my doing. The excitement of seeing the fae princess seemed to dim a little. Fear mingled with their awe, but a few foolhardy people still seemed to be on the awe side of the equation.

"Are those silver swords?" one man asked.

Several people were trying to restart their phones, instinct overcoming logic. Others were scrambling for pens.

"Why would my sword be silver?" I asked. "I wasn't *born* fae."

I was astounded that this question was still confusing to them. Someone had read just enough folklore to know that the fae were allergic to iron and steel, but skipped too many science classes. I wasn't born fae but bonded to one.

"I was born to a human. Witch by choice. Bonded to the prince," I said, loudly. That part was all true. I was also born to a *draugr,* but I wasn't sharing that tidbit.

"Does the prince use silver—"

"There is a publicist who schedules questions," I said, still using my crowd-control voice.

"Where is the prince?" another voice yelled.

"Sleeping," I said lightly.

"Does he mind you being a witch?"

"How is he in bed?" someone else called.

I scanned for that one. Eli was bold with me, but he was a private person. "Rattling a witch's gates isn't terribly safe, and neither is upsetting one."

I smiled so they'd laugh. Mostly all of them did. A few looked at me without even cracking a smile.

Then I drew one of my swords.

No one spoke.

"And intruding on the prince's privacy doesn't bring out my kindness." I summoned the injured roses toward me, and the rose hedge snapped a long, thorny vine out toward me. "Plus, uninvited guests upset the roses."

The vine paused as it touched my fingertips, as if in greeting.

Mine. My safety. My armor.

The vine continued to grow, thickening as it wrapped around my arm, crept across my chest and spiraled down my other arm.

The vines encircled my waist, and in the next moment, the vine cut itself away from the hedge. Now that it was separated, the two ends swirled around my legs in perfect matching coils.

In mere moments I was rose-and-thorn-covered, a nature-wrought, magic-altered armor. No weapon could cut through the rose vines when they were around me.

I knew what I looked like: sword in hand, blue hair twisted like tentacles as magic filled me, rose-and-thorn armored.

"Now, if you'll excuse me, this witch needs to ask you to leave peacefully." I smiled. "Enjoy our beautiful city. Buy a book on pirates or plagues. Our city has history on both! Have a chicory coffee. Listen to the amazing musicians. *Enjoy*."

I strolled forward, my vines lashing out into a fence that burst into blooms as I passed through the natural archway.

 ❧   4   ☙

Threats at both of my homes tonight. I pondered the possibilities. SAFARI, the hate group that existed to try to promote laws against *draugr* and fae, was always near the top of my list. The occasional upstart *draugr* who knew that my great-gran was the *draugr* queen could be trying to attack her by way of attacking me. Random relatives of dead folk I'd beheaded? Some obsessive interested in the stunning faery prince I'd supposedly entrapped? And of course, the Hexen Master I'd resurrected from the dead was out there, and his murderer, Chester, who was behind a number of questionable things in the world—and was developing a hatred toward me that I couldn't quite fathom.

My fan club was vast and varied.

I glanced back, scanning the crowd as if I could spot an instigator. Silly, perhaps, but the raw truth was that a certain sort of hatred included wanting to see your victim suffer. And sometimes that meant first-hand, not via photos or video.

"We have trespassing laws," Gary told the crowd sternly, peering at the tourists through the flowering wall of thorns.

"Blockading this residence or attempting unlawful entry will land you in jail if you are seen here again."

The officer who'd driven me to the house joined Gary. He held out old-fashioned Polaroid pictures. It might not be high-tech, but today that meant it was exactly the right tech.

"We keep a log on any perceived threats to our resident princess witch," Gary said in a lighter tone.

As the tourists and Officer Davis filtered away, I stepped up to the gate to my property, which opened at my approach.

The vines that covered the gate were seemingly absorbed into my body little-by-little, and tiny thorn-picks of blood dropped onto the soil inside the fence. It was a minimal amount of blood, but it hurt all the same. A thousand thorn pricks as the armor anchored to my flesh. Later, I'd need a tall glass of revitalizing smoothie—blood and herbs—to restore me from that blood loss, but it was a small cost for the layer of magical armor that now coated my skin.

"Gary?" I called as the remaining vines—those covering the rest of the fence—began to grow. Once the gate closed, it would again be thorn and rose covered.

Gary met my gaze. He had stayed outside the gate. "Crowe?"

I beckoned him forward, and the vines lashed out and laced together behind him. A thorn-coated wall started to expand, steering him forward.

When he crossed the threshold into my property, I felt the magic in the soil rise up.

"Hold still for a moment," I ordered.

My land read him as truly as any serum or technic invented by man or magic. If he had threat in his heart directed to me or mine, he'd not take a step closer. I trusted him enough to invite him in, but there were reasons no one came here without a level of trust I rarely bestowed. To enter with violence in heart would result in death. It was a bit of magic I'd recently added to our home.

The shock on Gary's face was enough to make me smile.

When the roses dusted him with deep red petals, I said, "Come into my home, and be welcome here, Gary Broussard."

"You're scarier than you used to be, kid." Gary shook his head, but he strode forward as if he was nonplussed by ancient magic reading his heart.

And though I'd offered him the mildest of formal invitations, and his words were mild, he still looked a bit gobsmacked as he crossed the lawn and approached the vine-draped house where my assistant was waiting.

By the time we went inside, I thought Gary would have something to say, but he was looking around like the mere thought of being inside my house was stunning.

"You okay?" I finally asked.

"Sure, kid. Sure." He cleared his throat. "Can I call you that now that you're all . . ." He motioned around at the hallway as if it was a clarifying word.

I knew what he meant, but I wasn't particularly pleased by it. "In a hallway? Inside? Walking?"

"A damned princess." He bit the words off. "You're a monster-beheading, blue-haired, smart-mouthed witch. I came to terms with all that, but you're not exactly making it easy on me these days. You know how much shit I got shoveled at me over potentially endangering the heir to Elphame? Not just in-house, Crowe. I got feds calling up the boss, and my boss . . ."

His words faded into a sigh as I stared at him.

"You, Gary Broussard, are my friend. And I like working with you, and I'm good at beheading fangers." I crossed my arms. "I'm still me."

He nodded, but he looked about as convinced as I felt.

Then the door to the main living quarters jerked open, and my assistant stood there holding onto what looked like a frozen Bloody Mary.

I stared at the drink and pressed my lips together.

"Oopsie!" Allie backed up. "Didn't know you brought company, boss." She held the frozen *actual* blood concoction out to me like it was a normal greeting. "Can I make you a cocktail, too? I cook when I'm stressed, so I made the boss a drink, you know? It isn't like she always drinks . . . err . . . I mean everyone drinks. Perfectly *normal*, right?" She shook the glass at me. "Bloody Alice, boss."

I closed my eyes and hoped I wasn't about to rattle poor Gary's brain. If he thought me being a princess complicated his life, he'd have a coronary if he discovered what exactly a Bloody Alice was or why I needed one.

"Lots of people drink, Ms. Chaddock," I muttered, pointedly not using her first name.

Gary looked at me. "Crowe, your assistant is going to make me think you're a lush or—" He stopped himself. "Are you Mrs. Chaddock? Widow of Alvin Chaddock."

Allie all but shoved the drink into my hand and tugged Gary into the house. "You knew him? My sweetie?"

"He donated to a lot of charities. His son, your . . ." Gary looked awkwardly at me.

I smothered my amusement in a long drink of my blood smoothie. Like a lot of rich old men, Alvin Chaddock married a woman who was the same age as his kid. I couldn't judge too much; I still had no idea how old Eli was. The question wasn't one he was at ease answering, so I let it go.

At a certain age, I guessed that numbers stopped mattering.

I wasn't sure how old that was for humans, but whatever people thought or accused, Alice Chaddock adored her late husband. *Still.* She'd tried to murder me as a result of her loyalty to him and his son, convinced me to enthrall her dead stepson, and continued to convince me not to behead him. Allie might be a bit intense, but she was one of the most loyal people I'd ever met.

"Tres," I interjected into whatever chatter Allie had been sharing. "Her stepson is Tres."

I met Allie's gaze. "So . . . why were there so many people outside the house? And how did you get trapped in here?"

Allie pouted briefly, which meant that I wasn't going to like the answer. "I reserved the cathedral like you said, to . . . err . . ."

"It's okay," I said. "NOPD needs to know sooner or later."

"Right." Allie gave one sharp nod. "So I reserved the cathedral, asked about setting up a perimeter, booking guards . . . you know. I let on that it was an important event. That I had a *royal* pain of a boss. Not that you're a pain that often, boss. Just trying to be hinty without being too subtle."

Gary's eyes were wide. "You're having the royal wedding *here?* You're. . . that's . . . you're Jewish."

Allie sighed.

"True," I admitted. "People are sometimes daft, though. They aren't thinking that a Jewish witch marrying a faery wouldn't actually be having an indoors wedding ceremony in a Catholic church."

"So, you aren't hiring guards?" Gary asked.

"Oh we are." Allie clapped her hands together. "I'm paying an embarrassing amount to the NOPD to pretend there's a royal wedding, and I'm going to donate the whole thing to some couple who can't afford a big ol' wedding. Like a fairy godmother!"

Gary stared at her and then looked back at me. "It's a distraction."

I nodded.

"And today's little crush of people was just the first bit of madness," he added.

"Yes . . .?" I admitted sheepishly.

Allie put her hands on her hips and launched into a mother hen lecture. "Gen deserves a wedding without paparazzi and tourists and haters and—"

"She does," Gary said, taking the sass out of her voice quickly.

"And the police will get paid the same as if it *was* there, so it's a win-win." Allie didn't sound nearly as chipper or flighty now. She sounded scary as she poked him in the chest with one manicured fingernail. "And you will help us with this ruse, Officer Broussard, or I know people who will make you regret it."

No one laughed, me because I thought she was as endearing as an angry mama bear and Gary because he was used to women with fierce attitudes. Alice Chaddock might be tiny and chirpy, but she was also the kind of woman who knew where bodies were buried, and in that moment, she was in full bridesmaid mode. This wedding would go off without a single error, or Allie might very well feed anyone who mis-stepped to proverbial dragons—or to the actual alligators since we were, in fact, hosting the real wedding out in the bayou.

"I'll happily be point person to coordinate the wedding at the cathedral," Gary said with a flicker of a laugh. "And I'll not tell a soul that the witch will marry her faery prince right here in our own version of a fairy tale castle. I'll nudge and raise a brow and be very subtle."

"Excellent." Allie hugged him. "Gen said you would likely help."

Whatever else she was, Allie was a part of my found family—and although *Allie* had no idea yet, I suspected she'd be literal family in time. The king of all fae had decided to marry her. They hadn't dated or anything, but fae relationship decisions were perplexing to me, even after magically marrying my own faery prince. Take Eli, for instance. For reasons only Eli knew, he'd met my blood-covered, sword-swinging, foul-mouthed self and thought "she's the one." He'd lived in exile, been my friend, and eventually my bonded spouse.

Weird courtship was a fae thing.

Unfortunately, so was the giant wedding celebration I was currently unable to keep avoiding. I had to plan at least one, but probably two wedding ceremonies—which meant that I pulled my notes out of my bag.

"Why didn't you tell me you were doing this tonight?" I asked.

"You're a terrible actress. I needed a scene. A real one. You delivered that because you were stunned." Allie shrugged like her answer made perfect sense.

It didn't, but neither did one of the wealthiest women in the city working as my assistant. Allie did what Allie wanted, and the rest of us just sort of coped as best we could.

"Let me get a drink for you while we get this part sorted out," I told Gary. "Allie, give him your official statement on the attempted break-in."

"Yes, boss." She walked over to sit primly on the sofa as if polite manners would hide the vicious streak she'd just revealed.

"It'll likely be all over the department within forty-eight hours," Gary said. "Don't be too subtle, Mrs. Chaddock. They need a few details to start gossiping."

I tossed back more of my Bloody Alice, as I wandered off to find a bottle of vodka and bowl of fruit.

Might as well multitask.

꙰ 5 ꙰

A few days later, I was feeling more capable about the wedding. Allie was working with my mother on the details—public and private ones. Contrary to the rumor mill we'd set in motion, I would not be having my ceremony inside *any* buildings.

Tonight, I was at a restaurant where I'd been meeting my grandmother bi-weekly. The interior was dimly lit, old-European ambiance with eloquence and age vying for dominance. On the wall were carved skulls and several paintings that were from lesser-known Renaissance artists. The chandeliers were old world oil fixtures, but that was not unusual in New Orleans. Flickering flames lit a lot of places in the city. I *suspected* that the décor was my grandmother's property. I *knew* the restaurant was.

"Ms. Crowe?" the waiter came by the table again. "Would you like to order? Or are you still waiting for the lady."

The lady, of course, was my great-times-great grandmother. She closed *Diablerie* for our meetings, allowing us both a privacy that we craved.

Beatrice was usually early, but tonight, I'd been here for an hour, and she still hadn't shown. Admittedly, she could be busy running one of her companies or beheading usurpers or whatever else she did. Still, I worried.

She hadn't mentioned any recent issues, and I tried not to ask too many questions—the secret to successful families, in my experience, was to avoid awkward topics. Sometimes it was belching at dinner, and sometimes it was "please don't send me heads in boxes." We agreed to disagree on the latter last holiday season.

Grandmother? I called on whatever "channel" it was that we used to speak at a distance. *Are you well, Beatrice?*

No answer.

I motioned for the waiter. If Beatrice wasn't replying, I was headed to the Outs to check on her.

But before the waiter reached me, Beatrice swept into the restaurant like a small storm. The red and black tablecloths all fluttered in the breeze created by her wake. There was *flowing*, and then there was the speed at which she did so. My bones tingled at the chill she radiated.

"Water," she said as the server paused at our table. To me she said, "My meeting ran late."

We were the only people in *Diablerie* other than the waiter, bartender, and chef.

Beatrice looked like a misplaced warrior. Knee-length leather wrapped her legs. She wore what resembled a traditional Scottish kilt, which was nothing more than a long swath of plaid fabric wrapped artfully around her. It was held at the waist with a length of snakeskin, as if the snake was biting its own tail. Leather gauntlets with metal decorations covered her wrists and throat.

Uncharacteristically, blood streaked her hair like dye, and bloody fangs were woven onto a cord that dangled around her throat. People were terrified of *draugr,* and with good reason. They were dead, and their existence was predicated on drinking the blood of the living. It made them closer to reptilian than human, although they all, in fact, started as human.

"Are those dripping?"

Beatrice smiled. "Someone questioned whether I was fit to serve."

I winced.

"I do dislike spurious challenges to my authority," she said mildly.

The waiter returned with water, as well two glasses of what appeared to be red wine. My glass *was* simply wine. Hers was not.

"Let's talk about flowers," Beatrice said. "Your mother thinks that we ought to ask Marcus if the fae have any bridal flowers of a traditional nature."

"Mmm."

"I think that he can do that in *Elphame*." Beatrice dabbed her lips with her red linen napkin.

"I think that my feet on the soil, and my family present to share my joy is all I want," I explained. "Honestly, I have no opinions on most of it."

"And the cathedral plans?"

"In order." I had no doubt that the wedding Allie was planning at the cathedral would be the dream wedding for whatever couple she'd privately approached. My wedding would be outside, though. In nature. That was the one unifying detail between the ceremony in the Outs and the one in *Elphame*. Well, that and my groom.

"Any word from Chester? Iggy?" Beatrice asked, as she did every time we met.

"Both silent." I sipped my wine. Chester was the oldest living human, and Iggy was a witch I'd brought back from the dead accidentally. The former had threatened me—and a very long time ago murdered Beatrice. The latter was either friend or foe depending on his agenda. "I think we're clear to have a crises free wedding."

She made an indelicate noise. "Between tourists and *men,* I have my doubts."

"You do realize that I'm *marrying a man*?" I asked lightly.

"Eli is acceptable." Beatrice shrugged. "I tire of beheading my enemies, daughter of mine. So often they are men. Our problems . . . so often . . ."

She stared at a spot beyond me. And for a flicker I thought an enemy waited there. Foolish of me. I would feel any dead presence, and all I noticed were her corpse-guards. She looked into her thoughts. I knew that the ancient witch *draugr* who had once been a mere mortal witch had been forced to carry children as Chester plotted to create a witch-*draugr* hybrid. Me. He had plotted to create *me* centuries before I was born, and it cost Beatrice her life. Add to that the fact that her descendant—my mother—was manipulated a couple decades ago to that end, and it was easy to see why Beatrice had some misandry.

"Cannot feed them to the dragons, cannot turn them into pigs," Beatrice muttered. "Your mother has asked much of me of late. I will be glad when the wedding has passed."

"I do appreciate you not feeding anyone to the gators," I said lightly.

"One pig and you mother threatened to move out." Beatrice held my gaze. "She has such patience, that woman."

I patted Beatrice's hand. "But you did get to rip the fangs from someone tonight . . . that's, err, something . . ."

She smiled, not quite a laugh but more cheerful now. "He was foolish to doubt my ferocity. A woman? A witch? A Jew? Does he think that *I* am stranger to challenges?"

"Underestimated isn't the same as defeated, though." I sipped my wine. "If there is any chance of co-existence with humanity, your path is the right one. Your allies see this."

"You give good counsel, daughter of mine. Perhaps we can stage a small coup after your nuptials. I have been eying what your nation calls Florida. They create so many conflicts."

I made a noncommittal noise, and this time Beatrice laughed genuinely.

By the time I was ready to leave, Beatrice and I had agreed

that we would allow my mother her way with the wedding, and I would talk to Mama Lauren if there was anyone who truly would be best served with a stint as a pig—excepting the King of *Elphame.*

AFTER I LEFT BEATRICE, I MET MY GROOM AT HIS BAR, BILL'S Tavern, for a drink. He had an incredibly capable manager, my friend Christy, but Eli was still on site frequently the last few weeks. It was Eli's bar, the reason we met and the place I had felt undeniably at home for several years. I used to think it was the ambiance: a polished wooden bar, low bar lights, and a remarkably good liquor collection. Turned out it was Eli.

"Crowe," the doorman called out to me as I approached the line waiting to get into the bar.

"No fair!"

"Hey!"

The doorman shut them all up with a glare. The news of the royal nuptials and the usual Halloween crowd in our fair city made for more of a crush than normal at Bill's Tavern. A part of me rebelled at all the unfamiliar faces as I stepped inside.

"Fangs," Eli murmured as he pulled me in for a polite hug. He was increasingly circumspect in public, and I wasn't sure if it was about protecting my privacy or about dissuading gossip.

I concentrated on retracting the recently acquired fangs. I didn't need them. I wasn't *dead,* so they were an unwelcome surprise. My *draugr* genes disagreed sometimes, though, and fangs extended. I developed an awkward lisp that could give me away, but other than that, it was fine.

Without another word, Eli motioned for a bartender, and in a matter of moments, we were walking to a roped off corner table with a bottle of tequila and a pair of glasses.

"And how is your grandmother?" he asked.

"Dressed in bloody fangs and grumbling at dealing with my

far-too-patient mother." I smiled. "I swear that Mama Lauren is the most reasonable of the bunch. Allie is bridesmaid-zilla with her desire that everything be perfect, and Beatrice is irritable. And your uncle . . . apparently he was irate that we were getting married in a church."

"A *church*?" Eli sounded like he might laugh. "He believed that?"

"Many people believe it. It's a historic building, beautiful and—"

"Catholic." Eli chuckled. "Do you think people are that gullible?"

I pulled out my phone and showed him a row of currently trending hashtags. I was simultaneously excoriated under the tags #badwitch and #BadJew and cheered under #faeryweddings and #witchybride.

"This is absurd," he muttered.

"Wait for the #hotfaery and #PrinceEli threads," I teased. "Apparently, there are plenty of people willing and eager to convince you to pick them instead."

He gave me a look that ought not be legal in public. "Impossible. I have everything I need right here."

He didn't look away from my eyes as he lifted my hand and pressed a kiss into my palm; his lips glanced over the edge of the callouses left there by countless hours with swords or axes in my hand.

"My warrior bride," he added. "My long-sought prize. My perfect dessert."

I sighed. "You make me feel speechless when you say things like that." I stepped closer and whispered, "Or like I ought to pull you into the office and ask you to ravish me."

"Good." He looked smug enough that only a fool would mistake him for human. No one does arrogant quite like the fae.

It felt like an absolutely perfect moment, right up to when the screams started.

"Death to monsters!" someone yelled before two other people shoved our bleeding doorman inside.

With a screech that was loud enough to cut through the chaos of a bar full of frightened drunks, a rust-bucket car came slamming into the front door. The hood of the car was covered in crucifixes, and the front window was missing.

Two people in hoods that resembled the ones worn on Mardi Gras floats crouched there with . . . high volume spray guns.

People screamed as they got doused in what smelled like plain water.

All the while, the radio of the car was cranked, and a Latin mass was playing loudly. The sound of a priest intoning prayers as the bar patrons were being doused with water was enough of an oddity that I had to wonder if this was someone's idea of a Halloween prank.

But prank or threat, I wasn't about to let it stand.

Eli was helping the doorman to his feet, and he and Christy were already handling getting people moved to the back of the building. The injured would heal, and even if there were *draugr* in the bar, holy water wouldn't do anything but make them wet.

Aside from the damage to the bar, this wasn't a dangerous situation. There were no fatal injuries. I wasn't feeling forgiving though.

My home.

My people.

I stomped toward the door, all while sending my grave magic out in waves that rippled and returned to me.

To me.

I could feel eyes opened in the soil. Ears listening for my call. Human and rodent and assorted pets. They were all aware of me. They were waking at my summons. No grave soil needed. For much of my life, I'd worked to develop control over my grave magic. It had been my focus since childhood, but since bonding with Eli, I was less about control—and more about testing my limits.

We come.

Mother.

We are yours.

We protect.

I invited the corpses to see through my eyes as I stared at the people who were here to cause me and mine harm.

"Get her!"

I felt something hit me, just as I heard the dead fall back to sleep.

Eli yelled, "Geneviève!"

But I was unable to reply to him, to the dead, to anyone.

$$\text{❄} \quad 6 \quad \text{❄}$$

"I knew time with you was going to be a wake snakes experience, Miss Crowe," a man said. The voice was familiar, but whatever knocked me out was intense enough that I couldn't focus.

"Wake snakes?" I echoed blearily. My brain felt fuzzy, and my mouth was parched. I tried to reach for my sword as I stepped forward, only to realize that there were metal restraints on my wrists and ankles.

I tried to force my eyes to focus to figure out where I was. I could smell air that felt stale, motionless, and *old*.

I can't see.

I can't move or see. I can speak.

I sent out a trickle of grave magic to see if I could figure out where I was—or summon the dead to my aid. Old age meant there had to be something or someone dead. If I could wake them, I could—

"Ah-ah-ah," the man said with a laugh. "Bad hexen! No uninvited armies."

I recognized that voice. I'd brought the ghost of the dead Hexen Master to life—and then I'd accidentally resurrected him.

He was as alive as I was, but as soon as I got free of the manacles on my arms, I'd set about changing that detail.

"*Iggy*. This is not okay." I tried to call upon the fae nature-affinity, tugging *that* magic to the surface, but that was equally futile. Nothing worked. Not a single magician flicker. I couldn't even pretend to be shocked, though. I was kidnapped by a Hexen Master so powerful that the oldest living human had killed him for amassing too much power. He wasn't likely to underestimate me. I'd been bound. Literally and magically. If I ever had a captive, I'd have to remember this . . . well, assuming I got free.

"What in the name of duck dongles were you thinking, Iggy?"

"I'm not sure why duck genitalia would be a factor, Hexen." Iggy laughed. "However, I was thinking we should talk, so I've brought you here to dis—"

"Phones, Iggy. Modern thing. No kidnapping required, so how about you release me?" I reverted to my former light-hearted manner with him, which was fine when he was a ghost. Right now? A lot less fine. I was angrier than a cat in a shower, but I thought I was hiding it fairly well.

"I know you too well, Hexen." Iggy chuckled. "You underestimated me. I shan't make the same mistake."

"So this isn't just a social call." I glared in the direction of his voice. I didn't need my vision to do that, although it was starting to bother me that I couldn't see. "What did you do to me? I can't see *anything* . . . or feel the dead."

"Bound you," Iggy said simply. "Eyes not working yet?"

"No."

I felt a glimmer of pressure as if someone kissed my eyelids.

When I opened them, I was expecting Iggy to be right there. He wasn't. He sat several yards away, on the opposite side of the room, looking remarkably piratical due to his surroundings. A chest, circa 1700s, was on the earthen ground at his side. What looked like a museum's worth of coins and jewels were heaped in it.

Ignatius Blackwood was more than a little intimidating now that he was alive again. No longer an old man, he still had his walking stick, topped with ebony handle almost as dark as the night, in one hand. It was more of an affectation now. He still wore the same elegant ring and watch, but his suit was no longer the vintage 1800s garb he'd worn when he was a ghost. In its place was a pair of what looked like designer trousers and a shirt that managed to be loose and yet still highlight more muscles than I recalled him having. I wasn't generally up on names, but my assistant was and this looked a lot like some of the John Varvatos pieces she'd added to Eli's closest. Whatever it was, the resurrected Hexen Master looked sharp and modern.

"Well? Do I pass muster?" he asked. "I've worked hard to restore my body to optimum health since you so kindly rejuvenated me."

"You look better now that you're alive," I allowed.

He'd been in his late-40s to early 50s and . . . well, *dead* when we met. I'd accidentally summoned him from the grave, and since the bit of magic I hadn't controlled very well, he looked a lot better. It was more than being restored to life or exercising. I tried to look past his surface for traces of magic, but my own magical abilities were locked out of my reach.

"Not everyone can pull off a magical facelift, nip and tuck, and turning back the decades," I guessed, but his pleased laughter was proof that I was right.

"Not all of us have the blood of the dead and the fae in our veins to make us youthful," he retorted.

Fear flickered at his words. Iggy didn't have to torment me. He could simply expose my heritage. "You're a monster, Ignatius Blackwood."

"Indeed I am." He bowed his head. "And a liar, Hexen, but as I said when last we parted, let there be peace between us. I truly do not wish you ill at this moment."

"Newsflash, Iggy Pops, kidnapping me isn't exactly how we

create peace these days," I tugged the chains that were restraining me.

"Would you have met me for dinner had I called?" He sounded more curious than mocking, which made it hard to maintain my outrage.

"No." I sighed. "Hey, I don't suppose you sent a driver in an SUV with tinted windows to try to smoosh me like a bug?"

"I did not." Iggy shook his head. "You think ill of me, Hexen, but I do not wish for your death. We have shared enemies. I seek to ally with you, protect you—"

"Leech off my magic," I interjected. Then I saw what I'd convinced myself was an illusion. The image of Baron Samedi, loa of the dead, hovered over him briefly, and grinned at me.

Then Samedi was gone, vanished as if the entire image was only in my mind. I supposed it could be a bit of smoke and mirrors, but that didn't seem like Iggy's style.

"Are my eyes working poorly?" I asked.

"No. Geneviève of Crowe, you see what my master allows. I made a vow a long time ago to one who is tied to death, one who leads the way, who can cure and kill. I serve at his pleasure. The transition between dead and alive solidified long-ago vows." Iggy gave me a tired smile. "Once upon a time, fair Geneviève, it was blasphemy to serve him, and so I blasphemed. I was born, like you, with an affinity for the dead. . . although I was alive, wholly and completely . . . unlike you."

"Who *are* you, Iggy?" I tugged on my restraints again, attempting to get comfortable as Iggy watched.

"I've worn many names, but I am but a man who is in your debt."

I shrugged and stretched, the chains jangling again as I tested how much reach I had. "Send flowers. A gift card. Oh! Allie set up a wedding registry at a high-end weaponry retailer and one at a blacksmith."

Iggy laughed. "I do like that woman." He met my eyes. "Vow

on your magic that you will not try to escape, and I shall offer you an equal vow that no harm will come to you while you're here."

"Mmmm. No. An eternity in your lair? Not exactly the future I'm planning."

"If you are left to roam, you will die, Geneviève of Crowe, and I find myself uninterested in that resolution." Iggy walked up to me and stood just out of reach. "I cannot allow you to meet that fate. It would not please Baron Samedi either."

Maybe it was living in New Orleans with a bunch of walking dead folk or going toe-to-toe with the king of *Elphame*, but the thought that the loa of the dead had an opinion on my life didn't freak me out as much as maybe it should've. Later, perhaps, it would. In that instant, however, all I could think of was Eli. He had to be worried, and more importantly, if I died Eli died. We were bound.

"Iggy, be reasonable! I cannot stay in your dirt pit, even though I applaud the piratical vibe. Very New Orleans history, there." I lunged as Iggy swayed closer, trying to at least catch an ankle to knock him off-balance. Hexen Master or man, a good length of chair around his throat and I could kill him.

Kill the man, end the spell. Even a baby witch knows that.

Iggy stepped back, ignoring my attempt at injuring him, and said, "My heart beats again. For this, I am in your debt. And I find that I like you. You remind me of your—"

"My grandmother?" I interrupted. "Seriously? That's a little gross, you know?"

He shrugged, not looking the least bit sheepish. "I waited over a century to be resurrected, to find someone strong enough to summon me. I played meek to lead you to trust me, to reach a point where you could be convinced to resurrect me. To restore me."

"I'm bonded to Eli. I *love* him," I reminded Iggy.

He brushed my hair gently. "He's granted you near-eternal life.

I'm grateful that you bonded to Eli, but I am unparalleled in strength and patience."

I laughed, pushing every mean, spiteful, angry bit of energy I had into it.

"Tell that to Eli, who waited *years* for me. Tell it to Chester, the human who murdered you. Tell it to my grandmother, who watched her family for generations." I spat at him. "I'm surrounded by patient people. I'm not impressed."

I didn't mention that I thought Chester was a terrifying creature—or that I hated saying his name. But I liked the flicker of rage in Iggy's expression when I said Chester's name.

I braced for an argument. I wasn't entirely sure if I wanted to debate because I was angry or because I was bored or because I was hoping Iggy would see reason. It didn't matter, though. Iggy simply strolled away into some dirt-walled tunnel, leaving me there in chains.

❧   7   ☙

I hadn't ever experienced the humidity of being in the earthen lairs, and I had to say that I wasn't loving it. New Orleans, admittedly, was damp in various ways. Humid air. Wet drizzle. Hurricane season. Bayou waters. There were plenty of ways that water was inevitable. In this pirate cave of Iggy's, the air felt thick. Moldy. Musty. But without the benefit of corpses of any sort that I could summon to me. The absence of the dead felt like a sudden loss of one of my primary senses. For years, I'd wished I could "turn off" my necromancy, but when it was gone after my bonding with Eli, I was miserable. Having it cut off now made me feel panic when I woke up in the same quiet darkened room. My magic was silent. I was still a captive.

This time, at least, I had a much longer chain on my ankles. My hands were free, and I was resting on a mound of blankets. They didn't smell terrible, but there was a damp earth scent that permeated them and the air itself.

At least I wasn't sleeping standing up. That was progress. My hands were free, too. I'd like to think that this meant Iggy was a fool, but he was obviously able to knock me out to change my restraints, so I wasn't arrogant enough to think he was foolish.

He'll make a mistake sooner or later. He has to.

I studied the rest of the room where I was caged. For a literal hole in the ground, it had its upsides. There were barrels that may or may not be filled with booze, crates of centuries' old liquor, and in the darkest corner, tucked behind the rest, a few free weights.

Who said you couldn't teach a dead man new tricks?

It appeared that my captor spent a not-insignificant amount of time here.

I'd always said that there was nowhere else I'd rather be than New Orleans. Plagues, floods, monsters. New Orleans didn't give up or give in, and I was proud of that. I hadn't meant that I wanted to be entombed under the city.

I tried again to reach for the dead, to reach for some sort of nature. I was inside the earth. That *was* nature. My magic was silent.

"Can you hear me?" I called to Beatrice, Eli, the dead.

No one answered.

Whatever Iggy had done when he bound my magic, it was damned effectual. I drifted back to sleep on my pallet of blankets. I might not be as strong as the Hexen Master who'd kidnapped me, but I wasn't going to stop fighting. That meant sleep.

And food.

That part wasn't as easily handled. Thanks to recent events, I was pretty reliant on my Bloody Allie drinks, and without regular access to fresh blood, I was going to get weaker and weaker.

Not helping.

I shoved that line of thought away. Sometimes in this world, all a girl could do was bop the gators that swam closest to the pirogue—or in this case, the kidnappers in the pirate tunnel.

. . .

ON MY NEXT WAKE-UP, I WAS GREETED BY THE SIGHT OF MY kidnapper draining blood from his wrist into a coffee mug that looked as old as the crates of liquor.

"Good morning, Hexen."

I said nothing, but it hit me then: I'd slept. *Twice* even. Since I went multiple days without needing even a catnap, I was sure that this was his doing, too.

"How long have I been here?"

"Two weeks." He glanced at me. "Fifteen days to be precise. I could tabulate hours, as well, but—"

"Why?" Muttering even that one word took more energy than seemed rational.

Cut off from Eli.

Cut off from the dead.

Cut off from nature.

The reasons were there, and I could think of them, but I couldn't understand why Iggy was doing this.

"Eli kill you," I swore blearily. "Bea...trice...too."

"Yes, yes, your calvary would try. And yet"—he made a point of looking around the cave-like room—"here we still are."

I glared at him, fighting to keep my eyes open long enough to do that.

"Bourbon?" He held up a bottle that looked almost as old as I thought he was. "There's port and sherry. Rum. You seem more like a bourbon-for-breakfast kind of woman."

I raised both middle fingers in his direction.

"Two fingers of bourbon it is!" Iggy gestured and the cork popped out the bottle.

Despite every bit of willpower that I knew I had, I looked at that bourbon splashing into the antique cup, twining around the blood in there, and I salivated like a starving dog.

Iggy walked over to me and crouched down.

I was too weak to reach the cup, too weak to sit up without his help, and I hated him just then.

He put the cup on the floor and pulled me upright. "Vow on your magic that you will not try to escape, Geneviève of Crowe, and I shall offer you an equal vow that no harm will come to you while you are here."

I coughed like I couldn't speak, and he brought the cup to my lips.

Ha! Fooled you! I thought as he tipped the cup and poured that beautiful elixir into my mouth.

Too slowly I realized that *I* was the fool in this situation. This was more than simple blood. I'd watched him, believed my eyes in my state of weakness and exhaustion, but Iggy had put other blood into the cup before I'd woken—and *that* blood was infused with his own magic.

"Mine to protect," Iggy murmured.

He held the cup to my lips, tipping it and me back so it poured down my throat even as I tried to close my mouth.

"My vow to you, Geneviève of Crowe, my apprentice. I Ignatius Blackwood, will guard your life and teach you." He stared at me as I grew stronger, watching his own magic enter my skin and bone. "To Death, we are committed. To this city, we are born again."

I jerked away, reaching up at the same time to grab the cup from his hand. In the next moment, I pulled back and smashed it into his throat.

Iggy fell backward, blood and bourbon dripping across his face, and as he reclined there, I rose up and kneeled down on his chest, pinning him.

Whatever binding he had placed on me was gone.

Geneviève! My grandmother's voice was a roar in my mind.

And louder still was Eli's: *Bonbon! Wife! Geneviève of Stonecroft!*

I am here, I thought-spoke to both. *Come to me. Please.*

I was not expecting them to arrive so quickly, but in less than five minutes, the wall bowed in. Dirt and rock and dust billowed in like a cloud.

And I was kneeling over a bloody, laughing man. In that flicker, I saw Baron Samedi again, winking at me as if the whole thing was a grand game. His hand—*Iggy's hand or Baron Samedi's, I wasn't sure*—grabbed my hip as if what was happening was something other than the truth.

To a lot of men, I suspect it would look like infidelity.

I was atop Iggy. Admittedly we were dressed and filthy, but Iggy looked pleased as a cat who'd already had more than a sample of the cream.

"Geneviève!" Eli plucked me from where I kneeled and moved us across the room in the same instant.

His hands were all over me, seeking injuries, verifying that I was there and real.

"You're alive," he said. "I knew you had to be. If not, I'd have died, but . . . fear does things. If anyone could find a way to spare me death despite being soul-bound, it would be you, bonbon."

My grandmother was less effusive, but her affection was equally obvious. She currently had my captor by the throat. "Daughter of Mine," was all she said to me. Her attention was on revenge.

Beatrice shook Iggy like a child's doll. "You dare touch my family, Iggy?"

I watched, and for a flicker of a moment, I thought that Iggy was about to die. I could summon his ghost and ask what in the name of—

"Hexen," he croaked. "Stop her."

And at his order, I was out of Eli's embrace and snarling at my grandmother as I jerked Iggy free of her hold. I wasn't fool enough to grab Beatrice, but I pulled him free of her grip.

❧ 8 ❧

Trickles of blood lined Iggy's neck from where Beatrice's fingernails scored his flesh, and he let them drip. A part of me wanted to lap up that blood, and that part warred with the bond I shared with my partner, my love, who was watching the Master Hexen with a quiet fury that made me wish I could say or do something to defuse the crisis.

"You dare?" Beatrice snarled. She was a vision of terror in her torn medieval gown. She'd been somewhere formal from the looks of that dress and the fire opal and diamond choker that she wore. The dress was filthy and torn, but she looked no less regal for it.

"Dare?" Iggy echoed. "I was summoned from death by this hexen. She called me from my grave, Bea."

To say that Beatrice was furious was underselling the level of rage she all but radiated. Beatrice paced like a caged predator, and her eyes turned red as if blood had actually filled them. "She is *my* family. Are you fool enough to start a war with me, *human?*"

"Human?" Iggy scoffed, straightening his shirt as if he wasn't at all intimidated by the rage rolling off Beatrice. Whether or not it was an act, I had no idea. He was powerful enough to hide me from the queen of the *draugr* in this part of the world *and* my bonded fae spouse. That took a level of juice that deserved a bit of arrogance.

"I'm not a bone to fight over," I started.

Iggy waved my words away. "That's what you choose to insult me with, Bea? *Human*? We both began that way. She didn't. You know she's *more* than us. If Chester gets ahold of her . . . " He took a breath, as if the thought he had was too dark to ponder. "I owe her for my life."

"So you bound her? Daughter of my daughter! *Mine*! What sort of payment is that?" Beatrice snarled, lip curled like an actual animal.

"Please don't bite him," I whispered.

"I'm not daft enough to drink a Master Hexen's blood carelessly! Did you learn nothing with the way you enthralled Chadwick? Or Odem?" Beatrice swung her rage-filled gaze toward me, and I was reminded that my *draugr* genetics originated from something far more primal than I liked to consider of late. We had developed a cultural love for vampires, and the *draugr* queen often played into that with her old-world dress and manner.

She was still the monster that humans had hid from for centuries.

She was still the creature that tore bodies limb from limb.

And I felt a prickle of fear.

"If you attack him," I said, sounding far calmer than I felt, "I'll have to defend him. Please don't make me do that."

It was as close to pleading as I'd ever come with any *draugr*, and the fact that she was my ancestor didn't take the sting of begging away.

"You've enthralled two *draugr* already?" Iggy prompted.

I looked at Iggy, but I didn't feel a whole lot like answering his question. If this was what Tres felt like because of his bond with me, I owed him an apology. I wanted to defend Iggy, protect him, and yes, a part of my mind that I wasn't admitting in public, wanted to lick the blood on his throat.

It's not real.

It's not my *desire.*

Instead, I said, "I'm not sure what you did, but I hold grudges like it's my fucking job, Iggy. You would be wise to remember that, to ponder it, and *undo this.*"

Beatrice straightened her dust-covered dress and seemingly straightened her temper in the motion. "He cannot. You drank spell-infused blood."

"Not by choice!" I looked at Eli. "I didn't bite him. I swear it."

If I was the easily embarrassed type, this would be a thoroughly mortifying moment, but I was in a room with a man I resurrected, my dead grandmother, and my beloved. And I was as blunt as a drunk co-ed sometimes. "He starved me and then there was a glass, well, a mug really with bourbon and—"

"I trust you," Eli said simply, cutting off my rambling explanation. Then he leveled a look at Iggy that would make a seasoned warrior piss his pants.

And I remembered that Eli could read me.

He can feel my desire for another man.

"Eli . . ." I reached out, and he squeezed my hand briefly.

Then he turned icy fury back to Iggy. "I recommend you start explaining your reasoning, Blackwood, because while I may not look as threatening as the young Lady Beatrice"—he glanced at her and bobbed his head briefly in respect before stepping toward Iggy—"I am not as tolerant. You are a *mayfly* in comparison to the fae, and you have attacked a sovereign nation by kidnapping and enslaving our future queen."

"I have afforded her my protection." Iggy frowned at everyone. "She is my—"

Before the word was even fully formed, Eli had Iggy pinned to the wall, using the *draugr* ability to *flow* that he'd gained after we bonded. The earthen wall had an indent in the shape of Iggy's body now. "No. She is very much not *your* anything."

I'd thought I'd seen Eli angry, but in that moment, I realized how much I owed him an apology. My gentle fae lover might speak like a poet and treat me as if I was made of the finest artisan-blown glass, but he was still a man with a possessive streak that made my knees weak and my pulse race.

And he'd felt my desire for someone else.

"My wife. My woman. My beloved." Each word was accompanied by a punch. "My warrior. My heart."

Iggy had two already-blackening eyes, and blood trickled from his mouth and nose.

"Do not mistake my words, Ignatius Blackwood: Geneviève of Crowe and Stonecroft is wholly mine until *our* mutual death, and any affront to her—which this was—will not be ignored."

Eli released the bloodied man, who leaned on the wall watching me with a wobbly grin.

"Geneviève, I demand—" Iggy's words once again died, this time because Eli punched him so forcefully that he collapsed and slid down the wall to a heap on the ground.

Then Eli grabbed a flask of bourbon and poured it over his blood-stained hands, so the blood was washed into the dirt.

"If you wouldn't mind?" he asked Beatrice.

"With pleasure." She pulled magic from the air and lit the blood-and-booze-stained earth to fire. It wouldn't spread throughout the cave, and for a flicker of moment I was glad. I didn't want Iggy to die.

I glanced at the unconscious man who had held me captive.

"He's still alive, Geneviève," Eli grumbled.

"I'm sorry," I whispered. "I swear I didn't . . . that . . . *I love you. Only you.*"

"I know." Eli swallowed and looked away.

Guilt filled me. I didn't want to care about Iggy, but I did. Maybe it was the bond—or maybe it was the laundry list of questions I had.

"No one else can tell me what I need to know about my

magic," I said quietly. "That doesn't mean I *like* his approach or *wanted* to be enthralled or—"

"It'll fade once his blood-magic is out of your system." Beatrice's tone was so cold that I was worried, and in that observant way of hers, she answered questions I didn't know how to ask: "He did the same to me. We shared a . . . few weeks . . . of . . . fondness."

"That's assault!"

She gave me a quelling look. "He gave me the blood at *my* request, Geneviève. We were experimenting. It was another time, and I was not unwilling in any way. Why he would do so with you without your consent is another matter entirely. Did he take liberties?"

It was Eli I looked at when I said, "No. I had his blood, and the silencing hold on me broke and"—I motioned toward the wall they'd imploded—"then you were here."

Eli gave a single nod. No one addressed the possibility of what would have happened if I hadn't broken that hold. I glanced at Iggy, verifying that he was breathing.

I shouldn't care.

In a calmer tone, Eli said, "Blackwood withheld your presence from my life for two weeks, Geneviève. He took you away from me. He held you prisoner when you would leave. That is not forgivable. *None* of it."

He looked back at Iggy, but unlike me, Eli watched the unconscious man as if debating whether or not to strike him again.

"Take me home?" I asked, pulling his gaze to me.

Another terse nod was Eli's entire response, but then he gestured for me to walk forward.

Beatrice stepped in front of me, walking over the rubble and roots as if she were gliding across a ballroom. I stumbled after her. I felt a level of confusion and exhaustion that was atypical.

Behind me Eli was a steady presence. One hand stayed flat on the small of my back as if assuring me that he was there—or perhaps assuring himself that I was. Either way, I felt like that hand was all that tethered me to the world.

Why had Iggy risked his newly-restored life?

What was his agenda?

There was one. I knew that with a certainty that defied everything else. He believed he was helping me, and I had no idea how. He'd not seemed particularly interested in me, aside from as a friend or a means to an end.

What was I missing here?

※ 9 ※

When we reached our home, the one that bordered *Elphame,* not my apartment, Beatrice took my face in her hands and held my gaze. "Do not forget who you are, Geneviève." She looked at Eli. "Or allow this wound with Eli to fester."

Then she kissed my forehead as tenderly as any mother ever did and, in a moment that left me thoroughly speechless, kissed Eli on both cheeks.

"I will handle your Alice and your mother," Beatrice said with a tone of voice that every Jewish mother could summon at will.

I smothered the smile that such a guilt-provoking tone brought to my lips. Beatrice had barely had the opportunity to be a mother, and both of the women she was going to "handle" were grown women. But seeing this moment of maternal exasperation was as endearing as seeing the gown-clad monster explode a wall to reach me.

"I am lucky to count you as family," I told her.

"Indeed," was all she said, but she looked pleased as a kitten in a basket of yarn for a sliver of an instant. Then she was gone as quickly as if she'd never been there. The *draugr* gift of speed was so remarkable as to mimic disappearing into thin air.

I took an uncomfortable breath before meeting Eli's gaze. "I don't want anyone but—"

"You are eternally my home, Geneviève of Crowe and Stonecroft. I share with you my hearth and lintel. May you find shelter in my heart and home." He led me to the keystone of the doorway, echoing words he'd said to me several times. "In this world and my home, you are mine to safeguard." He looked like each word was sharp glass on his tongue as he said, "And I failed you."

"No!"

"If you would seek shelter at another hearth, I will release—"

"You will not." I grabbed him. "You are eternally my home, Eli of Stonecroft. I share your hearth and lintel. I find shelter in your heart and home. *You are mine* unto death or beyond."

I felt my birth magic and our fae magic swirl around us, as if we were in the center of a hurricane. Wind whipped around us, and I was no longer certain that the earth was solid.

Arms around his neck, I pressed my lips to his. I wasn't sure if it was magic, love, lust or some twist of the three, but together we *flowed* into the house.

"Geneviève." Eli pushed me back onto the bed and pulled my dirt-and-blood-stained jeans down almost at the same moment.

"*Mine*." He breathed the word against my bare stomach as he kissed and bit his way up.

I plucked at his shirt, as I promised, "Yes. Yours. *Always* and eternally. Now, touch me. Two weeks apart is too long."

He laughed, low and joyous. "I would free you if you asked, Geneviève. It would kill me, but if that's what you w--"

"Not what I'm asking." I unbuttoned his trousers. "Not what I want *ever*."

I slipped my hand into his trousers and stroked. "This. I want this."

He leaned down and kissed me speechless.

My other hand slid under his shirt, shoving it up. As soon as it was over his head and out of my way, I kissed his chest, his shoulders, his throat. I nipped gently. "May I?"

"*Geneviève,*" he said.

"If you don't want me to since—"

"Bite me. Touch me," Eli ordered, voice low and rough. He shoved his trousers further down giving me unfettered access.

Then he ordered, "Show me."

I let my fangs slide into his skin, and the taste of his blood pouring into my mouth made me whimper even as I swallowed. All the while, I stroked him. Time seemed to melt as my world was reduced to the touch, scent, and taste of Eli.

Eli grabbed my wrist and pulled my hand away.

Straddling me.

Pinning my wrists over my head with one hand.

I felt the hard length of him as he thrust his hips against me. Not entering me, merely taunting.

"Who do you belong to, Geneviève?" he asked, a whisper in my ear since my fangs were in his throat still.

I moaned.

Eli pulled back, moving so his throat was out of my reach and his length was almost where I needed it. "I asked you a question."

I pulled my gaze away from the blood trickling along the column of his throat as he eased forward, barely inside me.

"Geneviève? Tell me." The demand in his voice, the same icy command he'd had in the cave made me try to push my hips upward.

Eli's hand gripped my hip and held me steady, all while his other hand gripped my wrists tightly.

"*You.*"

"Who?" he prompted as he slid home.

"You. Only you." I swore. "Eli of Stonecroft. *You.*"

"No doubts, Geneviève?" He had me pinned, unable to move, unable to do anything but wait.

"None. Please. *Please*." He held me immobile for several more moments, as if he needed to prove to us both that he had mastery of me.

I could only feel and beg. "More, Eli. Please. *More*."

He was quiet, breathing as needy as mine.

"I love you," I reminded him. "I'm here. I'm home."

I heard the strain in his voice as he half-ordered, half-swore, "No one will ever take you away from me, Geneviève."

Then there were no more words, as we spent the night reminding one another how perfectly we fit.

COME DAWN, I HAD TO DISENTANGLE MYSELF FROM ELI'S GRIP. Quietly, so as not to wake the sleeping prince, I whispered a spell for stealth, so the click of the door closing was muted.

Maybe it was a small bandage on a gaping wound, but I spent the next three hours planning details for the wedding ceremony that we would be having. Between Alice and my mother, the main pieces were pretty much in order—as if they had planned obsessively in my absence.

By the time Eli came into the room, eyes darting around in a panic that made my stomach twist, I had selected two wedding gowns, flowers, and finalized the remaining details.

"Tux for the wedding here or traditional fae garb?" I asked as he stood staring at me. "And did we want to have the royal guards attend both weddings?"

He opened and closed his mouth silently.

"And I was thinking that although I want our wedding to be private, we ought to do a drive by for the paparazzi." I realized I was talking nervously, too quickly and too obviously worried. "You. Me. Marcus and Alice. Maybe she'd get a clue that he wanted to make her his queen. I wish I could tell her or that you—"

"I respect the bargain you made, and as I was privy to the terms, I cannot disrespect you or the king by telling Alice. A faery bargain is sacred," he murmured quietly. "We'll deal with your plot to get around it later."

I met his gaze. "Can *I* create a faery bargain? I mean, since *we* bonded I have some of your fae traits."

Eli nodded, unusually speechless.

"I can then. Interesting." I pondered the language I wanted to use for a moment before asking, "What do you say to a faery bargain, Eli?"

The catch, of course, was that if a bargain is begun, the fae making the bargain knows what the bargainer most desperately wants. And I desperately needed to know what Eli most wanted.

Eli gave me a look that made me want to squirm as he pointed out, "If we agree to make such a bargain, you will know my heart's desire in this instant. Do you want that?"

"Yes, very much so. And I'll give it to you if . . ." I stalked toward him.

"If?" he echoed.

As much as I had enjoyed Eli's need to prove his dominance over me, I wasn't done with atoning. "Does that mean you would like to enter a faery bargain with me, Eli of Stonecroft?"

"Perhaps. What are your proposed terms?" he asked.

I took a deep breath as Eli's desire washed over me. *Eternity. My safety. Not taking the throne. Figuring out what Iggy wanted from me. Chester's death. A baby.* The noise of his mixed and varied desires was daunting. Several sexual scenarios flitted through my mind, and I made a note to examine those more closely later.

"This is how you knew what I liked," I mused.

He offered one of the half-shrugs that meant that he agreed but would not be admitting anything. "The fae do not lie, but that does not mean that we ignore those things we have in our arsenal."

He gave me a look that left me certain that we had always been headed to forever, even when I had the foolish notion that I might maintain my illusion that I could resist him.

"I will offer you a wish, Eli. One unrestricted request when most you want to use it," I said.

"If you do so, you are bound by law to comply." He stared at me, as if his will alone could impress clarity upon me. "Nothing and *no one* could order you otherwise."

"Yes." I took his hands in mine. "Not even your uncle the king, or Beatrice—"

"Or Blackwood," he added because that, of course, was the crux of the wish. We both wanted him to be able to use that wish to free me if the need were to arise.

I understood then that this—this ability to offer a bargain for the other person or for the bargainer to gain a coveted moment or exception to a law—was what he'd been doing all along. Our first faery bargain was for a kiss, which had led to our engagement. The first bargain made him my fiancé, but it allowed him to save my life. The second allowed us to stay engaged without rushing toward an actual marriage. The third led to our bonding.

Until this moment, he'd been giving me the power to control my fate despite the challenges that came from eons of fae tradition and law. And today I was giving him the power to overcome the Hexen magic that Iggy had used to entrap me.

"What terms?" Eli asked.

"I will grant you this wish, Eli, if you take me to Elphame and pronounce me your bride before all of *Elphame*."

"Now?"

"Now." I gathered my wedding plans and dress images. "Take me to your place of birth. I think it's time we had a wedding."

❦ 10 ❦

Over the next two hours, we made hasty plans to gather up my mother, my assistant, and my closest friends: Sera, Jesse, and Christy.

After my last trip to *Elphame,* I wasn't truly eager to leave New Orleans for the realm of the fae, but a mental clock was ticking louder and louder. Now that I was waiting to let Iggy's spell wear off, going to a land where he was not made welcome was all the more reason to get on with the ceremony.

"If I could invite you, I would," I told Beatrice as we stood at her estate, which admittedly seemed to have more feral pigs than it used to. I made a mental note to ask if they all *had* to stay in their porcine states. For now, I simply asked, "Will you have our ceremony here ready within the next week or so?"

"Of course, daughter of mine! I can finish without Fair Alice and Lauren." She sent a glare toward a man currently shaping vast topiaries. "I may find it easier in fact."

"Not all men are pigs," Eli said mildly.

"*You* are on two legs, Eli," Beatrice demurred. Then she offered a cold smile. "Please remind Marcus that as he would deny me the chance to see you wed in his world, I do hope he understands that he will not be welcome *here* on my land where the next ceremony will be."

Eli quirked his brow in her direction. "So, my wedding has become a contest, Beatrice? Truly?"

"Geneviève is more my child than any before her. You know this. Marcus knows this. Iggy knows." She patted my mother's cheek, as Mama Lauren joined our small group. "Lauren has *always* known. She created Geneviève from magic and will, carried a child that was both living and dead in her womb, and despite her ill-conceived affection for that worthless hyena of a creature who impreg—"

"Grandmother," Mama Lauren interrupted. "We agreed not to argue about Geneviève's fath—"

"Not my father," I grumbled. "He was a sperm donor. And I didn't agree not to point out that he was not worth the slime on the bottom of a toad's warty ass."

Mama Lauren looked around, as if someone would step in.

Jesse shrugged. "Don't like the dead."

"Except you Lady B," Allie added. "Right, everyone? And the boss, except Geneviève's not *really* dead, so are you insulted by the *draugr*-opposition, boss?"

I snorted. "What's my job?"

"Right." Allie clapped her hands and looked at the group. "So no, unless the job is a way to kill that part of you by projecting it onto—"

"Alice?" Eli interrupted. "We must depart. I expect that Geneviève would rather we do so without a psychoanalysis of her career path."

Allie grinned and no one did more than roll their eyes. We were family, a mismatched collection of weirdos who had turned friendship and genetics into something wonderful. And this family's shit-stirrer was Allie. Although she'd tried to murder me last year, Allie had more than earned her place at my side.

"Give Marcus my words," Beatrice said with a razor smile.

"Please try to not hex or eat anyone," Mama Lauren whispered.

Beatrice shooed us away with a placid look on her face.

Allie giggled, and I had a moment of gratitude that the queen of the *draugr* had a near-unparalleled fondness for me, but then Eli took my hand and we walked toward the glimmer in the air that was beckoning us to open it.

Allie, Sera, and Christy had been to *Elphame* once, and I suspected Allie had gone over on her own on several occasions. My mother and brother-by-choice had never entered the realm where the fae lived. I was more anxious than I probably ought to be, and Eli's steady hand in mine made me feel less like panicking.

"Only for this day and this time," he reminded our small group, as if he hadn't impressed the rules upon them repeatedly and carefully already. "Today and today alone, you may enter my homeland without restriction. To enter here without such assurances is to be trapped at the will and whim of the regent."

As we walked, a blinding slice appeared as if the air itself had been torn open. It glowed with a light and warmth that would make anyone want to run toward it, and I was glad to see that Jesse took both Christy and my mother's hands protectively. I flashed him a grateful smile as I motioned them forward.

Allie strode through first, as if she was far more at ease with that doorway than I realized.

Sera followed.

Then Christy released Jesse's hand, so she could step through the gateway in front of my mother and Jesse.

Once they were securely through, Eli and I crossed the passageway between this world and *Elphame*.

On the other side the air was as pure as air ought to be. No pollution. Nothing but the sort of air that the human world hadn't known for centuries now, except in the most remote corners.

"Welcome to my home," the king said to all of us, although his gaze lingered on Allie with the sort of proprietary gaze that she somehow *still* wasn't admitting existed.

I had theories as to why, but I'd made a bargain with Marcus not to get in his way . . . more or less. He had considered holding my assistant captive within *Elphame*, as was within his rights for any mortal entering his domain. Our discussion for her release was a combination of epiphanies and insults—and culminated with a vow not to disclose his intentions.

I hadn't found a good way to get around it, but damned if I hadn't tried.

"Nephew of mine," Marcus said with a warm voice. He embraced Eli before meeting my gaze. "Death Maiden."

I accepted his open armed invitation and whispered, "Cradle robber."

He laughed jovially, inviting curious looks from my entire group and a few shocked ones from his retinue. The royal guard was a fierce fighting force, and I'd had the pleasure of their accompaniment when I'd ended up trapped in a spa run by magic users and *draugr*.

A series of dipped heads met my gaze as I looked at the assembled fae warriors.

Then Marcus stepped forward to greet my mother. "It is an honor to meet the mother of my niece to be."

He reached out to lift her hand, expecting her to swoon or whatever it was most mortal women did. Mama Lauren was not most women, though. She turned his hand when he reached out and shook.

Marcus of Stonecroft was handsome and seemingly ageless. The fae didn't age like humans, so I had no real measure of his age —despite asking more than a few questions. Marcus had been king for a lot of years. He had been king when the world learned the fae were real, and he'd been king when they all retreated to *Elphame*.

And yet my mother—who had a few decades of knowing she

was raising a mixed species child, and that her own ancestor still walked our world as a blood-drinking, dead, warrior queen—was not easily impressed. She kept hold of Marcus' hand and whispered low enough that only the non-humans heard, "Young Alice may not see the truth of the words between your lines, but I do. The girl has no mother to speak for her, but that child is *our* family. My daughter and my grandmother are quite vicious, you know . . ."

The King of *Elphame* gave her a level look. "I see the trait is hereditary."

"I'm not opposed to outsourcing," she murmured.

Then the awkward moment passed, and everyone other than my mother was whisked away. I thought it best to keep Mama Lauren nearby in hopes of avoiding conflicts.

At Eli's house, my mother explored and then sat outside, marveling at nature as I once had. Unlike in the Outs, there were no random monsters—or the *draugr* or looter variety—roaming in the dark of night. There she'd always risen and slept with the cycle of the sun, and I thought she was enjoying the peace of being able to commune with nature under the moon.

❧ I I ❧

I slept. That was a weird side effect of whatever Iggy did. I sort of liked it, but it was obviously bothering Eli.

"Are you injured, Geneviève?" He was propped on one arm staring down at me. He touched my forehead carefully, and then took my pulse. It was sweet, if not for the reason. I'd bled all over him, been injected with venom, stabbed, shot, and magically depleted. I was, in sum, accident-prone.

"I don't think so." I didn't feel unwell. "Sleepier than normal, but I feel okay other than that. Honestly, my magic feels . . . *obedient*. It's not overwhelming or humming or anything. Maybe I just finally settled into my bones."

Eli didn't look convinced, but he took my hands and asked, "Shall we stand before the world and proclaim our love?"

I pulled him down and kissed him before slipping by him with a laugh and *flowing* to the main room. Out there, Mama Lauren was waiting with veritable baskets of flowers and hair pins.

I dutifully sat on an ottoman while she started twining blossoms into my hair.

Eli fixed coffee, glorious man that he was, for all of us, and said nothing as my mother fussed and jabbed and twisted my hair into something fitting for the future queen of *Elphame*.

"Boss?" Allie came in with a glass bowl of what appeared to be gemstones. "I have a gift from Lady B."

My mother looked at the cut-glass bowl. "I told her it was too much."

"What?" I looked closer, feeling the magic in the stones calling me. Carefully, I reached out a finger and felt the impossible flutter of ethereal wings.

Looking past the magic I could see gleaming emeralds of a Birdwing, rich sapphire of a Blue Morpho, translucent near-opal Amber Phantom, the ruby Red Lacewing, deep amethyst of the Purple Emperor. They were temporary, neither real nor living, but to create such an illusion was a degree of magical mastery that left me speechless.

The faux jewels were in a net that draped over my hair. The effect of flowers and gems on my already sapphire-hued hair was stunning.

"Time to go, Eli," Jesse called from the doorway. He walked inside and came to a dead stop when he saw me. "You're not as funny looking as you were when we were kids, Gen."

I flipped him off. Then I said, "You're shirking on your man of honor duties."

"What? I thought you said that over here—"

I snorted in laughter at his panic, even though Mama Lauren swatted me. "Geneviève. Behave. Both of you."

My childhood bestie and surrogate brother said, "Yes, Mama Lauren."

"Sorry," I said unapologetically. "But you should see your face."

"Wench." He rolled his eyes and turned to Eli. "Come on, man. Your bride is a vicious thing. You sure you want to do this? We could hit the beach and—"

"I have no doubts," Eli said loudly and clearly. "Eternity will not be enough to make me tire of Geneviève."

"Your life, man. She snores. Cuts her toenail in the kitch—"

"Liar," I said. "That's *you*."

Jesse walked over and stared down at me. "You're gorgeous, Gen. Strong. Kind. Fearless. He's a lucky man, and I'm proud to call him family."

Mama Lauren sniffled.

"No tears!" Jesse and I said in unison.

She gave us a watery smile, pulled me to my feet, and hugged us both. "My babies."

And Jesse and I both did that awkward man-pat on her shoulders. Weepy women were dangerous, especially mothers.

"Right, well, I'll be taking the groom." Jesse backed away quickly. "See you at the . . . wedding."

Once the two men were gone. Allie looked at us and said, "I'll go check on the other bridesmaids."

And then I was alone with my mother, who was still giving me a weepy smile.

"Let me get the dress," I offered and all but ran to the bedroom where the simple unbleached cotton and lace dress was. I'd seen the confectionary-looking dresses online and in stores, as well as in illustrations sent from *Elphame*. They were lovely, but they weren't me. So I'd chosen what looked like a long dress with a slit in case I had to run.

No, really. I understand people thinking I'm paranoid, but I was *just kidnapped and held in a pirate's lair. These things happened.*

So slit, simple, and natural.

Over that was a lace layer that went on a bit like a duster or a cardigan. It added the delicate layer that everyone else seemed to want, and I will admit it made me feel feminine. The hex-woven belt, shot with spun gold, was the only truly extravagant item, but it was commissioned by Eli. He brought me the materials and asked me to create a wedding sash.

He wore a matching one.

I walked toward my mother with the belt in hand. "Will you?"

Silently, aside from stray sniffles, she wrapped it around my natural waist and tied it so that it hung down. It would sway as I walked, but that was fine.

The last touch was the butterfly veil that draped over my hair. My face was uncovered, but the net of gemstones on my hair added a weight to my step. This was it. My wedding. A flicker of panic rose in my throat.

"You love him." My mother kissed my cheek. "And he loves you."

I nodded. We were already bound unto death, but it felt somber to proclaim my tender feelings in front of the whole of *Elphame.* These were mine, and I hating feeling exposed.

We walked toward a field where it felt like the world had gathered. Thousands of faeries gathered. A path of blossoms led me toward Eli, where he stood waiting. My mother walked me to him.

"I give you my child unto your safe-keeping." She took his hand in hers, and then she took mine in her other hand. She pulled them together, so our hands were clasped.

Then Mama Lauren stepped back. Loud enough for all to hear, she pronounced, "There are two paths. One together. One apart."

My bridesmaids and Man of Honor all stood. In this ceremony, they were my witnesses. It was a fae thing.

"Before these witnesses of your life and past, I urge you to choose."

King Marcus and assorted fae stood.

Marcus walked to a central bower of closed flower buds. "Do you bring me a queen of our people, Eli of Stonecroft?"

For a long moment, no one spoke.

Then Eli looked at me. "I offer you my throne, my homes, my last drop of blood, my final gasp of air."

I swallowed.

"Will you join me, Geneviève of Crowe?" He stared into my

eyes as if there was any chance that he'd find doubt.

There wasn't.

"I go where you go," I said. "Your people are mine. Your ancestors are mine. All I have to offer in return are my last drop of blood, my last breath of life, and . . . both my grave magic and my blades, for you already have my heart, my body, and my soul."

No one remarked on the modification of our vows, but I was a witch. I would add those aspects to my vows.

Eli smiled. "I will walk whichever path you allow."

I looked at the two paths—away from or toward the king—and then I grabbed Eli's hand and ran toward the king. Hand-in-hand, we *flowed*. It was not a trait I would share so openly in the world of my birth, but here I was willing to show them what I was. If I was going to do this, accept the responsibility of a throne, I was going to be clear on what they were getting as a queen.

Marcus didn't quite muffle his muttered expletive, but Eli looked joyous.

"I was in a hurry," I said loudly.

Laughter fluttered around us, and my groom joined in.

"Are there any objections?" I asked the assembled crowd. "Not to marrying Eli. That is done. But to me being here as your queen-in-waiting alongside him?"

No one objected. Instead, as one, they curtsied or bowed. And I felt a wave of acceptance that was foreign in my life.

"No delicate maiden," Marcus said. "A warrior queen fit for your warrior king."

The butterflies-made-jewels took flight and dispersed.

Still with our hands intertwined, we both knelt—although protocol was such that only Eli was to kneel. I was merely to bow my head.

Then the King of *Elphame* placed crowns gently on both of our heads. "I give you Eli and Geneviève of Crowe and Stonecroft, my heirs."

❧ 12 ❧

Returning to New Orleans was bittersweet this time. I had felt a connection with the land of my husband, and I'd enjoyed yet another mini-honeymoon with him. However, being the officially presented heir and being tour guide for my friends and mother was exhausting.

When we stepped through the gate from *Elphame* to our human-world home city, we paused at Beatrice's estate long enough to deliver my mother there. Jesse and Christy stopped by his mother's home in the Outs, which left Sera and Allie in the car with Eli and me.

"It's not so bad there, is it?" Allie asked Sera. They were both in the backseat of the car we were using. It was modified for fae, of course, but much more spacious than Eli's convertible.

Sera smiled. "It's beautiful."

I'd seen her dancing with one of the fae guards she'd met over the summer. And more than once, I saw them walk away together. Allie, on the other hand, was all but chasing the king away with a rolled-up newspaper. Two of my friends seemed liable to be enmeshed with fae, although neither one quite understood how serious their flirtations were.

"You know, Sera, often the fae select their mates based on weighing criteria that only they know." I tried to stare at Allie as I said it. "Eli chose to marry me years ago. He waited and waited, carefully getting closer . . ."

"True." He reached over to the passenger seat and squeezed my leg. "Worth the wait."

Allie perked up. "Well, I think that's just sweet. Patience and all . . . I can't believe how oblivious you must've been."

I opened my mouth to point out that this was kettle-pot statement because she was somehow not catching on that the King of *Elphame* had her in his sights. No words came. Just a garbled noise as if I was choking. The peril of the faery bargain with Marcus was that I literally couldn't comment.

"Allie . . ." Sera started. "The king looks at you like Eli looks at Gen."

Allie looked at Sera like she was a swamp rat with a piece of trash. "Why would you say such a thing?"

"Because Gen seems to choke when she tries," Sera said, watching me. "Something is preventing her from speaking clearly. Roisin says that's what happens if there's a bargain."

Allie looked between us like Eli and I were betrayers or like Sera was a mad woman.

"Some traditions are magically binding, Alice." Eli shrugged, but he squeezed my knee in a way that I knew meant 'it's fine.'

I was, obviously, frustrated that I couldn't say anything, but at least Allie had a bit of a clue now.

"Well, that devious bastard . . ." Allie muttered.

And finally, I exhaled. Marcus might've led her on a bit of a con, but now that Allie knew his intentions, I almost felt sorry for him.

Testing the boundaries of the faery bargain, I said, "Poor Marcus."

Allie gave me a look that could strike fear into seasoned

warriors but all she said was, "I'll be needing a bit of a holiday boss. I'll let you know when."

"Oh?"

"Mmmhmm," she said. "I'm overdue for a trip home to Tennessee."

Eli flinched a little, maybe in empathy for his uncle or maybe at the knowledge that an angry Alice was a terrifying thing to ponder.

"Wedding first," Sera pointed out.

"Of course!" Allie leaned back in her seat.

Prim and proper expression back in place, Alice Chaddock could pass for a sweet Southern lady in that moment. Butter wouldn't even melt in her mouth.

And in that instant, any hope I had of Eli avoiding the throne because his uncle would marry and have a child vanished. The King of *Elphame* had no idea what he'd sparked when he pissed off Allie. I couldn't imagine her forgiving him and marrying him.

ANY THOUGHT I HAD OF THE KING OR ALICE OR ANYTHING ELSE faded as we neared the cathedral. The entire block was filled with tourists. It was like Mardi Gras met Superbowl met Halloween.

"What in the name of sweet baby Jesus is that?" Allie gestured to an effigy that I suspected was to be me because of the garish witch's mask and blue wig. The thing was strapped to a crude post on the street corner. Wood was piled all around it, and what appeared to be tailgaters with coolers were hooting and hollering like it was a pre-game party.

"I think they're . . ." Sera glared out the window. "They're planning to burn you at the stake."

"Well, 'Die Witch Bitch' isn't the cleverest slogan I've ever—"

"Bonbon." Eli interrupted, as he pulled the car to the side of the street to watch the madness. "I do not find this amusing."

The truth was that I didn't either. I felt several dead presences in the crowd, *draugr* who undoubtedly were not sanctioned to be there by the reigning queen—who was, incidentally, hosting my wedding at her home.

I let my grave magic roll out, feeling the age of the enemies stoking the hate. No one under two centuries.

As I realized that the fervor was being stoked by political enemies of my grandmother's, my temper slipped a bit more.

"Do you trust me?" I asked.

"Always," Eli answered.

I reached over and kissed him. "I shall see you at the wedding tomorrow. . . or before. Take my bridesmaids home?"

Eli nodded. He obviously *could* fight, and if I needed him, he would come. Being a few blocks away would be better right now though. I let my grave magic rise up, settle into my bones and skin.

"If you need me—"

"I always need you," I reminded him. "But there are times when your fae energy does not like what I will do."

Sera interjected, "Gen, maybe you could talk to them. . ."

"Hate doesn't listen to words." Eli looked back at her. "SAFARI exists to bring death to fae and *draugr*. And SAFARI is either involved or behind th—"

"*Draugr*," I interrupted, gesturing toward the pockets of dead that I could feel in the crowd.

"For fucking real?" Allie said.

Eli laughed. "I would feel terrible for my uncle if he didn't create his own bed, as you say."

"Made your bed, lie in it, Prince Eli. That's the phrase. But that man would be so lucky as to lie in a bed with the likes of me," Allie muttered. Then louder, she added, "We'll be at the house, Boss. Go give 'em hell."

"Try talking to them, at least," Sera asked, grabbing my arm.

"That's the plan," I told them both as I got out of the car and grabbed my sword and dagger from the trunk.

Sharp things. Never go anywhere without them.

As soon as my beloved and my friends were a block away, I had sheathed my weapons and untethered the grave magic that wanted to be released. It felt like a monsoon surging through a hose. Too much. Too forceful. A part of my mind whispered that my own magic would tear me apart.

Another part stretched like a fighter about to get a little exercise after a dull season.

Come out, come out, wherever you are. I summoned the dead, felt them knit bone and flesh together. Heard their voices as one loud symphony in my mind.

"To me." I spoke the words into the air, let magic whip my order across the city.

No part of me was fae in this moment.

No part of me was human.

I was Death Magic given form, and this was *my* city that had been invaded. I strode across the street toward their signs and crude mockery of me. This was hate and ignorance. This was fear whipped into violence. And I had no fucking time for it.

"Do you follow the dead so eagerly?" I said, projecting my voice as I swung up into a balcony on one of the historic homes that had been preserved well.

"It's her!"

"Death to witches!"

"Burn her!"

"You would come to my city with violence at the behest of *draugr*?" I called out. At the same time, I summoned the *draugr* there to me.

I wasn't sure how many of them I could beckon with will and magic while I was raising the dead, but no time like the present to test my limits, right?

One fanger, the youngest, all but threw himself at my feet.

"Well, don't you look human," I murmured. Louder, I ordered, "Teeth. In fact show them what you were like before you were leashed."

And he flashed fang like a child on Halloween.

Then promptly started hissing, slobbering, and generally acting like a newborn fanger.

Apparently, my magic went a little *too* far. Oops.

Tourists screamed, and more than a few took pictures . . . because of course, they did. Social media was its own sort of monster. Why fear death right here hissing and growling if you could pause to photograph it for your feed?

Elsewhere in the crowd, my magic pressed the same command on the other *draugr*.

The eldest of the lot *flowed* to stand in front of me. She was dressed like a Viking playing dress-up as a Goth. An awkward mix of fur and leather and jewelry on a fighter's body that ought to be holding a sword, not a metal chair.

I guess violence is the mother of improvisation or something like that. . .

She swung the folding camp chair at me like it was a bludgeon.

"Stop it." She smacked it into a tourist who went flopping into another, and in short order, we had a riot on our hands as well as an angry dead lady with a camp chair.

"I feel you in my head," she complained, rubbing her temple.

I snorted. "You won't be feeling your head on your dumb shit shoulders if you don't turn around and get out of my city."

"*Your* city?"

"Mine to protect."

Another older dead-dude showed up then, *flowing* up to her side. This one had a golf club.

"Seriously?" I almost regretted drawing a sword, but talking wasn't getting anywhere.

I gave talking one last try, though, and said, "Get out of my city. Don't make trouble for me or Beatrice, and I'll let you keep your heads."

"Your days are limited, child," the golfclub-swinging *draugr* said. "You—"

He stopped talking as my sword sliced through his vocal cords.

Then my army of the dead arrived. Before me and all around us were literal walking corpses that had been knitted together in their moldering graves to do my bidding.

"Remove them from my city unless they swear loyalty to me," I ordered my undead army.

I felt another dead presence to my side and turned, expecting to find one of the other *draugr*.

Instead, there stood Iggy. "Hello, Hexen."

"Take a number, Iggy." I was unexpectedly impressed as a third dead guy appeared and took up the golf club like it was a rapier. He actually took a fencing stance and motioned me forward.

"I swear, some people think that just because I'm a witch I'm going to be a shit swordfighter." I was more longsword or single-hander than rapier, which was suited for thrusts not slicing *and* thrusting like a longsword. "I don't have time for this. I need to sit through a manicure yet."

"A manicure?" Iggy said as he watched me fence with the *draugr*.

"Wedding tomorrow," I called to him. "You aren't invited."

Iggy sighed and with a gesture, the *draugr* froze. Literally. He was encased in ice. "Fix that, Miss Crowe."

I beheaded the fencer and strode into the crowd hunting the other three *draugr*. Even if they weren't starting a hate-Gen party, they were obviously not great people—even by my slightly laxer standards for dead folk these days.

"You are a vexing creature," Iggy pronounced as he walked at my side. "I try to offer you shelter and safety, and you chose this . .

." He paused, drew a knife from his hip and hurled it into the throat of a *draugr* mid-*flow*.

I was reluctantly impressed.

"You choose a *melee* over the sanctuary I offered you," Iggy continued, dodging a pair of 17th century corpses dragging a literal sack of yelling tourists away.

"Leave them at the gate, please!" I called to my army.

Then I turned back to Iggy.

"I'm just tidying up." I motioned to the chaos. "I don't want the monsters—human or *draugr* —running around starting shit on my wedding day."

The formerly-dead Hexen Master frowned. "In my day, we kept women safe. Perhaps not dead women like Beatrice, but aside from her, women knew that they were to stay safely locked away while men sorted out the conflicts."

I paused. "That's why you *kidnapped* me? To keep me safe?"

"I'd heard rumors of this"—he gestured at the chaos around us —"and I wanted to keep you free from harm, talk to you about training, explain the dangers of Chester and . . . well, I do enjoy your company. I had thought that perhaps you would be receptive."

I stared at him.

"It is not an impossible hope," Iggy said, sounding far too sure of himself for someone I had exactly zero interest in as anything other than a magical mentor.

"Bite my freckled fanny," I grumbled.

Then I *flowed* away, forgetting for a moment about the cameras everywhere.

"Oh Hexen," Iggy called.

Then with a snap of his figures, lightning flickered around in a beautiful web to various phones and cameras. People dropped suddenly hot electronics, circuitry fried.

"Blessed nuptials," Iggy said as he strolled past me a few moments later. "You obstreperous woman."

❧   13   ❧

Later that night I slipped into bed with Eli. The dead were safely nestled back in their graves, and the *draugr* I hadn't beheaded were gone. The tourists who arrived in my city with hatred in their heart were escorted to the city's gates. And Iggy had crawled back into whatever cave he lived with his antiquated notions.

"How was work?" Eli murmured after kissing me hello.

"Dead," I quipped.

Eli, proving yet again that he was the one for me, smiled. "Indeed."

I filled him in, and then snuggled into his arms to rest a bit. It was a bit alarming to suddenly need sleep more often, but that was another question for another week. Tonight was for pre-wedding snuggles and sleep.

THE NEXT MORNING, WE WOKE TO THE MAGICAL ALARM THAT let us know that Allie was here.

"Breakfast!" she called as she let herself into the house.

"Did you forget to lock the door?" I grumbled to Eli.

"I gave her a key," he said cheerily.

Then he escaped my grumpy morning-mood to start to ready himself for the day while I met the chirpy "Helloooo, my bridal birdie" of my assistant.

I swore she was cheerful just to piss me off sometimes.

"Come on," she said, knocking on the bedroom door. "We need to head out so we can get you all beautified. I have a whole team meeting us there."

I jerked open the door. "You're lying, right?"

"Nope."

We arrived at Beatrice's estate. Reflexively, my magic reached out to the dead in the soil, absences in pockets of space. There were a number of graves here. Three women in the bayou. Six more men in the ground closer to the house. A child in a grave. And a tangle of bones in a field . . . sixty. . . maybe up to eighty bodies.

It was as if I greeted them when I visited, reaching out, finding them. Knowing where they were. In the city, the dead were always easy to find. New Orleans was a city of graves. Out here in what was once called Slidell, the dead were often hidden.

Except the *draugr*.

My sense of the dead was always humming at Beatrice's home. Her guards were not *all* walking dead, but they were present enough that I felt hyper-alert the first few times I'd been here. Now, after several visits over the last year, I was getting used to their "signatures." I could identify some of the guests by the way my magic recognized them.

Beatrice swept out the door, and despite her elegant gown, she still looked like she was a moment from declaring war. She was draped in a midnight blue gown with a hundreds of small glinting gems that gave her the appearance of royalty—which she was among her kind.

She wore no shoes. In fact, a pair of employees at her door were collecting and tagging all shoes. There would be no footwear allowed at my wedding.

Fortunately, this was a small, private event, and none of my guests were the sort to disagree. They knew me.

"Your dress awaits," Beatrice said, motioning us forward.

The hallway was covered with a carpet of moss and flowers. Magic or patience could be responsible. I didn't ask which it was. I merely followed her to a medieval-looking room where dresses were hung in waiting.

Light blue and green dresses waited for my bridesmaids. And for me, a mid-tone blue gown that was cut to look a bit like a mermaid's tail. The material was dyed several shades lighter than my hair. Simple, but narrowing at the calf to highlight my shape. It was fancier than I'd thought I wanted, and there was nowhere to hide a sword.

"I'll slaughter the world for you," Beatrice reminded me, noticing my anxiety. "Wear the dress. Relax for these hours."

I nodded and slipped into the dress.

Beatrice stared at me. "I have sent Alice's people away to tend the bridesmaids. I know that is not 'your style.'"

I muffled a laugh.

Then she leaned forward and placed a circlet of gems on my hair. "This is not a veil. It is not a fae crown. It is in place of those things."

Carefully I met her eyes in the mirror. The crown was obviously a gift, but I could not help but suspect that there was more to it. "You're not telling me everything."

Beatrice waved my words away, reminding me of every time my own mother made such a gesture.

"Today is not the day to speak of *everything*," Beatrice said. "Later you may question me."

I nodded.

"Today you celebrate your love before your family, yes?" Beatrice fussed with my hair.

Behind me, by way of the mirror, I saw my mother, who had just walked into the room. The three of us stood there for a moment.

Then Beatrice kissed Mama Lauren's cheek. Then mine. "You are my greatest achievements in these many centuries of un-living existence."

Before we could think to reply, she *flowed* out of the room.

"She loves the way she can," Mama Lauren said. "I remind myself of that often when she is imperious."

"Sounds like you," I teased.

Mama Lauren swatted my arm lightly. "You are lovely, despite that sass."

"Because of it?" I asked.

"Perhaps." My mother's smile was agreeing, even if her words were tentative. "From my long-ago bargain . . . to this wedding, there has never been a risk too great when it came to your happiness."

We talked and finished getting ready in what felt like minutes, although it was almost two hours later that we walked out of the room and toward the courtyard.

I watched as Allie, Sera, and Christy walked toward Beatrice, who was officiating. Then, Jesse stepped forward. My "Man of Honor" had chosen to wait at the front with the ring. He was also in place to hold my bouquet of vibrant flowers.

Halfway up the aisle, then, was my groom. My already-husband. My bound-unto-death fae prince. Handsome in every way I could dream—and mine. Eli was everything I never dreamed to find.

My mother escorted me toward him, and I could not look away.

"Breathe in and out, Gen," Mama Lauren whispered.

"Trying." I smiled at Eli. "He steals my breath."

I knew there were guests as well, but in that moment, I couldn't tell you who or why they were here.

My mother and I reached Eli's side, and she said, "I give my heart into your possession, Eli. Guard her. Love her."

"I shall," he promised.

"I trust you." She stepped away.

As I placed my hand on his arm, I was trembling. This was it. The last ceremony. The final exchange of vows.

"Three exchanges," I whispered, thinking about the rule of three.

Eli smiled as we walked toward Beatrice.

She looked at us, smiled, and said, "The couple would like to say a few words in the presence of witnesses."

"Eternally yours," he swore. "I've waited years to be able to call myself the luckiest person in either world, Geneviève Crowe."

"I was oblivious so long, I'm glad you thought I was worth the wait."

Friends laughed.

"My heart, my hearth, and my hand are yours, Geneviève Crowe. Unto death I shall live and fight at your side. And in us, the future of my family is bound." Eli stared into my eyes. "It is my privilege to love you, and my great joy to be loved by you."

"My heart, my hearth, and hand are yours, Eli of Stonecroft. Not even death could tear me from your side." I swallowed. "I love you and will be honored to be mother to your child one day, partner on the throne of *Elphame,* and the sword at your side."

Then Eli gave me a wicked smile. "I accept your faery bargain, Geneviève of Crowe and Stonecroft. Your terms are acceptable to me."

I laughed at his going off script this time. "So mote it be, Eli of Crowe and Stonecroft."

Beatrice shook her head at our impromptu modification and then asked, "Do you take this person to be your spouse, your partner, your equal in all ways?"

"Unto death," Eli said.

"Unto death," I echoed.

"By the powers granted me by familial law, as well as my court and kin, I pronounce you wed." Then she swept her arms open and stated, "May I present Geneviève and Eli of Crowe and Stonecroft."

EPILOGUE

everal hours later, I found Beatrice outside in her courtyard as dawn was approaching. Everyone else had left, so only family remained. If this had been my first wedding, perhaps I'd have been long gone, but this was the third such event if you counted my bonding—which I did.

"Grandmother of mine," I said quietly, staring at a pig with the jacket. "Does that pig seem familiar?"

"I warned him." She took a delicate sip of the shiraz she was drinking. A bottle and empty glass sat on a pub table with a linen tablecloth. "Drink?"

"You warned the pig . . .?" I gestured toward the angry-looking pig as I accepted a glass of wine from her.

As she poured my drink, Beatrice gave me that look that said I was a little dim. Then her frown of irritation twisted into a cold grin of victory. "Piggy Iggy."

"Ignatius, the Hexen Master, is . . . a pig." I stared at him as he rolled in the water and muck that Beatrice's caterers had poured out into the garden. It was fascinating because I could see Iggy's intellect in the pig's expression, but he was still, in behavior, a *pig*.

"I invited him for a drink, during which I warned him that I was not going to tolerate affronts to my family," Beatrice said in a prim voice, as if centuries had faded from her. Her diction was less crisp as her emotion quarreled with her elocution. "A woman expects more from former paramours. Did I ask for eternity? Did I ask for fidelity?"

"No," I guessed.

"Precisely. I asked for simple respect, and yet he failed. He ought to have understood that making eyes at—"

"Making eyes," I echoed with a forcefully suppressed laugh.

Beatrice waved her hand and stared at me. "It was unseemly, Geneviève."

"To make eyes at me," I clarified, as a member of the catering team chased Iggy away from the door.

"Boorish. He was being boorish." Beatrice cracked a smile. "So . . . *voila*. He is a *boar*. It is a pun, you see? Your mother was telling me of puns."

"Mama Lauren knows you turned Iggy into a . . .pun-pig?" I asked carefully.

My centuries-old grandmother studied her nails as if she were a teenager caught in a lie. "Not precisely. If she weren't so *ethical*, I could tell her. I thought it was best not to mention before the wedding."

So, I did the only possible thing I could--I gave in to my laughter and pulled her into a hug. Then I whispered, "If you were around when I was a kid, I think Mama Lauren would've grounded us both."

When I pulled back from hugging her, she asked, "Piggy Iggy is better than a head in a box, yes? I did not kill him. He is a temporary pig."

She gestured with her glass before topping off both our drinks.

And I thought back to her holiday gift last year: a silver foil-wrapped box with bold blue ribbons. In the box was the severed head of a man who'd shot at me with the broach of a draugr who'd attacked me jabbed into the forehead of the dead man.

"Equally unexpected," I allowed.

Then the wickedest smile came over her. Fangs glinting, she said "We have a family tradition then . . ."

Quashing thoughts of what sort of gifts followed severed heads and pigs, I nodded. "We do, indeed. Perhaps the holiday season will be more interesting for it."

She lifted her glass to me. "To defeating our enemies with festive spirits!"

I lifted my glass to hers. "To family."

She smiled at me, and then she toasted Piggy Iggy with a malicious grin.

As I drained the glass, I couldn't decide whether Eli or I landed the most terrifying in-laws. Fae King or *Draugr* Queen? Both were ferocious.

Either way, I felt certain of both the love and the strength we had at our sides. Whatever came next, we were not alone in facing it.

EXCERPT OF THE WICKED &
THE DEAD

The Wicked & The Dead
AVAILABLE now!

Chapter 1

Autumn in the South was still both humid and hot. New Orleans was always a wet city. Wet air. Wet drizzle. Beer soaked streets. *Other* things spilling out from behind trash bins. Sometimes, the heavy air and frequent rain was just this side of too much.

Most nights, there was nowhere else I'd rather be. We were a city risen from the ashes, over and over. Plagues, floods, monsters. New Orleans didn't stop, didn't give up, and I was proud of that. Tonight, though, I watched the fog roll out like a cheap film effect, and a good book in front of a warm fire sounded far better than work. The nonstop rain this month would wash away evidence of the things that happened in New Orleans' darkened corners, but I could prevent bloodshed. It was more or less what I did. Sometimes, I spilled a bit of blood, but if we weighed it all out, I was fairly sure I was one of the good guys.

More curves and sass than actual *guys*, but the point held. White hat. Dingy around the edges. I blame my persistent nagging guilt.

A *thump* on the other side of the wall made me pause.

Could I hurl myself over the wall into Cypress Grove Cemetery? It wasn't the *worst* idea ever—or even this month—which said more about my life than I'd like to admit.

I listened for more sounds. *Nothing.* No scrabbling. No growling.

I needed to be on the other side of the wall where tombs were lined up like miniature houses. The tree branches I'd used last time were gone, probably trimmed by someone who saw their potential. Now, there was no graceful way to hurl myself over the ten-foot wall.

Every cemetery in the nation now had taller walls and plenty of newly-opened space for the dead. Cemeteries had become "stage one" of the verification of death process. Honestly, I guess graves were better than cold storage at the morgue. The lack of heartbeat made it impossible to know if the corpses would walk again, and those of us who advocated for beheading all corpses were deemed callous.

I wasn't sure I was callous for wanting the dead to stay dead. I knew what they were capable of before the world at large did.

At least I was prepared. A moment or so later, I shoved a metal spike into the wall, cutting my palm in the process.

"Shit. Damn. Monkey balls."

A ripple of light flashed around me the moment my blood dripped to the soil. At least the light was magic, not the police or a tourist with a camera. While the laws were ever-changing, B&E was still illegal. And I was breaking into a cemetery where I might need to carry out a contracted beheading. *That* was illegal, too.

It simply wasn't a photo-ready moment—although with my long dyed-blue hair and nearly translucent skin, I was far too photogenic. I won't say I look like I've been drained of both blood and color, but I will admit that next to a lot of the folks in my city, I look like I've been bleached.

I fumbled with my gloves, trapping my blood inside the thick leather before I resumed shoving climbing cams into gaps in the wall. Normally, cams held the ropes that climbers use. Tonight, they'd be like tiny foot supports. If I were human, this wouldn't work out well.

I'm not.

Mostly, I'd say I am a witch, but that is the polite truth. I am more like witch-with-hard-to-explain-extras. That smidge of blood I'd spilled was enough to send out "wakey, wakey" messages to whatever corpses were listening, but the last time I'd had to bleed for them to rest again, I'd needed to shed more than a cup of blood.

I concentrated on not sending out a second magic flare and continued to insert the cams.

Rest. Stay. I felt silly thinking messages to the dead, but better silly than planning for excess bleeding.

At least this job *should* be an easy one. My task was to find out if Alice Navarro was again-walking or if she was securely in her vault. I hoped for the latter. Most people hired me to ease their dearly departed back in the "departed" category, but the Navarro family was the other sort. They missed her, and sometimes grief makes people do things that are on the wrong side of rational.

My pistol had tranquilizer rounds tonight. If Navarro was awake, I'd need to tranq her. If she wasn't, I could call it a night—unless there were other again-walkers. That's where the beheading came in. Straight-forward. Despite the cold and wet, I still hoped for the best. All things considered, I really was an optimist at heart.

At the top of the wall, I swung my leg over the stylish spikes cemented there and dropped into the wet grass. I was braced for it, but when I landed, it wasn't dew or rain that made me land on my ass.

An older man, judging by the tufts of grey hair on the bloodied body, in a security guard uniform had bled out on the ground. Something—most likely an again-walker—had gnawed on the security guard's face. Who had made the decision to have a living man with no special skills stand inside the walls of a cemetery? Now, he was dead.

I whispered a quick prayer before surveying my surroundings. Once I located the *draugr*, I could call in the location of the dead man. First, though, I had to find the face-gnawer who killed him. Since my magic was erratic, I didn't want to send a voluntary pulse out to find my prey. That would wake the truly dead, and there were plenty of them here to wake.

Several rows into the cemetery, I found Alice Navarro's undisturbed grave. No upheaval. No turned soil. Mrs. Navarro was well and truly dead. My clients had their answer—but now, I had a mystery. Which cemetery resident had killed the security guard?

A sound drew my attention. A thin hooded figure, masked like they were off to an early carnival party, stared back at me. They didn't move like they were dead. Too slow. Too human. And *draugr* weren't big on masks.

"Hey!" My voice seemed too loud. "You. What are you . . ."

The figure ran, and several other voices suddenly rang out. Young voices. Teens inside the cemetery.

"Shit cookies!" I ran after the masked person. Who in the name of all reason would be in among the graves at night? I ran through the rows of graves, looking for evidence of waking as I went.

"Bitch!"

The masked figure was climbing over the wall with a ladder, the chain sort you use in home fire-emergencies. Two teens tried to grab the person. One kid was kneeling, hand gripping his shoulder in obvious pain.

And there, several feet away, was Marie and Edward Chevalier's grave. The soil was disturbed, as if a pack of excited dogs had been digging. The person in the mask was not the dead one in the nearby grave. There *was* a recently dead *draugr*.

And kids.

I glanced back at the teens.

A masked stranger, a dead security guard, a *draugr,* and kids. This was a terrible combination.

The masked person dropped something and pulled a gun. The kids backed away quickly, and the masked person glanced at me before scrambling the rest of the way over the wall—all while awkwardly holding a gun.

"Are you okay?" I asked the kids, even as my gaze was scanning for the *draugr*.

"She stabbed Gerry," the girl said, pointing at the kid on the ground.

The tallest of the teens grabbed the thing the intruder dropped and held it up. A syringe.

"She?" I asked.

"Lady chest," the tall one explained. "When I ran into her, I felt her—"

"Got it." I nodded, glad the intruder with the needle was gone, but a quick glance at the stone by the disturbed grave told me that a fresh body had been planted there two days ago. That was the likely cause of the security guard's missing face. I read the dates on the stone: Edward was not yet dead. Marie was.

I was seeking Marie Chevalier.

"Marie?" I whispered loudly as the kids talked among themselves. The last thing I needed right now was a *draugr* arriving to gnaw on the three dumb kids. "Oh, Miss Marie? Where are you?"

Marie wouldn't answer, even if she had been a polite Southern lady. *Draugr* were like big infants for the first decade and change: they ate, yelled, and stumbled around.

"There's a real one?" the girl asked.

I glanced at the kids. I was calling out a thing that would *eat* them if they had been alone with it, and they seemed excited. Best case was a drooling open-mouthed lurch in my direction. Worst case was they all died.

"Go home," I said.

Instead they trailed behind me as I walked around, looking for Marie. I passed by the front gate—which was now standing wide open.

"Did you do that?" The lock had been removed. The pieces were on the ground. Cut through. Marie was not in the cemetery.

Shaking heads. "No, man. The ladder the bitch used was ours."

Intruder. With a needle. Possibly also the person who left the gate open? Had someone wanted Marie Chevalier released? Or was that a coincidence? Either way, a face-gnawer was loose somewhere in the city, one of the who-knows-how-many *draugr* that hid here or in the nearby suburbs or small towns.

I pushed the gates closed and called it in to the police. "Broken gate at Cypress Grove. Cut in pieces."

"Miss Crowe," the woman on dispatch replied. "Are you injured?"

"No. The *lock* was cut. Bunch of kids here." I shot them a look. "Said it wasn't them."

"I will send a car," she said. A longer than normal pause. "Why are *you* there, Miss Crowe?"

I smothered a sigh. It complicated my life that so many of the cops recognized me, that dispatch did, that the ER folks at the hospital did. It wasn't like New Orleans was *that* small.

"Do you log my number?" I asked. "Or is it my voice?"

Another sigh. Another pause. She ignored my questions. "Details?"

"I was checking on a grave here. It's intact, but the cemetery gate's busted," I explained.

"I noted that," she said mildly. "Are the kids alive?"

"Yeah. A person in a mask tried to inject one of them, and a guard inside is missing a lot of his face. No *draugr* here now, but the grave of Marie and Edward Chevalier is broken out. I'm guessing it was her that killed the guard."

The calm tone was gone. "There's a car about two blocks away. You and the children—"

"I'm good." I interrupted. "Marie's long gone, I guess. I'll be sure the kids are secure, but—"

"Miss Crowe! You don't know if she's still there or nearby. You need to be relocated to safety, too."

"Honest to Pete, you all need to worry a lot less about me," I said.

She made a noise that reminded me of my mother. Mama Lauren could fit a whole lecture in one of those "uh-huh" noises of hers. The woman on dispatch tonight came near to matching my mother.

"Someone *cut* the lock," I told dispatch. "What we need to know is why. And who. And if there are other opened cemeteries." I paused. "And who tried to inject the kid."

I looked at them. They were in a small huddle. One of them dropped and stomped the needle. I winced. That was going to make investigating a lot harder.

Not my problem, I reminded myself. I was a hired killer, not a cop, not a detective, not a nanny.

"Kid probably ought to get a tox screen and tetanus shot," I muttered.

Dispatch made an agreeing noise, and said, "Please try not to 'find' more trouble tonight, Miss Crowe."

I made no promises.

When I disconnected, I looked at the kids. "Gerry, right?"

The kid in the middle nodded. White boy. Looking almost as pale as me currently. I was guessing he was terrified.

"Let me see your arm."

He pulled his shirt off. It looked like the skin was torn.

"Do not scream," I said. My eyes shifted into larger versions of a snake's eyes. I knew what it looked like, and maybe a part of me was okay with letting them see because nobody would believe them if they did tell. They were kids, and while a lot had changed in the world, people still doubted kids when they talked.

More practically, though, as my eyes changed I could see in a way humans couldn't.

Green. Glowing like a cheap neon light. The syringe had venom. *Draugr* venom. It wasn't inside the skin. The syringe was either jammed or the kid jerked away.

"Water?"

One of the kids pulled a bottle from his bag, and I washed the wound. "Don't touch the fucking syringe." I pointed at it. "Who stomped on it? Hold your boot up."

I rinsed that, too. Venom wasn't the sort of thing anyone wanted on their skin unless they wanted acid-burn.

"Venom," I said. "That was venom in the needle. You could've died. And"—I pointed behind me—"there was a *draugr* here. Guy got his face chewed off."

They were listening, seeming to at least. I wasn't their family, though. I was a blue-haired woman with some weapons and weird eyes. The best I could do was hand them over to the police and hope they weren't stupid enough to end up in danger again tomorrow.

New Orleans had more than Marie hiding in the shadows. *Draugr* were fast, strong, and difficult to kill. If not for their need to feed on the living like mindless beasts the first few decades after resurrection, I might accept them as the next evolutionary step. But I wasn't a fan of anything—mindless or sentient—that stole blood and life.

Marie might have been an angel in life, but right now she was a killer.

In my city.

If I found the person or people who decided to release Marie—or the woman with the syringe--I'd call the police. I tried to avoid killing the living. But if I found Marie, or others like her, I wasn't calling dispatch. When it came to venomous killers, I tended to be more of a behead first, ask later kind of woman.

The Kiss & The Killer

The next installment in a new faery and fanged world written by the author of the internationally bestselling Wicked Lovely series...for readers of Patricia Briggs, Chloe Neill, and Jeaniene Frost.

HALF WITCH, HALF KILLER, WHOLLY UNSUCCESSFUL AT EVERY Faery Bargain so far...

After an accidental engagement, overcoming attempted murder, and discovering a family secret, Geneviève is ready for things to settle down, but carnival season in New Orleans is not the best time of year for "normal."

As the *draugr* mix with the locals and tourists, and bodies start to pile up, Geneviève is enlisted by the New Orleans Police Department to hunt *draugr* all while trying to navigate this latest faery bargain amidst the swirl of parades and parties of carnival season.

When Eli Stonecroft, the faery who has claimed her heart despite her best attempts, offers her a new faery bargain--she's smart enough to say no . . . right up to the point when she has to decide between dealing with the consequence of this faery bargain or facing the killer alone.

WHAT READERS SAID ABOUT BOOK 1:

"I loved The Wicked and The Dead! A sassy, ass-kicking heroine, a deliciously mysterious fae hero, and a wonderful mix of action and romance. Add that to Melissa's usual great world-building, and I'm already looking forward to book 2!" – Jeaniene Frost, NYT Bestselling Author

"Wow! You all seriously want to read this. It's an urban fantasy - very cool twist on vampires - with a heroine simultaneously so kickass, warmly human, and passionate about the world that I want to be her. I also want to be her because of the insanely hot Eli, her fae love interest. . . .Get in on the ground level with this series, because it's going to be an auto buy. Highly recommend."-- Jeffe Kennedy, award-winning author and SFWA Board Member

Available Now

The Fanged & The Fae: A Faery Bargains Collection

Three novellas in a book length collection:

"Blood Martinis & Mistletoe" (Set after book 1)

Half-dead witch Geneviève Crowe makes her living beheading the dead--and spends her free time trying not to get too attached to her business partner, Eli Stonecroft, a faery prince in self-imposed exile in New Orleans.

A walking-dead relative and a deadly but well-paying job make the holidays a lot more complicated than anyone needs. With a killer at her throat and a blood martini in her hand, Geneviève accepts what seems like a straight-forward faery bargain. Eli's terms might make the holidays a little more bearable, but if she can't figure out a way to escape this faery bargain, she'll be planning a wedding soon.

"DAIQUIRIS & DAGGERS" (SET AFTER BOOK 2)

A fun spa weekend away with friends in a city free of monsters, what could be better? Gen's necromancy had been on the fritz, so a recharge sounds perfect–until she arrives in San

Diego to discover that either the spa is too steps beyond weird or there's magic afoot

"CHAMPAGNE & COMMITMENTS" (SET RIGHT BEFORE BOOK 3)

Half-dead witch Geneviève Crowe makes her living beheading the dead--and trying to make sense of accidentally ending up a faery princess when she ended up bonded to Eli Stonecroft, a faery prince in self-imposed exile in New Orleans. But bonded for eternity isn't enough for family and friends--of her future citizens. It's time to plan a wedding ceremony. Unfortunately there isn't enough champagne available to deal with an undead-great-grand-mother, a faery king who's trying to romance Gen's assistant, and a city where Halloween is a holiday worth dying to enjoy.

ABOUT THE AUTHOR

Melissa Marr is a former university literature instructor who writes fiction for adults, teens, and children. Her books have been translated into twenty-eight languages and have been bestsellers internationally (Germany, France, Sweden, Australia, et. al.) as well as domestically. She is best known for the Wicked Lovely series for teens, *Graveminder* for adults, and her debut picture book *Bunny Roo, I Love You*.

In her free time, she practices medieval swordfighting, kayaks, hikes, and raises kids in the Arizona desert.

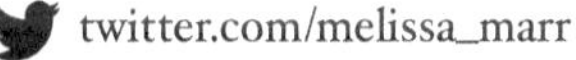 facebook.com/MelissaMarrBooks

twitter.com/melissa_marr

goodreads.com/melissa_marr